Murder,
al fresco

Murder,
al fresco

Frances Patton Statham

Bocage Books

To

Emily, Helen, and Sue

Copyright © 2012 by Frances Patton Statham

ISBN: 0-9675233-8-9

Cover design by: Steve McAfee

Cover painting by: Erin Hill

Manufactured in the United States of America

First Edition: December 2012

www.bocagebooks.com
bocagebooks@mindspring.com

10 9 8 7 6 5 4 3 2 1

Murder,
al fresco

 *Prologue*

"*D*id you get the key?"

"Yes. It's hidden in my apartment where no one can find it."

"Good."

Lydia Garson Burnside, the aristocratic, white-haired matriarch, sat up in her hospital bed and nodded in satisfaction at Joie Chang, her longtime housekeeper.

"But nothing's going to go wrong tomorrow," Joie assured her. "I'm told that angioplasty is quite a safe procedure."

"I know that, Joie, but I have to be careful to protect my granddaughters. Only if something happens to me and they come after either Carley or Morgan are you to give them the key. You'll know when it's time. Promise me."

"Of course, Lydia."

"Then, you'd better go. Carley's waiting downstairs to take you home."

Once Joie left, the nurse came in, carrying a tray of small white paper cups. "Time for your sleeping pill, Mrs. Burnside," the nurse ordered, taking one of the cups and handing it to Lydia.

The hospital regimen was just as bureaucratic as another organization she was acquainted with, and it would not do to be listed as uncooperative. So, as the nurse watched, Lydia duly took the medication and then settled down for the night.

Several hours later, a man dressed in a white coat entered the darkened room. He worked quietly so that he would not disturb the sleeping woman. Taking a syringe from his pocket, he injected a lethal dose of lidocaine into her IV bag. When he had finished, he smiled and vanished from the room. In less than ten minutes, Lydia Burnside would die of a massive heart infarction, and then she would no longer be a threat.

 *Chapter 1*

"You should have seen it coming, Carley," her twin accused. "After all, it didn't happen overnight."

"Well, I haven't had as much experience with faithless husbands as you have, Morgan."

"You're certainly right about that. But at least, I didn't wind up completely poverty stricken."

"I've got to hang up, now. The light's turned green."

Carley Burnside's cell phone had rung just as she'd stopped at a red light in Fairhope, Alabama. As usual, Morgan was running late — this time for their appointment at Goose's office in downtown Mobile.

George Godwin Goosens, III, attorney-at-law, had been one of their grandmother's best friends, as well as her executor. But no one ever called him anything but *Goose,* one of those nicknames given to him in the first grade nearly sixty years previously and more than likely destined to follow him to the grave.

That was the problem with living almost one's entire life in the same town, Carley thought. Everyone knew entirely too much about everyone else. She resented terribly this insular grapevine, especially since she had been the gossip filler of conversations until Lucinda Bledsoe took over as the hottest topic on everyone's lips.

In fact, she had just come from Lucinda's new property in Point Clear, farther down the bay. Goose had given her name to Lucinda as a possible landscape designer, but

Carley had turned down the commission, even though she needed the job. Now, she was not looking forward to explaining her reasons to Goose.

Gran's death had come at the worst possible time in Carley's life. She still had not gotten over her husband's sudden request for a divorce. To make matters even worse, he had also seen to it that Sherrie, the other woman, had jumped several rungs in the corporate ladder of the architectural firm where he was a junior partner.

With that coup, Carley, who had been the undisputed star of the landscape side of the firm, was placed in an untenable situation. Her award-winning designs seemed to have been forgotten as the senior partner, Arthur Regan, explained, "You realize, of course, that it would be much too awkward for you to continue working at Regan, Barnes, and O'Reilly, especially with Sherrie on the job. But we will certainly recommend you to other firms."

Right. Well, she wouldn't hold her breath for that to happen.

The fog obscured the sides of the long causeway over Mobile Bay, and Carley had to concentrate on the brake lights in front of her. Soon, she was off the bridge and headed toward Cathedral Square downtown.

It had been a week since the funeral, and Goose had summoned Carley and Morgan for the reading of the will. The two were the only heirs, although there was little left to inherit. But through the years, they had received more important things than money from their paternal grandmother. It was Gran who had taken them in hand when they had suddenly become orphans at the age of twelve.

If she had determined to mold them in her own social image, she had done so with love—imparting the necessary skills that would assure their places in Mobile society, while arming them with enough education to make them self-sufficient.

That had meant dancing school, cotillions, being kind to

her friends—especially the Mardi Gras committee, who oversaw the selection of the Court—and pushing them toward all the volunteer work that looked good on their résumés and college transcripts.

Although Carley and Morgan were identical twins, blonde and green-eyed, Morgan was much more adept in the social world. She had a certain flair that caused heads to turn, whereas Carley was more conservative, preferring flowers and gardens to dinner parties. Her hands showed it, too—while Morgan's smooth, long fingers had never touched a trowel or bulb planter.

Carley suddenly smiled, remembering Gran and the secret that she had kept from Mobile society for twenty-five years. Her investment club had actually been a poker club with Goose, Edward Raines, and Henry Wetherbee. Each Wednesday night, the four had met while the Methodist Prayer Meeting suppers were taking place only a mile from her English Tudor, half-timbered house. But since the Burnsides were Episcopalian, she wasn't missed. Yet, it did seem strange that none of her female friends had ever breached that particular secret. And it seemed even stranger to Carley that she and Morgan had been cautioned never to mention the club. It was almost as if something more clandestine were going on than a mere poker club disguised as an investment club. In the end, Carley finally decided that she had read too many mysteries in her childhood, and she attributed her questioning to an overactive imagination.

She turned on to Government Street, where a number of beautiful old historic houses were shaded by huge, moss-hanging live oaks. The only good thing about the Civil War was that the federal shells bombarding the city from the bay had been mostly duds, and so little damage was done to the residential areas. Many of those same houses that survived the cannons had been faithfully restored and now function-ed as business or law offices.

Goose's office was in one of the most lavish houses on the street, with its white-columned porch and green staghorn ferns at the beveled-glass double doors beckoning clients inside. But Carley had seldom entered that front door.

She pulled into the driveway in her red Toyota truck and drove on to the graveled parking lot in the rear. The truck, with her landscape design logo emblazoned on the side, was one of the few things that she had kept after the divorce, since it was clearly in her name.

She walked up the steps and tapped on the back door of the office as her grandmother had always done. Far from being considered a tradesman's entrance, the back door had a special significance, indicating the closeness between visitor and occupant. Soon, Goose, himself, opened the screened door.

"How are you, darlin'?" he asked, giving her a big bear hug.

"It's been a difficult week, Goose."

"I know. I still can't believe Lydia's gone." As the two passed by his assistant's desk, he said, "Agnes, I'd be pleased if you could get Carley and me a cup of coffee, and maybe some of those orange-chocolate cookies that she likes so much."

Goose must have realized that Carley needed comfort food. Coffee, too, since she had not stopped for breakfast.

"Morgan called. She's going to be a few minutes late," Carley informed him.

"Then we'll have time to chat on our own until she gets here."

Goose was a wonderful old white-haired gentleman — among the last of that genteel world of earlier Mobile that was fast vanishing with the influx of new industries. But make no mistake; he was still one of the major power brokers.

Agnes was almost as old as Goose, but she had recently colored her hair a bright strawberry blonde and had started working out every Saturday at the new yoga sanctuary next door to the art gallery.

"How is the yoga class, Miss Agnes?" Carley asked as Agnes brought in the silver tea service with bone china cups and placed them on the coffee table between the cordovan leather chairs.

"Coming along quite well. It's a great de-stresser."″

"Then, maybe I need to check it out."

Agnes smiled and discreetly left the room.

The first thing that Carley had noticed when she walked into his office was Goose's antique mahogany desk, which was usually cluttered with papers. Today, all the papers were gone. In their stead was a deck of cards, carefully splayed into a fan-shaped design.

Puzzled, Carley looked again at the desk, but then Goose quickly diverted her attention. "So, how did the appointment with Lucinda go?"

"I turned down the job, Goose. People keep putting up unpleasant signs around her yard. And I just couldn't see my landscape sign as a companion to all the graffiti."

"Well, I can't say that I blame you," he admitted.

Lucinda was also one of Goose's longtime clients, but she had not taken his advice in her most recent endeavor.

Instead, this seventy-two-year-old widow had married her thirty-six-year-old chauffeur and handyman, who had spent time in prison. Rumor had it that he had murdered someone.

Lucinda was from a fine old family that had first settled at Dauphin Island and made a fortune in shipping and timber. This unfortunate marriage had caused an immediate estrangement from her family and friends. Miffed, she had sold her home in the city and purchased property farther down the bay. But her new neighbors were equally aghast. Soon protest signs had begun appearing all along her driveway.

Goose reached for a cookie. After he had taken a bite, he said, "Carley, you know Boris Cavanaugh, don't you?"

"Not personally. But anybody who passes through Fairhope knows of his artists' colony. Why do you ask?"

"Because of something he said last week, he might be a potential client for you. I could give him a call while we're waiting for Morgan."

"Goose, I really appreciate your trying to help me out, but I'd rather you didn't."

"And why not?"

"I need to find work on my own."

By that time, he had already risen from his chair and headed toward his desk. "Just this one call," he insisted.

"Then, I think I'll go and talk with Agnes while you make it." Carley took her coffee cup and another cookie with her and stepped into the hallway.

Almost immediately, she heard the reckless crunch of Morgan's Jaguar on the gravel, and then a door slam. So, carefully balancing her coffee cup, she changed directions and walked into the foyer toward the front door. Morgan never entered back doors.

"I do wish Goose would pave his parking area," her twin complained immediately. "Pea gravel is so hard on good shoes."

Morgan was wearing the perfect color to enhance her blonde looks—a sherbet green silk Mizrahi suit, with matching high-heeled sandals.

"I see that you're wearing green today, too," Carley said with a smile.

Examining her twin's white slacks and navy blue linen blazer, Morgan in all seriousness said, "I'm sure that Raymond can get the grass stain out of your slacks. He's really good."

It was a standing family joke—Carley's propensity for ruining her clothes. Even dressed for a party, she couldn't seem to resist pulling up one last weed, as she left her yard behind.

"Hello, Morgan. Good to see you."

During the exchange, Goose had come into the hallway. "It's all settled, Carley. I've set up an appointment for you to see Boris. Now, you two come into my office."

"What was that all about?" Morgan asked.

"A potential job."

"Oh."

Without being asked, Agnes had another coffee cup ready for Morgan and, within a few moments, Goose became the family executor, explaining the contents of their grandmother's will.

"As you both know, Lydia left a small insurance policy for each of you. The only tangible property she had were the two houses."

"*Two* houses?" Morgan and Carley chimed at almost the same second.

"Are you counting the old carriage house in the backyard?" Carley asked.

"No. That's considered part of the Mobile property. She also owned a small villa in France, which she rented out."

"Well, that's certainly news to us," Morgan said. Carley agreed.

"And since there are two of you, each will inherit a house."

When Morgan became thoughtful, she always bit her lower lip. "Did she specify who gets which one?"

"Not exactly." Goose coughed, as if slightly embarrassed. "You know how Lydia always enjoyed games of chance."

"Oh, no." Carley suddenly realized why the cards had been spread out on the desk. "We're going to draw for them."

Goose nodded. "So we might as well get on with it." He paged Agnes, saying, "You can bring in the video camera now, Agnes."

As much as Carley loved the large old house in Mobile, she was aware of the repairs that it needed, especially to the slate roof. The property in France would more than likely need some upgrades, too, but the idea of owning a villa in Europe was instantly more compelling.

Although their grandmother's death had been a shock, it was not unexpected, since they'd known about her heart for a long time.

But Carley thought that it had been particularly callous of Bob and Sherrie to announce their marriage in the *Mobile Register* only one day after Gran's obituary had appeared. If the villa became hers, then there was nothing to keep her from leaving Mobile behind. For the first time in weeks, she felt a rush of enthusiasm.

She had already worked in Europe as a former member of the firm — to develop a community park in Brussels, and an environmentally friendly playground near Amsterdam.
If she had a European base, then she was sure that she could find other work there, while allowing time for her personal wounds to heal.

With the camera recording the event, Goose explained the procedure to be followed. Facing the camera, Goose said, "Today is Friday, July 12, —. In my office are Carleton LeMoyne Burnside and Countess Morgan Burnside-Bramante, heirs to the estate of the late Lydia Garson Burnside. According to her last will and testament, and with the desire not to show partiality to either of her granddaughters, the decedent has stipulated that her two heirs are to draw cards for the two houses, which constitute the bulk of her estate.

"On my desk is a deck of cards, face-down and in no particular order. The decedent has also stipulated that two draws are to be made; the first to determine which house is to be considered, and the second draw to determine who wins that house. The granddaughter with the lower number in the second draw automatically receives the other house."

"My God!" Morgan exclaimed. "She's still playing games beyond the grave."

Carley laughed at the ludicrous situation, so like Gran to devise.

"Who goes first?" she asked Goose.

"The draw will be simultaneous. So both of you step behind my desk and face the camera," he instructed. When the two had done so, he continued. "Now, each of you may pick up a card."

Morgan and Carley reached at the same time—Carley, with her right hand and Morgan with her left. "What's yours?" Morgan asked, looking down at her own card while she waited for Carley's reply.

"The queen of spades. And yours?"

"The ten of diamonds. So I guess you'll decide which house we'll draw for."

"The villa in France," Carley immediately responded.

Again they drew cards while the whir of the video camera indicated that their every move was being recorded.

Carley was afraid to look at her second card. Instead, she clutched it to her blazer while she said a silent prayer. *Oh, please. Let me get the villa.*

"Hold up the cards for the camera, please."

They did so, while Goose explained, "Carley has drawn the jack of clubs."

She held her breath and waited. "But Morgan has drawn the ace of spades. So let it be recorded that Morgan receives the villa at Milly-la-Forêt, while Carleton inherits the Mobile house."

How disappointed Carley was! Instead of running away, she was destined, by the luck of the draw, to remain in Mobile.

 *Chapter 2*

*T*hat day, when she inherited the English Tudor house, Carley had not intended inheriting the investment club, as well. But five days later, she invited Goose, Edward, and Henry to the house for one last game of poker, in honor of her grandmother.

It was not as if she were a stranger to the group. Occasionally, she had filled in when one of them was out of town. Henry had recently retired from the banking business, and Edward was at loose ends after selling his company to a Swiss conglomerate. Only Goose was active—in law practice. But all three were still known as members of the city's "Mobility."

After grumbling about the greed of now defunct corporations and a few words about the economy, they soon settled down to the real reason for getting together.

Amid a few tears and an occasional emotional voice break, they remembered Lydia.

As they played poker, the three men regaled Carley with reminiscences of past years and what their friendship with her grandmother had meant. She suspected that all three had been in love with her at some time in their lives.

Toward midnight, when the game had broken up and Carley was seeing them to the door, Edward said, "I'll bring the beer next Wednesday."

"And I'll stop by the deli for cheese and chips," Henry

offered. "And maybe some more trail mix."

Goose looked at Carley and grinned.

"Sure. Next Wednesday, then." What else could she say? She suddenly realized the void in their lives.

Yet, was she any different? When a person is no longer part of a couple, or part of a firm, one's social life evaporates until new alliances can be formed. But when you're thirty-one, you don't really expect your new social life to revolve around your grandmother's contemporaries. Yet, Carley loved them all.

She locked the door and then went to the kitchen to hand wash the four empty beer steins. Years ago, Goose had brought them back from Austria. He'd even had them etched as a joke with the words, *Wednesday Night Investment Club.*

The sudden, lonely quiet caused her to shiver, despite the heat of that summer evening. The house seemed so empty. Morgan had flown to Italy the day after the reading of the will to pick up her daughter, Cristina. The seven-year-old was spending part of the summer with the Contessa Bramante, her paternal grandmother. Now, it was time for her to be reclaimed.

When Morgan had made the brilliant marriage to the heir of an ancient Venetian family, after having her previous marriage annulled (she didn't count the first one), it had seemed that she was destined for a story book life.

Everything had gone extremely well for the first few years, but when Cristina was four years old, Morgan had called Carley in the middle of the night. "I found him in bed with another *man*," she screamed.

"Oh, no, Morgan. I'm so sorry." The untimely call had awakened Carley's husband Bob, who was not pleased. "What are you going to do about it?"

"Divorce the *bastardo*. Wouldn't you do the same?"

"Morgan, let me call you later, when we can talk at length."

In the end, the contessa intervened. So Morgan and

Gianni merely separated to keep the scandal from affecting Cristina and the good name of the Bramantes.

Putting the beer steins into the cupboard, Carley shook her head, as if to erase the memory of that disturbing telephone conversation and its aftermath. When she'd snuggled back into the spoon position with her husband, she remembered thinking how lucky she was. Bob would never betray her the way Gianni had betrayed Morgan. How wrong she had been.

As she left the kitchen, she realized how quickly life could change in the space of a few months. From being a happily married woman with a satisfying career, she was now single and jobless. She owned an aging house that carried on conversations with itself during a storm. She was also the caretaker of her grandmother's two Maltese cats, Li-Po and Cho-Cho. They had been willed to Cristina if she wanted them, but Carley had an idea that Morgan would choose to ignore that bequest. As for the poker club, she would just have to wait and see what evolved.

Yet, if she had learned anything at all under Gran's tutelage, it was to get on with the future and not cry over the past. She would start anew — beginning tomorrow — with the job interview that Goose had arranged.

Carley walked through the house, turned out the lights, and climbed the stairs to her bedroom, with Li-Po and Cho-Cho directly behind her.

Later, with the cats purring on the pillow beside her, she turned on the television set and surfed the channels.

Since the divorce, she had gotten into a bad habit of leaving on the television until she went to sleep. Sometimes in the middle of the night, she would be startled by a loud commercial, and she would wake. So she tried to find an innocuous program designed to put her to sleep.

Unfortunately, her plan didn't work. In the middle of the night, the decibel level rose dramatically, causing her to awake and sit up.

Disoriented, she sleepily gazed at the screen. A late night

televangelist was peddling prosperity handkerchiefs to his viewers. Why did that sound so familiar? Of course. This was evidently where Alva Patillo's daughter, Gaddi, kept getting her supply. She had even given one to her grandmother, which Carley had found unopened the day before the funeral.

Smiling to herself, she decided that if her financial position didn't get better soon, she might be a candidate, herself.

The program finally put Carley back to sleep. Yet it was an uneasy rest with weird and troubling dreams. And so by morning, Carley was happy to feel the sun on her face and realize that she had survived another night.

One good thing about cats, she decided, is that they are so self-sufficient. While she had her morning coffee, Li-Po and Cho-Cho, who had already eaten, eyed her from the twin hammocks attached to the underside of an old hutch in the breakfast room. She had gotten the idea for the swing design from Martha Stewart one morning when she had stayed at home with a bad cold and watched TV. She'd had no inkling that the finished project would be so successful.

Thinking of projects, Carley nervously crossed her fingers. In less than two hours, she would be in Fairhope and facing the formidable Boris Cavanaugh. It was unfortunate that she had forgotten to send her three pairs of white slacks to Raymond for cleaning.

 *Chapter 3*

*T*he massive wrought iron gates of the estate called *Cavallegria* loomed before her. Carley had driven her truck about a quarter of a mile off the Fairhope road and through a heavily wooded area of scraggly timber before the double gates suddenly appeared, blocking the entry to the property. She stopped her truck and walked over to the intercom to press the button, as Goose had instructed.

"Identify yourself," the gruff voice boomed, causing her to jump. In her best, business-like voice, she answered, "I'm Carleton Burnside. I have a 10:30 appointment with Mr. Cavanaugh."

She stood there in complete silence, waiting for a response. The only answer was a slow swinging of the right gate, opening just wide enough for her truck to squeeze through. She hurriedly got back into her truck, revved the motor, and shot past before the gate closed again.

Sprinkled throughout the compound, she noticed a number of small dwellings—typical French Colonial shotgun cottages that reminded Carley of some in the older quarters of New Orleans. They had been called that for years, because of the arrangement of rooms on each side of a main hallway. A person could stand at the front door and shoot straight through to the back door. Yet, from what she could see through the trees, the cottages were well preserved and would provide adequate space for their seasonal occupants.

After a few windings and turns, the road finally straightened to reveal an unusual white stucco structure with sharp angles—a gargantuan house with red-tiled roof—a Mizner-like mansion that had almost been swallowed up by hanging moss, trees, and tortuously twisted vines.

That sight made Carley's heart quicken. It was every landscape designer's dream. The grounds desperately needed attention.

Before she had a chance to use the lion head doorknocker, the weathered cypress door opened. Filling almost the entire opening stood Boris Cavanaugh, dressed in a flowing white robe, with a white beard to match. He looked as if he might have stepped out of a Carravaggio fresco, painted on some Renaissance chapel wall.

"You're a woman," he barked.

"Yes. And you're an artist, I understand."

He stared at Carley, taking his time, as if he were examining a prospective nude for his art class. "Well, come in. I suppose that since you're already here, I can at least give you a few minutes."

She followed him through the marbled foyer, down a long hallway, and finally into his studio at the rear, where he offered her a seat opposite the canvas he was obviously working on. He took up a brush, dabbed at one of the pigments on his palette, and slashed it on the canvas. "The paint is drying too fast for me to stop," he said. "I'll be finished soon."

Carley knew when to keep quiet. But while she waited, she silently swore at Goose, who had made the appointment for her. Had he deliberately not told Cavanaugh that he would be dealing with a woman?

Finally, Boris wiped his sable brush with a pigment-stained rag, put it in a beaker of liquid that smelled of orange blossoms, and then turned to Carley. "So what ideas do you have to keep Mother Nature from strangling this compound?"

She resented the superior, impatient tone of his voice.

Since she suspected that she was already out of the running for the job, she was determined not to be intimidated. "Before I respond to your question, Mr. Cavanaugh, I have one of my own."

"Yes?"

"Do you pick up a canvas and start painting willy-nilly before you know the subject of your painting?"

"Willy-nilly? What kind of word is that? I always know my subject well, young woman."

"Well, when it comes to landscape design, I'm that way, too," she responded. "I have to know my subject thoroughly before I make plans. And since I haven't walked over your estate or discovered your preferences or how extensive you want the renovations to be, then I have no instant plans to offer you." Carley smiled apologetically.

After a long silence, Boris said, "I suppose you want me to take you on a walking tour of the property."

"Or we could go in my truck."

"We'll walk." He went to an adjoining door and yelled, "Wingate, put another plate on the table. We have a guest for lunch."

As he turned, Carley realized that he had a slight smear of red on his caftan. For a brief moment, she began to feel a little better about this ogre of a man. Perhaps he had a human side, after all.

That thought was instantly dispelled by his next actions. "Before we leave the studio, come and stand before my canvas."

The sun poured through the skylight above, bathing the canvas in reflected light.

Strong, primary colors—reds, blues, and yellows—had been slashed diagonally across the canvas, interspersed with glittering, beaded skeletons of animals that had been tied to moss-covered tree limbs. The center one had been used as a vase for a large Venus-fly-trap, with an unsuspecting beetle lighting on its cusp.

The violence of the painting shocked Carley. This was no

Georgia O'Keeffe look-alike of flower petals, sanitized bones, or desert sunsets. Instead, the canvas spoke of struggle, of loss, of desecration.

Boris seemed to enjoy her reaction. "As you can see, I'm no pale, pathetic impressionist. And I want no pale, pathetic landscape. You understand?"

She merely nodded.

Boris led the way through a rear double door, and the two emerged into a jungled growth that had encroached upon the remnants of a stone patio. A broken urn lay on its side, a victim of a severed tree limb that had evidently fallen during one of the electrical storms, so prevalent during the obsessively hot days of summer. It, too, lay on the ground.

"I want a high wall enclosing this area," he said. "And in it, a garden that I can see from my studio window."

"Similar to the house itself, or in a contrasting material?"

"Whatever will give me the most privacy."

They continued walking along a shell-lined path to another building — a dining hall, built in a compatible design to the main house. Low places in the pathway contained little puddles of water, which Carley sidestepped.

"This is where my students eat. Also where I conduct seminars and critiques. I'd like to have a good view of the bay from here."

"Where is it?"

Boris pointed in a westerly direction. "About three hundred yards from where we're standing."

If he had not mentioned it, she never would have known that the water was so near. It was completely obscured by rampant growth.

"Well, aren't you going to write down anything that I've said?" he asked, frowning at her.

"Mr. Cavanaugh, I'll remember our conversation in context to the land," she explained. "If I'm so busy scribbling, I won't be able to absorb half of what I'm seeing."

Carley had long admired the work of Frederick Law Olmsted — not as the landscaper of Central Park and the 1893

Columbian Exposition in Chicago, but as the designer of a more Southern orientation. In planning the vast estate of the Biltmore House, as well as the Druid Hills section of Atlanta, which he had never finished, Olmsted had been attuned to a new rhythm, a new understanding of working with a regional nature that oftentimes refused to cooperate with more Northern standards.

Boris, with his long strides, seemed to be testing her physical endurance. He did not know that she ran several miles a day, so although Carley took three steps to his two, she kept up the pace as they explored the lay of the land.

They walked for over an hour, with little conversation and seemingly little rapport.

Yet, as Carley drank in the landscape, her mind became busy with endless possibilities, with transformations that nature required to be reined in, without harming the natural growth, while making the landscape friendlier to the people who inhabited it.

Boris Cavanaugh had become a legend along the Gulf Coast. Tremendously wealthy, he was still considered an eccentric. He had abruptly sold the family business and turned his inherited estate, Cavallegria, into a school for emerging artists, both young and old. And his avocation had become his obsession. So much so, that he had neglected the once beautiful property.

Finally, Boris and Carley returned to the house. This time, they entered through the front door. A European-style mat with house slippers was located directly inside the door, and with good reason. Their shoes were dirty with sand and debris, so it was only natural to remove them.

Boris indicated a pair of soft terry cloth slippers for Carley. She put them on, even though they were many sizes too large. They reminded her of the Hungarian spa at Lake Ballaton, where German tourists came down to breakfast in bathrobes and slippers before going on to the mud baths. Carley was grateful that it had not been raining. Otherwise, she might have been offered a robe, too.

"The powder room is to the right."

"Thank you."

Although he was spare with words, at least he had a sense of hospitality. Carley not only needed to wash her hands, but to comb her unruly hair that had responded to the high humidity of the near tropical landscape.

Boris was nowhere to be seen when she re-emerged into the hallway. No one seemed to be in the large dining room, so she headed toward the delicious smells emanating from the kitchen.

"Hi! You must be Wingate," she said, almost bumping into the thin, elderly man, who was carrying a soup tureen. "I'm Carley."

A decided scowl met her attempt to be friendly. The man seemed to resent her intrusion even more than the artist for whom he worked. "Mr. Cavanaugh seldom has guests for lunch," he said. "Usually, there are just the two of us."

"Then, I feel honored to be included today."

"Wingate, you must be more cordial to Ms. Burnside," Boris admonished from the threshold. "She might easily be around for quite a few weeks."

Boris indicated the chair where she was to sit, in what Carley assumed to be a family dining room. It was much smaller than the large, elegant one nearest the foyer. Soon the three of them were partaking of a delicious bouillabaisse, the ingredients from the recent jubilee along the coast.

No one ever questioned the largesse that came to the coast every few years, when all species of fish, crab, and shrimp suddenly cast themselves by the thousands along the inlets and beaches. It had been called a *jubilee* from the earliest days of settlement. From childhood, Carley had heard the excited call while citizens rushed with their baskets and buckets to dip up what the sea had given to the land.

"Wingate is an artist, too," Boris announced. "He's currently carving a bis pole."

She had never heard the term. "A *bis* pole? What is that?"

Wingate seemed unwilling to enlighten her, so Boris explained. "Wingate spent several years in New Guinea, studying the artistic side of the aboriginal culture, especially among the warrior-headhunters. The artists always used a mangrove root to carve the ancestral pole, and the headhunters provided the shrunken head to wedge into the structure."

A serious Wingate finally responded. "When I finish, Boris has promised to find a permanent place in the landscape to plant the pole."

"And will it also have a head lodged in it?" Carley asked, seeing the silent, amused exchange between the two men. She had learned her lesson in Boris's studio and was on to their game.

"He hasn't decided," Boris answered. "But it *will* have all the other attributes, such as a canoe and, of course, the crowned prow of the ancestral *asmat*, which is a symbol for male fertility."

At that moment, Carley was sorry that she had turned down the Bledsoe project.

"Are you also using a mangrove tree for your bis pole, Wingate?"

"Yes. But not the scrawny type from the Florida coast. I imported several large ones from Southeast Asia."

"I suppose that, in the overall landscape plan, Mr. Cavanaugh, you'll expect me to include a site specifically designed for the bis pole."

"What about that, Wingate? Would you like a garden site all your own?"

"Well, I would need to be consulted on the selection."

"Certainly," Carley replied.

"Time for coffee, Wingate," Boris suddenly announced.

The man took their empty soup bowls and the remainder of the French bread into the kitchen. Once he had disappeared, Boris asked, "How soon can you start?"

"That depends upon our coming to terms with price and the amount of work that you want done." Carley tried not to sound too eager. "I can have a preliminary report done by Tuesday. If you approve, then I'll order a survey and draw up a master plan."

He waved his hand. "I don't need to be bothered with details, young woman. Take everything to Goose. If he approves, he can sign the contract for me and pay the bills. But I want the work to begin exactly two weeks from today. That's when my students arrive."

Surprised, Carley said, "Will all the noise and work not be distracting to the artists?"

"The more noise and bedlam the better. Like putting a grain of sand in the oyster, I have decided on a new experiment—to see the pearls created amid the distractions. It's been far too quiet in the compound for the past few years."

"Well, I can guarantee that there will be plenty of noise."

Wingate returned to the dining room with coffee. Twenty minutes later, wearing her own shoes, Carley was driving out of the estate, while wondering what she had gotten herself into. She was not absolutely certain that she had the job. But Boris had given her the code to open the gates at will. That, at least, should count for something— unless he decided to change the code.

 *Chapter 4*

When Carley returned home, she noticed that Joie Chang, her grandmother's housekeeper, had come back from visiting her sister in California. There were three fresh bamboo shoots in a vase on the kitchen table, and her breakfast dishes had been washed and put away in the cabinet.

In her will, Gran had specified that Joie could have the free use of the apartment over the carriage house in the back so long as either granddaughter owned the property. Joie was not obligated to do any work in the house, and luckily, Carley was not obligated to pay her, since Joie had her own side business as a *feng shui* consultant with a local real estate company and several of the architectural firms that often worked with Eastern business investors.

But the habit of coming into the house and doing a little cleaning was too ingrained for her to change overnight. Carley just hoped that the woman had not tried to rearrange her current office space for a more auspicious *chi*, which she had done in her bedroom when she was a teenager. She had never really forgiven her for throwing out her psychedelic *Kiss* poster.

During the divorce proceedings, when she had first returned to Gran's house, Carley had chosen a small cubbyhole at the end of the upstairs hallway to serve as her temporary office. With confidence, she had set up her computer, her filing cabinets, and design software — fully expecting that her new telephone number and web site would be extremely busy with prospective clients rushing to hire her. That had not proven to be the case.

She soon realized the truth. It was going to be harder than she thought to start over.

Now, with such a short deadline for the Cavanaugh project, she would have to work around the clock. She was never at a loss for creative ideas, when it came to design. So that didn't bother her. Carley's main concern was in becoming her own contractor and gathering together a reliable work crew to put the plans into action.

Who, among the people that she had worked with before, would be willing to risk working for her, now that she was *persona non grata* with Bob's architectural firm?

She had so little time to assemble a prospective landscape crew for the heavy work. But she knew that she would have to start on that immediately, even before she finished the design or got the final okay.

This was a first— for a client not to be interested in seeing the initial rendering or the estimated cost of the project. Though Boris Cavanaugh had made it clear that he didn't want to be bothered with the details, she knew that he was aware of how tough Goose could be in watching after his interests and seeing to it that costs did not get out of hand.

With Goose, friendships stopped at the checkbook. He might help Carley find a job, but then she was entirely on her own to succeed.

For the setup costs, Carley would have to dip into the insurance money that Gran had left her. She hoped that it would be money well spent.

When she walked into her minuscule office, she closed the blinds against the western sun that was already beginning its penetration through the tree leaves outside the upstairs window and then settled down at her desk.

With one cat, Cho-Cho, perching on the needlepoint work stool at her feet, and Li-Po taking forty winks on the window seat cushion, Carley lost all track of time. It was only later when the grandfather clock downstairs began to chime a number of times that she realized how long she had worked at the computer.

It had grown dark and, aside from the clock, the house was unusually silent. Even the cats had deserted her. She stretched, switched on the overhead light, and turned off the computer graphics.

On the spur of the moment, Carley picked up the telephone to call Joie. If she had not already eaten, she would welcome her back by inviting her to share a sandwich and dessert. Carley also had an ulterior motive.

Fifteen minutes later, Joie was in the kitchen. She had already eaten dinner, but she accepted the invitation for coffee and dessert. So while Carley ate her sandwich, Joie chatted about her trip.

"Ella wants me to move back to California to live with her."

"But you've lived in Mobile for so many years," Carley protested. "Wouldn't you miss all your friends here on the bay? Besides, I was hoping that you would agree to serve as a consultant on my upcoming project."

Joie's expression did not change. "So someone has hired you?"

"I think so. At least, if the plans are approved."

"Then, I suppose there's no hurry in making a decision about moving."

Lydia's sudden death had put Joie in an awkward position. She knew about the will, but she had to make sure that Carley truly wanted her to remain.

Joie listened as Carley began to talk about her plans for a contemplative Oriental garden as one aspect of the overall garden design. But when she told her of the bis pole, Joie frowned.

"This man, Wingate, has no business carving such an ancestral pole," she said. "It's the same as singing a Native American's personal song. You will have to hide it in an inauspicious place."

They sat for another hour, discussing the project. By the time Joie left, it was too late for Carley to telephone anyone. But somehow, she felt that bouncing ideas off Joie had been quite productive. She also knew a lot of gossip.

One of the things she had learned from her was that Jake Fuentes, a valuable member of the landscape crew, had quit working for Bob's firm after falling out with Sherrie. Jake was temperamental, but Carley had always gotten along well with him. She put him at the top of her telephone list for the next day.

Carley had a restful night, but the cats' contented purring woke her long before the sun had come up. For the first time in ages, she felt an eagerness for the day to begin.

She hurriedly went downstairs, opened a can of cat food for the Maltese twins and made some coffee for herself. She didn't even take time to get dressed. Still in her flimsy Versace nightshirt that Morgan had given her for her birthday four years previously, Carley settled down at the computer.

Not long after the chimes downstairs struck the half-hour, Carley called Jake. He was a bear about his sleep, and she didn't want to antagonize him by calling too early. But since he usually left his house at six o'clock, she didn't want to miss him.

"Who's calling at this ungodly hour?" a foggy voice demanded, after the phone had rung a number of times.

"Jake, it's me. Carley. Did I call too early?"

"Sure did."

"Well, shake yourself awake. I need your help."

"Let me get on my trousers, and I'll be right over."

"It's not that kind of emergency, Jake," she assured him. "I'm bidding on a rather large landscape job, and I want to know if you'll be available as the project foreman."

"Who else is bidding on it?"

"I'm the only one, so far. If the plans are approved, then I have the job. But we'd have to start in less than two weeks."

The silence stretched an inordinate length of time. "Are you still there, Jake?"

"I'm thinking."

Finally, he responded. "I was supposed to go to Jackson to help out a friend for the next couple of weeks, but I could put that off 'til later. *If* you get the job," he added.

"I should know something definite by next Thursday."

"Well, call me as soon as you know for sure."

"Thanks, Jake. I really appreciate this."

"Okay." He broke the connection, but Carley didn't mind. His tentative commitment was all that she needed to hear.

She celebrated by slipping on her sweats and taking an extra long jog through the neighborhood.

For the entire weekend she worked, estimating the costs of labor, materials, and equipment for each segment of the plan. She wanted to make the design visually exciting. The detailed drawings could come later, once she had the exact dimensions. For that, she needed the survey. Carley decided to take a chance and get the survey done even before the initial plans were approved.

Shortly before noon on Monday, Carley had enough of the master plan done to present to Goose for his approval. Without taking time to eat lunch, she went to the bank and withdrew funds to put into her meager business account. Then she drove to Goose's office and left the landscape portfolio in Agnes' hands.

She had decided that it would not be good to mix business with hospitality when Goose came to the house for the Wednesday night poker game. It was better to leave the portfolio at his office.

Carley never liked to eat on the run, but she had so little time left to drive to Cavanaugh's place, where she was to meet Ed Burns, the surveyor. So she stopped at a fast food window and ordered a hamburger before getting on the bridge.

By the time she arrived at the turnoff to Cavallegria, Ed

and his Latino helper, Juan, were already waiting by the side of the road.

Short, stout, and freckled from the sun, Ed was a history buff and was quite knowledgeable about Mobile and its surrounding coastal areas.

Carley motioned for Ed to follow her down the narrow sandy road. Before they reached the wrought iron gates, a silver Lexus came barreling down the road in the opposite direction and nearly ran both pickups into the ditch.

Carley recognized the car immediately. "Hell's bells, Sherrie!" she shouted after her. "Are you trying to kill us?"

Her anger soon turned to alarm. What was Sherrie doing on Boris's property? Was she also bidding on the landscape project? If so, how had she heard about it? Carley's spirits sank, and the possibility of losing the contract nagged at her for the rest of the afternoon.

Once the two trucks had driven into the compound, which seemed unusually quiet, and Juan was removing the surveying equipment from the bed of the truck, an interested Ed looked around. "This is certainly a big property," he said.

Carley agreed. "You probably know its entire history, but I haven't been able to discover much about its earliest French settlers."

"Actually, you're not alone. About the only things left of the original settlement are the legends that have been handed down through the years. Even the Mobile Tricentennial Committee has some key pieces missing from its history."

"Then, wouldn't it be wonderful, when we start digging and grading, if we found some really interesting artifacts?"

"Might be better if you didn't. It could delay you for months, with archaeologists crawling all over the place before you could move a single grain of sand."

His comment brought her back to reality. She didn't need any delays. That is, if she actually got the go-ahead on the job.

While Juan and Ed took precise measurements, Carley walked over the property for the second time.

She'd always had a vivid imagination, but standing at water's edge, Carley could visualize the ships of Pierre LeMoyne d'Iberville traveling up the bay to Mobile Landing three hundred years previously.

Mobile was a proud city—with her French and Spanish ancestry and her celebration of Mardi Gras even older than the one in New Orleans. But what a shame that the man who had become governor of the Louisiana Territory, and had done so much for Mobile, had suffered the misfortune of dying of yellow fever in Cuba.

His legacy of trade and culture between Mobile and Havana had lasted for nearly two hundred and fifty years, only to have it come to an abrupt end with Castro's rise to power.

Carley shook her head to clear the past from her thoughts and to focus on the present. But she only saw the specter of the ambitious Sherrie, who loomed like a pelican, intent on filling her pouch from another's lean catch of the day.

 *Chapter 5*

𝓗er grandmother had always told Carley that she possessed a good poker face, but on that next Wednesday night, it was difficult for her to maintain her composure. All the time that she was playing, she was anxiously waiting to learn what Goose had thought of her landscape plans. But she was determined not to bring up the subject with Henry and Edward present.

"Carley, it's your turn. Are you going to raise?" Henry asked.

"Oh, sorry." She forced herself to pay better attention to the game, but the cards had not gone right for her, and she had lost most of her chips.

"Anybody ready for another beer?" she asked.

"Count me in," Edward said.

"The same here," Goose said.

"Me, too," Henry added.

As she got up and reached for the empty beer steins, Goose said, "Here, Carley, let me help you." He took two of the steins and followed her into the kitchen.

He spoke in a low voice. "I might as well tell you the bad news first, Carley."

Goose was deliberately bringing up the subject that she had been so careful to avoid. "You mean, you didn't like my plans? I didn't get the Cavanaugh job?"

"Oh, no. I think your plans are brilliant. Boris will be

quite pleased with them, too, I'm sure. You have the job."

"Then, what's the catch?"

"You won't be the only one working on the property. He's also hired someone else."

Carley stopped pouring the beer into the third stein, and waited for Goose to explain.

"Boris has commissioned a new boathouse and dock to be built at the same time."

"Well, the crew and I can easily work around that. So what's the problem?"

"Your former husband Bob is the architect who designed the boathouse. So you'll be running into him from time to time."

She spilled some of the beer. "How could Boris do this to me?" she wailed. Before Goose could come up with an answer, she suddenly remembered Boris's words about putting the irritating grain of sand in the poor oyster's shell. The artists were not the only ones at his mercy.

"Is this going to make a difference?" Goose asked.

"Of course it is. But I'll just have to find some way of ignoring the *bastardo*," she said, using one of Morgan's favorite words.

"That's my girl, Carley."

"Hey, you two. Where's the beer?" a voice called.

"Coming!" Carley shouted back and hurried into the den with Goose directly behind her.

From that moment on, her life had an urgent purpose, marred only by the possibility of having to deal with her ex-husband on the job. Armed with the survey, she was able to complete the master plan. Jake assembled the work crew, and Carley contacted the heavy equipment firm, Hings and Popple, to set up the rental of the grading machinery. With each subsequent step, she gave a copy of the plans to Goose for his files.

He also became the conduit between C. Burnside, LLC and Bob's architectural firm.

In her overall design, Carley had decided to build a tall observation deck in the shape of an obelisk, so the artists would have a magnificent view of the bay. It would be much like a hidden duck blind, except that the artists would be painting the waterfowl, instead of shooting them.

Because of the structure, she needed to know the siting of the new boathouse and dock, so there would be no mutual encroachment. But she certainly was not going to ask for the plans, herself.

Less than a week before the artists were to arrive and the landscape work was to begin, Carley and Jake Fuentes left Mobile on a rainy Friday morning to visit a wholesale plant nursery in the Florida Panhandle. Carley had always found the best buys and most unusual plants off I-10 at Garden-Gator. Artie Ingle, the owner, also ran an alligator farm next door, hence the name.

Jake had already seen the proposed plant list. Since he had an innate talent in selecting the best plants out of an entire field, Carley always liked to have him along. The two also had that rare rapport that if one saw something that he or she liked better, then neither had a hesitation in switching and reserving that plant, instead.

The moment they came across a particular blood-red plant, they knew that it had happened again. It was an amaranthus caudatus, better known by its common name — *Love-Lies-Bleeding*.

"The plant's perfect, isn't it?" Carley said to Jake. When he nodded, Carley said, "Reserve six gross for us, please."

In her mind, Carley could see the stucco wall beyond Boris's private studio. It would enclose the contemplative garden, using a curved concrete bridge structure, white boulders, a minimum of plant material, and white sand throughout, raked to resemble a meandering stream.

The only other color in the garden, beyond a dark green juniper, would be a small red Japanese maple, and now, as a seasonal blaance, the mass of blood red Love-Lies Bleeding.

True, the garden would demand a daily raking with a fifty-pound rake to keep the neat design in the sand stream, but it would be worth the effort because of its beauty. Carley took pleasure in visualizing the diabolical Boris, himself, doing the work. She suspected, though, that he would delegate that chore to someone else.

At the nursery, Carley noticed that Jake stepped gingerly along the paths and looked as much to the ground as to the plants, but she said nothing. Finally, she could see the relief in his eyes when it was time to get back into the truck and head for home. Their previous experience at Garden-Gator had not been the best. An alligator had crawled through the fence and wandered into the plant nursery. It had been a narrow escape for both of them. That was why Artie had stayed with them on this visit.

On the way back to Mobile, Carley stopped for gas. It was one of those independent stations with a small restaurant attached. She stuck her credit card in the slot and asked Jake to get the receipt after he'd finished pumping the gas.

She then went inside the restaurant and found a table for the two of them, since they were both hungry. She had not realized what attention they would be getting from the other clientele. Jake was extremely swarthy and weathered from working in the sun. His long salt and pepper hair was scraped back in a ponytail, whereas Carley's hair was blonde and loose. They were a decided contrast in both looks and dress. Yet Jake was her friend and fellow worker, and the two had done a super day's work together.

Carley was determined to ignore the stares, but the two did not linger. They finished eating and then, like Willie Nelson, they hit the road again.

 *Chapter 6*

By the time Carley returned home, it was late and she was too tired to drive her truck to the back. Instead, she left it in the driveway and unlocked the side door that led into the mudroom off the kitchen.

All she wanted was to take a quick shower and then crawl into bed. But first, she needed to file the project plant list in her office cubbyhole.

As she turned on the light at the head of the stairs, her heart gave a decided thump. The hallway was bare. Gone were her computer, printer, desk, and filing cabinets. Even her needlepoint footstool was missing. What had happened? Had the house been burglarized while she was gone? Or had Joie been at work in her absence?

She raced into her bedroom — the one she had occupied from the time she was twelve years old until she and Bob had gotten married. At first, it looked as if nothing had been touched. Then, she looked more closely at the furniture. It wasn't hers. It was Gran's.

Retracing her steps down to the first floor, she rushed into Gran's bedroom, which was adjacent to the living room. Her furniture was all there — looking as if it had been sitting there for ages, rather than for the last six hours or so.

Li-Po and Cho-Cho had already made themselves comfortable on the bed. They looked up at her, then closed their eyes and started purring in contentment.

Carley marched to the telephone and rang Joie's number. She certainly had a lot to answer for.

"You're the mistress of the house now," Joie argued. "It would not do for you to remain in your childhood bedroom."

"Well, couldn't you have waited to talk it over with me, instead of moving everything behind my back?"

"I was only following your grandmother's instructions."

"You mean, you would have done this to Morgan, if *she'd* been the one to inherit the house?"

"Morgan would have moved into the master bedroom on her own. She would not have needed my help."

"But why couldn't you have left my office where I had it?"

"Once you had a job, you needed a more auspicious space for success. Besides, it will be much cooler for you downstairs."

"Joie, I'm too tired to go on a search tonight. Just tell me where my office is, so that I can check to make sure everything is hooked up and working."

"It's in that nice little sitting room behind the den. You have a wonderful view of the garden and fountain through the screened porch. It's the best place in your *ba-gua* for wealth and success."

Carley was too beaten down to argue. She left the plant list on the bedroom dresser and stripped while walking to Gran's bath.

Later, when her head finally hit the pillow, she quickly went to sleep.

The next morning, before Carley had even gone into the kitchen to make coffee, she went to check out her office. Actually, the cats raced ahead of her, as if they had prior knowledge. She didn't mean to imply that they had ever exhibited any psychic qualities. They were just being cats — attempting to lead the parade through the house and just missing having their tails stepped on.

The first thing that Carley noticed, while standing at the

threshold of the small sitting room, was Gran's beautiful, red phoenix screen that now occupied the southeast corner of the room. It was balanced at the opposite corner by a cachepot containing the schefflera, her large green plant that evidently had been embezzled from the breakfast room. On one wall, Joie had hung a mirror that reflected her computer from across the room.

All in all, it was a beautifully arranged setting, but Carley still resented Joie's interference in her life. She didn't need to be *feng shui*-ed.

What should have been a leisurely Saturday morning rapidly changed into a hectic, troublesome day. Shortly after her neighborhood run, the grading equipment company called to tell her they could not guarantee their commitment on the days she had reserved their services. Regan, Barnes, and O'Reilly had priority.

She understood immediately. An arm had been twisted by someone in Bob's architectural firm and she had been blacklisted.

Dejectedly, Carley realized that her entire project was at risk. It would be almost impossible to find a replacement this late.

With the economy on the downside for everyone, it had become a cutthroat reality. Small, independent players were not allowed into the game.

Just as she was ready to hang up, the man at the other end of the line lowered his voice and said, "But I might make a suggestion. Confidentially, of course."

"Yes?"

"Some of our equipment was leased to Barnie Overton at Ocean Springs. You might sub-contract with him, since I hear that he's almost finished his project. And he has several more weeks on the rental."

"Do you have his telephone number?"

The man hesitated. Then his voice rose to its original level. "I'm so sorry for the mix-up. But thank you for thinking of us."

Carley was left with nothing but a dial tone. Slowly, it dawned on her. Someone must have come into his office, and the man didn't want to risk losing his job.

Barnie's number proved to be quite elusive. She tried the Coastal Directory, the online Yellow Pages, and the white residential pages. He was not listed in any of them. Completely frustrated, Carley decided to drive to Ocean Springs herself and locate him, since she had so little time to settle the matter.

As she backed her truck onto the street, she noticed that an unfamiliar car was still parked under an old oak farther down the way. Something about that car bothered her. Was it her imagination, or was it the same one that had trailed her on I-10, when she and Jake had gone to the plant wholesaler? Lately, it seemed that almost everywhere she had gone, the same car was not far behind.

Once she had passed it, she looked in her rear view mirror. The gray car pulled out, and the back of her neck began to tingle. To double check that it was following her, Carley suddenly turned onto Old Shell Road and headed for the nearest gasoline station. The same car turned onto Old Shell Road. She was beginning to get paranoid.

After filling her gas tank, Carley decided to return home, rather than getting onto the expressway. If, in fact, someone *were* following her, then she wasn't going to make it easy for him or her.

Fifteen minutes later, from her office, she called her grandmother's former housekeeper.

"Joie, do you have any plans for today that can't be broken?"

"I was going to the grocery store for tofu. But that's about all. Why?"

"I've decided, on the spur of the moment, to go to Ocean Springs. And I was hoping that you'd go with me."

Joie hesitated. "I don't know..."

"We could stop for a nice lunch on the way," Carley offered as an incentive.

It did not take Joie long to make up her mind. "So when would you like to leave?"

"As soon as you can get ready."

"Give me about twenty minutes, then. I'll meet you by your truck."

Carley nervously cleared her throat. "Actually... actually I thought we might go in Gran's car, and you could drive."

After a few seconds of silence, Joie said, "What's going on, Carley? What's wrong?"

"Don't think that I'm losing my mind, Joie. But I'm almost certain someone has been following me for more than a week."

"Are you talking about that gray car down the block? The one that doesn't belong to anybody on the street?"

So she had noticed it, too. That gave Carley some comfort as to her mental health, although the idea was disturbing.

"That's the one. Is it back?"

"Let me look out the window." Joie, from the upper level of the carriage house, had a better view of that part of the street. "Yes, it's parked there again."

Carley had no idea why anyone might be stalking her, but she needed to be careful, nevertheless.

Talking with Joie, she felt as if the two were co-conspirators, devising an elaborate plan to elude a possible danger. Before she hung up though, she knew that she would have to make a stab at an apology for her previous night's behavior.

"By the way, Joie. You did a great job with my office. So I forgive you."

Shortly thereafter, she slipped into the garden and then hid in the back seat of Gran's vintage black Cadillac. Joie backed the car out of the carriage house. Carley barely saw her red Toyota truck as Joie moved down the driveway and, with a bump, pulled onto the street.

"Is the gray car following us?" she asked.

"I don't see it."

Later, when they were on the expressway, and Carley had taken over the driving, she congratulated herself for having eluded whoever might be following. Unfortunately, she did not see the other car, which had begun its steady surveillance only several hundred yards behind Gran's Cadillac.

 *Chapter 7*

Sherrie Rushton had always been jealous of Carley Burnside—of her looks, her talent, and especially of her manner that caused all the doyennes of society to fall all over themselves to entertain for her the year that she had been a debutante, along with her twin, Morgan.

But Sherrie was getting back at her at every turn, now that she had inherited enough money. The first thing she had done was to have the best plastic surgeon in New Orleans reshape her face—to straighten her nose and give her a better chin. She had actually taken a picture of Carley to him and said, "I want to look like this."

Then, she had lightened her mousy brown hair to a shade that was remarkably similar to Carley's. She didn't care that it was expensive to maintain. The liposuction had done wonders, also.

For the past two years, she had worked hard at Regan, Barnes, and O'Reilly to undermine Carley's work and to prop up Bob's ego.

Both had paid off spectacularly. She now had Carley's job and was married to her former husband. Sherrie should have been exquisitely happy, but something still nagged at her. Carley, just like those two cats, seemed to have landed on her feet again. That's what made it all so unsettling. When she'd heard that Carley had gotten the landscape job at Cavallegria, she had gone to Boris to ask him to reconsider and let her have the job, instead. But he had brushed her off as if she were a carrier of West Nile virus. They would both be sorry, that was for sure.

The P.I. that she had hired to follow Carley was an unsavory character, willing to do almost anything, if the price were right. He would do what it took to keep her from even starting the project. Of course, it would have to be short of murder. Sherrie couldn't condone murder. After all, she still had certain principles.

Unaware that they were still being followed, Joie and Carley continued along the highway toward Ocean Springs, until it was time to stop for lunch. They looked for their favorite place, but when they reached the restaurant, it was closed for renovations. So Carley kept driving. Several miles farther, she saw a sign reading *Giverney's.*

"What about that one?" Carley asked, pointing to the French restaurant.

"I was hoping for some good seafood," a hesitant Joie said. "I'm not in the mood for heavy sauces today."

"Neither am I," Carley agreed. "At least, we can take a look at the menu. If it doesn't suit us, then we'll drive on."

As she turned into the driveway, Joie said, "It has a well-placed front door."

Carley smiled. From Joie's comment, she knew that the restaurant had passed inspection.

The menu also passed inspection, and soon they were sitting at a pristine white, linen-covered table and enjoying a wonderful meal of seafood, spinach salad and, finally, a melt-in-your-mouth gateau.

It was as if the stress of the morning had never existed. The slower pace, combined with the low-key atmosphere of the restaurant and the casual conversation, served to banish any hint of danger.

"Wasn't this a wonderful meal?" Carley exclaimed, after she'd scooped up the last little cake crumb.

"Yes, I'm so glad we stopped here."

"Even though we've lingered far longer than I'd planned. We'll have to hurry to make up for lost time." Carley signaled for their waitress. "May we have our check, please?"

"Oh, it's already been taken care of."

"There must be some mistake."

"No. The gentleman who was seated at the far window table paid for your lunches. With a nice tip, too."

Carley turned her head to acknowledge the stranger who had been so generous, but the table was empty.

"What did he look like?" she asked. "Young? Old?"

"Fortyish, I'd say. Nicely dressed, but in rather a hurry. He only ordered a bowl of soup."

"Well, thank you very much. Everything was delicious."

"Come again," the waitress urged.

Rocky Donovan sat in his car across the street and waited for the Cadillac to pull out of the restaurant parking area. He was rather enjoying himself, at Sherrie's expense.

He had sent her the bill for his new clothes, and now she would also get the restaurant tab for Carley Burnside and the Oriental woman that she was with. Rocky was sorry that he hadn't ordered a steak, but it would have taken too much time. He'd make up for it later.

He loosened his tie and congratulated himself on putting a bug on the old Cadillac, as well as the truck. This Carley Burnside was a slippery one, thinking that she could bamboozle him by switching vehicles.

Of course, that meant that, somewhere along the way, she must have suspected that she was being followed. But that made the game even more fun. For him, a little fear on the part of an attractive woman always upped the excitement of the stalking.

Once they started out on the highway again, Carley and Joie were both silent for a number of miles. The festive mood in the restaurant had not come with them. Carley was thinking of how she could find Barnie. Who would know how to get in touch with the man?

"So what do you *really* plan to do in Ocean Springs?" Joie finally asked.

There was no need to dissemble. She could never hide anything from Joie. "I have to find a man—Barnie Overton. If I want to stay on schedule, or even begin the Cavanaugh project, he's the only one who can help me."

Carley proceeded to tell her about the problem with the grading equipment. Once she had finished, Joie said, "I'm not surprised. Bob was always a jealous husband."

Carley immediately challenged her comment. "You must be mistaken, Joie. As many times as I had to work late with other men, he never seemed to mind."

"I'm not talking about that kind of jealousy. I'm referring to professional jealousy. Just think back. How many awards did you receive, while working with the firm?"

"Oh, seven or eight."

"And how many did Bob receive?"

"The architectural firm received a number of..."

Joie interrupted. "That didn't count with him. He wanted to be recognized individually. And he soon felt in direct competition with you."

"But we were a team," Carley protested. "He helped to design the buildings; I designed the grounds."

"It was a shame that he didn't see it that way. And I'll tell you something else. The main reason he married Sherrie, besides her flagrant chasing after him, was that she will never be any more than just adequate in her job. So he won't ever feel threatened."

Carley couldn't believe what Joie had just said. It was a completely new idea for her to mull over.

"Your grandmother and I talked about it a number of times. We were both surprised that the marriage lasted as long as it did."

Carley didn't want to discuss her failed marriage with Joie. She turned her attention to the highway and watched for the turn-off to Ocean Springs.

Known as Old Biloxi, Ocean Springs had alternated with Mobile and New Orleans as the capital of the Louisiana Territory in the early days when d'Iberville first landed. As she traveled along the route, Carley began to think of the cassette girls, or dowry-chest girls, who had been sent from France to marry complete strangers. How had their marriages fared? Any better than hers? And how far up the coast had they sailed?

She mulled over her earlier conversation with Ed, the surveyor. Despite his caution, she was still hoping to find an artifact or two from those earlier days on Cavanaugh's property. It certainly was not out of the question.

Stopping first at the Visitor's Center, located in the old L&N Depot, Carley was relying on her experience with other coastal towns, where longtime residents knew almost everybody and how to reach them.

But when she asked about Barnie, the elderly volunteer, who was staffing the information desk, said, "Oh, you won't find him around here. Strange, but somebody else came in a few minutes ago, talking about him. Said he was over on Horn Island this week, working at the Preserve."

Disconcerted at the news, Carley said, "I really need to see him as soon as possible."

"Then, why don't you go over to the National Seashore Office on Park Road? They have chartered boats to the barrier isles from time to time. If you're lucky, you might get a seat on one of them."

Carley followed the man's suggestion, but she was not lucky.

"The next Horn Island boat won't leave until Monday. But we still have tickets for Ship Island," she was told.

Carley knew that Ship Island was always a favorite with tourists because of Fort Massachusetts, an important masonry fortification of the Civil War. But she had no desire to visit that deep channel island. It was Horn Island she was intent on.

Seeing her disappointment, the woman at the desk said,

"If it's urgent for you to get to Horn Island this weekend, you might check at the Walter Anderson Museum to see if they have any tickets left for Sunday's excursion."

"What's the connection with the museum?" Carley asked.

"Horn Island was where Anderson isolated himself when he was having his mental problems. Off and on for years, he painted almost every bird and animal on the island. Lots of people are just plain curious to see if they can recognize the landscape he used in his paintings."

On the way out, Carley grabbed a bunch of brochures from a kiosk near the door. Once she and Joie were back in the car, Carley said, "We have to stay through tomorrow."

"But we didn't even bring a toothbrush," Joie protested. "And what about the cats?"

She answered the second question first. "I left plenty of water and food to last another day. And we could go to the drugstore to buy toothbrushes."

She handed the brochures to Joie. "See if you can find a hotel or motel where we can stay for the night."

"Don't you think you'd better go to the museum first?"

"You mean to see if any tickets are left?"

"Yes."

"I'm on my way."

Carley found Washington Avenue and the parking lot of the museum. "Okay. Let's go in. Keep your fingers crossed, Joie."

She always felt an aura of excitement every time she stepped inside an art museum. That Saturday afternoon was no different. Carley was immediately surrounded by vivid colors of plants and animals calling for attention from the large canvases on the walls.

She asked at the front desk about the boat tour, and the docent directed her to the gift shop. Walking down the hallway, strung with Anderson's magnificent paintings that held a vague likeness to some of the early Australian aboriginal art, Carley was so interested in them that she almost bumped into a man standing by the display case at the gift shop entrance.

"Sorry," she said and veered to the right. The man walked on, making no acknowledgment of her apology.

When she went inside to inquire about the Horn Island excursion tickets, the woman in charge shook her head.

"I'm afraid that we have only one ticket left. If you had come in only five minutes ago—"

Disappointed, Carley looked at Joie.

"Go on, Carley. Buy the ticket. I'll find something else to do tomorrow."

"Are you sure?"

"Yes. Actually, I get a little seasick, so I'll have a better time on land, browsing in the shops and galleries. And maybe I'll come back to spend some time here. There's some interesting pottery I glimpsed when we first came in."

With Joie's blessing, Carley purchased the last ticket.

They didn't linger, since they needed to find a room for the night. Returning to the car, Carley said, "Do you see a suitable hotel in any of the brochures?"

"This bed-and-breakfast looks nice," Joie replied, pointing to a picture in one of the ads. "And it evidently faces the water."

"What's the telephone number?"

Carley pulled out her cell phone and dialed, as Joie called out the numbers. There was no vacancy.

"Okay," she said, "select another one."

The second bed-and-breakfast had a vacancy. Carley immediately reserved a double room for that night, even though the quoted price was rather exorbitant. But with such a busy coastal resort for boaters, golfers, and gamblers, she felt lucky to have found *any* place to stay on such short notice.

 *Chapter 8*

*T*he grandfather clock in the Victorian vestibule of the *Golden Crane* chimed five o'clock by the time Carley and Joie arrived with their small cache of purchases.

One of the first things they had noticed from the parking lot was the metal weathervane atop the cupola of the white, two-story house. It was in the shape of a crane and, as a gentle breeze from the Gulf pushed it back and forth, the weathervane reflected the golden glint of the afternoon sun. So it was aptly named.

Once Carley had registered for the night, Agatha Sommers, the slightly plump but pleasant owner, handed her an old-fashioned, oversized metal room key.

"I'm sorry that all the rooms with a view of the water are taken," she apologized, "but you have a nice garden view. Some people actually prefer being on that side."

"I'm sure the room will be quite nice," Carley reassured her.

"Just go up the steps, turn left, and your room is the second one on the left. Once you've freshened up, do come downstairs to join the other guests for a glass of wine in the common room. We'll be gathering at six."

Joie looked at Carley as they climbed the steps. "I'm not much for socializing, are you?"

"No. I'd rather take a shower and then find some place to eat dinner," Carley replied.

"Sounds good to me," Joie agreed.

The room was spacious enough, with two beds, a private bath, and French doors leading to the upper porch overlooking the flower garden. Carley had never shared a room with Joie before, and she was hoping that the woman was a quiet sleeper.

It didn't take long for Carley to shower away the heat and stress of the busy summer day. While she waited for Joie to do the same, she dug into her purse, found her compact and powdered her nose. With a little lip-gloss and a quick comb-through of her hair, she was ready.

Her one regret was that she would have to wear the same clothes she'd worn all day, but she'd seen no need to splurge and buy another outfit that humid afternoon.

It had been far more important to purchase sunscreen, water, and bug repellent for the boat trip. Her navy linen blazer, white shell, and slacks would just have to do for the next twenty-four hours.

Judging from the sounds emanating from below, the social hour had begun promptly. Acting as if they were two fugitives, Carley and Joie shut the bedroom door, locked it, and tiptoed down the stairs. They had almost made their getaway, when Agatha spotted them. "Oh, there you are. Do come in and meet some of the other guests."

Her grandmother's upbringing took over, forcing Carley to smile and enter the crowded room. Mrs. Sommers's hand on her arm was also a deciding factor that kept her from running in the opposite direction. Joie had no recourse but to follow.

When introductions began, Carley became overly cautious. However remote the possibility that someone might connect her to the real reason for being in Ocean Springs, or her proposed trip to Horn Island, she was determined to remain deliberately vague. She immediately introduced Joie as a *feng shui* expert, effectively transferring attention to Joie.

From the safety of a tall palm near a window, Carley watched while Joie fielded a number of questions by several of the interested women gathered around her. Their elderly husbands looked on with an amused air.

Ten minutes later, Agatha, however, found her. "Come and have another glass of wine," she urged.

Carley, looking at her watch, politely declined. It was time to rescue Joie. Quietly, she approached the circle and said, "I'm sorry to break into the conversation, Joie, but our dinner reservations won't wait."

"Oh, I didn't realize that it was so late."

Carley took their two wine glasses, set them on a silver tray, and then smiled at the adoring group as she guided Joie out the door.

"You owe me one," Joie seethed in a low voice.

A car had parked so closely to Gran's oversized Cadillac that it was difficult for Carley to maneuver out of the space. She had to try twice, before she was successful.

"That driver parks like my sister Ella," Joie commented. "Lines don't mean much to her, either."

The *Sea Horse* was crowded and had a completely different ambiance from the restaurant where they had stopped for lunch. The tables were too close together, and the smoke from the lounge had already permeated the nonsmoking section.

But the signs on the walls were amusing, and reading them helped to pass the time until the waitress brought their food to the table.

"I think I've seen that sign before," Carley commented. *Unattended children will be used for bait.*

To Carley, it was interesting how a mere sign could suddenly short-circuit the brain. It was even more interesting to see how Joie had picked up on her thoughts.

"How is Cristina?"

Carley sighed. "From her last letter, she doesn't sound very happy. She said her mother is talking about putting her in a boarding school in Switzerland for the fall."

"Why would Morgan do that?"

"I suppose because of renovating her new property. It's an old millhouse and needs a lot of work."

The stuffed Shiitake mushrooms came, interrupting their conversation. They did not revisit the subject of Cristina until much later in the evening, when they were sitting in rocking chairs on the upstairs porch of the *Golden Crane*.

Rocky Donovan had sat in a secluded corner of the garden, waiting for it to get dark. The damned mosquitoes were giving him a fit, and he was certainly going to charge Sherrie overtime on this one. But he had kept his eyes open, observing the comings and goings. Seeing the maids arrive, he made his move.

He had already discovered the room number where Carley Burnside and Joie Chang were staying. It helped to have the eavesdropping equipment with him. Now, all he had to do, while the maid was inside, replenishing the linens, was to slip the sticky tape into the doorjamb, so it wouldn't lock properly. That way, he could get inside the room after she had made her rounds. He was relying on the two occupants not returning until he had finished.

He strolled into the house, as if he were a guest, walked up the steps to the second floor, and down the hallway. He nodded to the maid, who was already unlocking the first door on the left. Then later, when she had entered Carley Burnside's room, Rocky returned. He had just slapped on the transparent tape, when the maid suddenly reappeared from the bath. She looked at him with a frown.

Thinking fast, Rocky said, "I'm going out for a while, but would you please put an extra bar of soap in 210? My wife is a little picky."

She didn't seem to understand. So he pointed to a bar of soap on her cart and then to the room several doors away.

The maid brightened and nodded her head.

"*Gracias,*" he said, and pulled out a bill from his pocket, causing her to give him a big smile.

Later, after the maids had gone, he removed the two

boxes of saltwater taffy from the cooler in his car, and retraced his steps. The cooler had been a good idea, since the taffy would have melted from the heat. Once inside, he found the upstairs hallway deserted. Everyone seemed to be out to dinner.

Rocky worked quickly, finished his task, removed the tape from the doorjamb, and turned the inside lock, shutting the door behind him. Now, he could go out and celebrate with a big steak. His work was done for the night.

When Carley and Joie returned to the *Golden Crane*, the other car was gone, so Carley had a much easier time parking Gran's car. When she and Joie reentered the vestibule, Agatha looked up from the desk and smiled her approval. They had been considerate guests, arriving before the midnight curfew, when the front door would be locked for the night.

In their absence, a maid had put fresh towels in the bath and turned down the coverlets on the beds. As a bonus, she had evidently left a small box of saltwater taffy on each bed.

Since Carley didn't care for taffy, one of the few sweets that she didn't like, she gave hers to Joie, who put the extra box in the drawer of the nightstand, to eat the next day.

Later, with her rinsed out underwear hanging in the bath, and a rather large terrycloth robe, that she'd found in the closet, wrapped around her, Carley sat on the dark, deserted porch with Joie. Below, in the garden, the steady sound of a mosquito zapper vied with the croaking of tree frogs to entertain them, while Joie sampled the saltwater taffy.

With her thoughts returning to Cristina, Carley confided, "I have a small problem, Joie."

"Tell me if I'm right," Joie said. "You're still thinking about Cristina. And instead of boarding school, she'd rather come back to Mobile and stay with you for this coming school year."

"How did you guess? Or are you psychic?"

"No. Just observant."

"Then, you realize my dilemma. I dearly love Christina, and I don't want her to be unhappy."

"The responsibility for the child is not yours, Carley. Even if you're willing to take it on. It's up to Morgan to decide on her education."

"I suppose you're right."

A pesky mosquito buzzing about their heads diverted their conversation.

"The zapper in the garden doesn't seem to be working," Joie commented, slapping at the insect on its second reconnaissance around their chairs.

With that observation, they both agreed to go inside. Carley latched the French doors behind them and, under the light of the bedside lamp, she glanced at her watch."Gosh! I didn't realize that it was this late. It's well after midnight."

"So, we'd better get on to bed. You're going to have a long day tomorrow."

Soon they were in their separate beds, with only the small nightstand between them. Joie immediately went to sleep. Carley could tell by her soft breathing. But she remained awake for another hour, puzzling over the feeling of being watched at the seafood restaurant. Each time she'd looked up, a dangerously handsome stranger, seated at a nearby table, had quickly averted his eyes, as if he did not want to be caught staring.

Then, there was the other one, a much older man, dressed in a seersucker suit. He'd come into the restaurant, scanned the tables, lingering on theirs, and then, just as quickly, disappeared. From a distance, he'd resembled Henry Wetherbee, except that he was bald.

Almost everyone knew that Henry wore a toupee. Since she had never seen him without it, Carley couldn't be absolutely certain that it was Henry. Besides, what would one of Gran's poker buddies be doing in Ocean Springs, Mississippi on that particular night?

Carley finally decided that she had been mistaken. She

was glad that she had said nothing to Joie at the time. Henry would have given some sign of recognition, instead of hurrying out of the restaurant as if he didn't want to be seen.

She finally drifted off to a fitful, disturbing sleep. All through the night, Carley dreamed bizarre dreams of Henry and the other poker players. Edward had taken over Henry's toupee, and rather than being at Gran's house, they were all marooned on a gambling casino boat in the Sound, while the piercing eyes of a stranger looked on. For Carley, it was a long, troubled night.

 *Chapter 9*

By eight o'clock the next morning, Carley was up and ready to face the day. Because of the high humidity, her underwear was still damp. Luckily, she was able to blow dry it with the hair dryer, yet another luxury of the *Golden Crane.*

While she was dressing, Joie went downstairs to bring up their breakfast tray of juice, Danish, and coffee. Carley didn't have much time, since she needed to get to the docks by 9:00.

"Now, you're sure you'll be all right for the day?" she asked Joie.

"Oh, yes. I saw a little Episcopal church around the corner. I might go to the services this morning. One thing for sure, I'll find a nice place for lunch, and then I'll shop for the afternoon. You remember that Oriental store that we passed on the way here?"

Carley nodded. "I caught only a glance, but the window display looked interesting."

"It was Chang Antiques." Joie smiled in amusement. "Who knows? I might even find a relative today."

They finished their breakfast and soon it was time to get to the dock.

When they arrived, the dock, flanked by an avenue of palm trees, was particularly crowded. Boats of every kind were visible almost as far as the eye could see—offshore gambling casino boats, permanently anchored in the Sound, as well as fishing boats, yachts, catamarans, and, of course, the tourist boats.

Looking out at the Gulf, Carley felt its soothing influence. She loved the different shades of blue, the variations of light and dark, indicating where the sandbars and reefs were. Even though people had told her that water has no color, that it is really the reflection of the sky, that fact did not lessen her appreciation for its beauty.

Rocky swore when he saw an apparently healthy Carley arrive at the dock. She evidently had not eaten any of the candy. Otherwise, she'd be too sick for the trip. Sherrie had been wrong about the sweets.

He would have to think of some other way to keep Carley from Barnie and the equipment she needed. Besides having no boat ticket, he'd had enough of mosquitoes and alligators to last a lifetime. He narrowed his eyes, searching the crowd queuing up for the boat to Horn Island.

His gaze stopped on three young men with backpacks. He pulled out his wallet and approached the shabbiest looking one....

At first, with so many boats, Carley wondered if she would ever find the correct one. Then, she saw the colorful placard, indicating the line to the museum excursion. She turned around and waved to Joie, who was standing by Gran's car. Joie returned her wave and then got back into the Cadillac.

On the boat, *The Flying Pelican,* there was a combination of young and old, in every style of dress. Some were foreign tourists; others were art students, Carley soon discovered. The young man she sat beside on deck, a Gary Massey, was on holiday from an art institute in Florida. Dressed in Dockers shorts, a faded blue denim shirt, and hiking boots, he looked to be in his twenties, had a short beard, two rings in his right eyebrow, and wore a weathered backpack that held his bottled water, mosquito repellent, and other supplies.

"We went to the large museums in Europe last year," he commented, pointing to his two friends, Drew and Nobby, a short distance away. "This year, we decided we would stay in America and visit the regional ones."

"It's a great deal of fun, isn't it?' Carley commented. "I did much the same thing one summer when I was still in school. But I was visiting West Coast gardens, instead—all the way to the Butchart Gardens in Canada."

"Are you going to camp out overnight?" Gary asked.

"You mean, on Horn Island?"

"Yes."

"Oh, no. I'm just going over for the day. What about you?"

"We're planning on staying for several days and doing a little sketching."

The tour guide began her talk, with the megaphone sound reverberating across the water. It was impossible to carry on a personal conversation, so most of the group became quiet and began to listen.

"When Walter Anderson, the artist, wanted to escape from civilization, he would get into his skiff and row the twelve miles to Horn Island, with his paints, his gun, and his fishing pole— "

Carley found the talk fascinating and began to wonder why so many brilliant minds become so troubled, when they're surrounded by the stresses of society. But did that not happen to most people at sometime in their lives—this need to get away to their own Walden Pond? It was too bad that a wilderness area was not a mere three miles from home, as it was in Thoreau's day. Running away, now-a-days, Carley decided, took a lot of planning.

Yet, the one-hundred-and-fifty-mile stretch of barrier isles along the Gulf was perfect for a present day escape into the wilderness, especially on Horn Island, with such varied vegetation—from the sandy beaches where one could fish, to the inlands ponds, lagoons, and tidal marshes that served as nurseries and breeding grounds for rare and endangered species. Of course, there were hazards too—mosquitoes, as well as cottonmouths and alligators.

It did not take long to arrive on the island that had gotten its name because of a lost powder horn in earlier days. As far as Carley could see, there was nothing but white sand, sprinkled with stands of sea oats and pieces of driftwood strewn about.

She had not realized how desolate the island would look, and she began to wonder what sort of work Barnie had been hired to do in this wildlife refuge.

As the passengers disembarked from the boat, they were given instructions and choices—to explore on their own, or follow a guided tour. A lunch would be served onboard at noon, and for those who wished to return to the mainland, they would have to be at the dock promptly at four o'clock.

Carley's main goal, of course, was to locate Barnie. So, armed with a map of the island, she struck off on her own. She chose a sandy path that wound along the beach and then turned inland past saw palmettos and slash pines.

"Hey, Carley! Hold on!" Gary called.

Surprised, she stopped and waited for the three students to catch up with her.

"You want to join forces for the rest of the day?" Gary asked.

Carley was not the bravest woman in the world, especially around snakes and alligators. In the short time of being on the island, she had discovered that she would have to be careful, also, to avoid the spiny cactus and stickers that impeded her path.

"Why not?" she said. "But sometime during the day, I need to find a man who's working at the Preserve."

"No problem. We'll just select a camping site, unload, and then be off to explore."

Carley waited for the three to complete their setup not too far from one of the scrub trees about fifteen yards inside the campsite on the windward side of the island. A few minutes later, when they returned, Gary held out two leather leg protectors, much like the old puttees of World War I vintage.

"Here, snap these around your ankles. You wouldn't want a snake to crawl up your pants legs."

She accepted them with thanks.

"Now, let's go and find *the man*," one of the other students said, acting as if they were all off on a great adventure.

"What does he look like?" Drew asked.

"I have no idea," Carley replied.

Barnie proved elusive. Carley did find a work site and some grading equipment, but no Barnie. That was probably too much to expect. After all, it was a Sunday morning, and even the rustic Ranger Station was closed. However, Carley *did* leave a note pinned to the bulletin board hanging on the sheltered porch of the station.

They explored the island, with the art students stopping from time to time to capture a quick camera angle of unusual scenery—a white pelican, an American kestrel, a twisted slash pine, a slender-leafed Clammy Weed.

They bumped into other tourists with cameras, acknowledged their presence with a smile, and then walked on, occasionally dodging a snake sunning itself on the path. All during that time, Carley searched for some sign of Barnie.

At intervals, the four stopped to spray themselves with insect repellent and to drink from their water bottles. It was dreadfully hot and humid, and Carley had early on taken off her linen blazer and draped around her waist. Even her T-shirt was wet with perspiration, and her underwear that she had so carefully dried that morning was damp again. Also, she could feel the wisps of her hair curling, as tree leaves do during a long drought.

By noon, she was glad to get back to the excursion boat, with its striped awning a protection from the direct rays of the sun. The long walk had made her both hungry and thirsty. She checked with the boat captain, but Barnie had made no contact with him during the time that Carley had been searching.

After lunch, she parted ways with the three students. She had only a couple of hours left to find Barnie, and although they meant well, Gary and the other two had slowed her in her search. She suspected that she had hampered them, as well.

Later, when Carley retraced her steps to the porch of the closed Ranger Station and studied the bulletin board, she found that Barnie had seen her message and left a reply.

She was elated that she had finally made a connection. His note gave her directions to a crew bungalow where he was staying. It seemed to be quite a distance, almost on the opposite side of the island. She glanced at her watch and then began the trek inland.

As she trudged along even more rugged landscape, she was sorry that she had given back the leg protectors to Gary. She was also worried about the distance.

Carley soon stepped into a bog, ruining her shoes. But that was the least of her worries. The marshy area was large, and it took her a long time to find her way around it and get to more solid ground.

She kept walking. By the time she finally reached the site marked on the map, she could see no bungalow, or building whatever. Only the keel of an old rotting boat was barely visible through the overgrown tangle of vines. Her heart plummeted. The entire episode had turned into a wild goose chase. Surely, Barnie had no cause to deceive her. But if not Barnie, then who had found her note and written a bogus reply?

Reversing directions, she began to unravel her way toward the dock and the boat. But it didn't help when halfway back, she was suddenly faced in a standoff with an unusually large, scaly alligator. It was companion to the one on the museum wall, with its rainbow scales catching the glint of the afternoon sun. Only, this was no painting. This particular alligator was the real thing. The makeshift walking stick that she had picked up on the trail was no match for such a behemoth.

The alligator blocked the narrow pathway, with the waters of the marsh on both sides. It would be futile to attempt to get past while the reptile remained where he was. She also didn't want to do anything to antagonize him.

Carley tried to remember Artie's advice at Garden-Gator. She froze and waited for the monster to make the first move. After a number of minutes that felt like eons, the alligator finally disappeared into the marsh grass. Waiting awhile longer, to make sure that he had really gone, Carley then began to jog down the trail.

Shortly thereafter, a high-pitched sound of warning bells penetrated the island. Carley glanced down at her watch. "Oh, no," she croaked, loud enough for the Great Blue heron in the nearby tree to be startled and take flight. How could it be four o'clock already? Not only had she missed Barnie, she was also in danger of being left behind by *The Flying Pelican*. She picked up speed — forgetting what might be lying across her path.

But when she finally arrived at the pier, hot, exhausted, and sweaty, the Sunday excursion boat to the mainland was already disappearing over the horizon.

Chapter 10

"Well, guys, do you have room for another camper?"

"Carley! What happened? You miss the boat?" a surprised Gary asked.

"In more ways than you can imagine."

As soon as they indicated a space for her on one of the spread out sleeping bags, she plopped down, and then proceeded to tell the three the trick that had been played on her after they had parted ways earlier.

The sun was beginning to set, making a picturesque post card of the barrier isle. Smoke from the camp cooking fire rose upward and was then cast aside by the prevailing wind, as Gary, Drew, and Nobby continued to roast their hot dogs, suspended on long green sticks.

The juice dripping onto the open flames sizzled and gave off a wonderful aroma that vied with other campfire odors at the wilderness site. Carley tried to suppress the rumbling of her empty stomach, but she was not successful.

Nobby, who seemed unusually subdued, took a bun, deftly slid his cooked dog off the stick onto the bun, and said, "Here, Carley. Take this one."

"Oh, Nobby, I couldn't. Thank you anyway."

"I insist. And there's mustard and ketchup over there," he said, indicating a makeshift table made from driftwood not far from their sleeping bags.

"So, tell us the rest of the story," Drew said.

"Well, it's not a total disaster," Carley replied, while

spreading mustard and ketchup on her hot dog bun. "About forty-five minutes after the boat disappeared, and I was sitting on the beach and trying to decide my next move, a rusty old barge chugged into sight and dropped anchor."

Nobby, listening intently, began to roast another hot dog.

Carley suddenly smiled. "You'd never guess who was on it." She didn't wait for an answer. "The very man I had come to find. I have a ride back with him to the mainland tomorrow morning, along with the grading equipment. That was lucky, wasn't it?"

The three agreed.

"My only problem, besides being stranded here for the night, is that the friend who's waiting for me is probably frantic, since I didn't come back on the excursion boat."

"Didn't the barge have some sort of communication, ship to shore?" Gary asked.

"It didn't work," Carley replied, not wanting to go into every little detail. Neither did she tell the students that she had been invited to sleep on the barge that night with Barnie and the grungy looking captain. She had felt that she would be safer in the wilderness camp.

But she *had* negotiated with Barnie on the sublease of the equipment. Since he had finished at the Preserve, he had even agreed to do the grading on the Cavanaugh project.

Barnie Overton paced up and down on the deck of the old barge. He had come up empty handed. The island was entirely too large to excavate the entire fourteen miles. Because he knew that the smugglers had been forced to bury their treasure so hurriedly, Barnie had bid extremely low on the Preserve project, to dredge the lake and clear the rampant vegetation that was threatening to overrun some of the nursery ponds.

Unfortunately, the Ranger had become suspicious, and once he had finished the contracted part of the work, the Ranger had given him an ultimatum to get the equipment off the island by that Monday morning.

He'd already heard talk about Carley Burnside—that maybe she had inherited something even more valuable than her grandmother's house. Maybe a map.

At first, seeing the woman on the beach, and thinking that she was after the treasure too, he'd become alarmed. But it was only the equipment she was interested in. Still, she would bear watching. What better way to do that than to work side by side with her at *Cavallegria*? The smugglers would be getting paroled soon, so time was running out to find the treasure by himself. At the moment, his best bet was sticking close to Carley Burnside. Perhaps, this time, his luck would change.

Much later that night, after Carley had crawled into the sleeping bag that Gary had loaned her, a slight snoring from one of the students vied with the bellowing of a prowling bull alligator in the marsh. Then, when she heard someone approaching, she sat up immediately.

"Carley, are you asleep?"

"Nobby?"

"Yeah," he whispered. "I want you to know how sorry I am about the way things turned out today."

"It couldn't be helped, Nobby. So no harm's done."

"No. It *could* be helped. You see, it was my fault."

"What do you mean?"

"Some guy came up to me and offered a hundred dollars to keep an eye on you and make sure you didn't find the man you'd come to see. *I* was the one who wrote the bogus note that caused you to miss your ride back to the mainland."

"Oh, Nobby. How could you?"

"I just thought it was a harmless thing for a quick buck or two..."

"...And students don't ever have much money," she finished for him.

"The man said he was a friend, paying you back for a practical joke on him. And I really didn't see any harm in going along with the game."

"I'm glad you told me, Nobby. But I'm curious. What did he look like?"

"He was in his forties, maybe. Medium height and weight. Nothing much distinctive about him. He was wearing dark glasses, so I couldn't see the color of his eyes."

"Where did you meet him?"

"At the dock. Before we got on the boat."

"Did he get on the boat, too?"

"No. He just pointed you out and then left."

So Carley had not been paranoid after all, feeling that someone had been following her. Who could it be? And how had the man known that she was looking for Barnie?

The entire episode made her uneasy, but she was so tired after not getting a good night's sleep the previous night, that she told Nobby to forget it and, within a few minutes, she drifted off, despite the lumpy, hard ground. She didn't wake again until the sun erupted through the trees with startling shards of light.

By the time Carley met Barnie, who had already seen to the loading of the equipment onto the barge, she felt completely unkempt. It hadn't helped, scuttling around to find a safe place to pee amid the flora and fauna. Her clothes were dirty and wrinkled, and her only effort at improving her appearance was a quick rake through of her hair with her fingers.

Nodding a good morning, Barnie was kind enough not to mention her disheveled appearance.

"Ready to go?" he asked.

"Ready," she replied.

Carley had never ridden on a flat-bottomed barge before. It really wasn't that bad, except that it was so slow and cumbersome. She had been warned to stay safely away from the machinery, in case the cables snapped. So she held on to the railing and watched for some evidence of the shoreline.

When they were approximately halfway to Ocean Springs, she saw a small motorboat speeding toward them, with one passenger. As it approached on the port side, she began to wave frantically. "Henry! Henry Wetherbee!"

Henry looked back, and Carley didn't know who was more startled at seeing the other. He suddenly stood in the small boat, and then realizing his mistake, he just as suddenly sat down again. Soon, the boat veered, changing course. Avoiding the wake of the heavier vessel, the boat began to follow the barge.

Not returning to the same dock where Carley had taken the excursion boat, the barge dropped anchor, instead, farther down the cove in a more commercial area.

By the time Carley had said her good-byes to Barnie, Henry was already waiting on land. "My God, Carley! What happened to you? We've all been frantic."

"It's a long story, Henry. But how did you know where I was? Did Joie call you?"

"No. We were both at the dock yesterday at the same time. When you didn't come back, I hired the motorboat to come and search for you first thing this morning."

"That was kind of you, Henry. But tell me, have you been following me lately? And were you at the *Sea Horse* restaurant two nights ago?"

"Yes. But I was in disguise, and I was hoping that you wouldn't see or recognize me. You've got to be more careful, Carley," he cautioned. "There's something underhanded going on. And that's why the three of us in the club decided we'd take turns looking out for you."

"Does it have anything to do with the Cavanaugh project?"

"Partially. And maybe something else, too. All we know is that you have some enemies out there, Carley."

Immediately, she felt a great affection for Gran's poker buddies. Yet, at the same time, she was angry that someone was trying to sabotage her life—as if it weren't complicated enough.

Since she had left her cell phone with Joie, she borrowed Henry's, and called her own number. Joie answered.

"This is Carley. I just wanted you to know that I'm okay and back at the cove."

"Thank heavens! Did Henry find you?"

"We rather found each other. Are you still at the *Golden Crane*?"

"Yes. Do you want me to come and pick you up?"

"No. Henry will give me a ride. But don't check out yet. I desperately need a bath before driving back to Mobile."

Carley waited beside Henry's car while he went inside Tullie's Bait and Rental to settle the bill for the boat. When he returned, and they were driving to the B&B, Carley related the events to Henry.

Finally, she grinned, in spite of herself. "By the way, the Cavanaugh project can start on schedule. I not only sub-contracted with Barnie Overton for the equipment, but he's agreed to work on the project, too. By the time someone finds out, he will already be on the job. For that, I can exchange spending *one* night in a mangy sleeping bag."

"You'll have to admit, Carley," Henry cautioned, "Lady Luck was with you this time. But she might not be so generous in the future."

When Carley arrived at the bed and breakfast cottage, she was glad that no one was in the common room. She slipped up the stairs and knocked at the door.

"Joie?" she called out.

When Joie finally opened the door, and Carley took one look at her, she found herself repeating the same question that Henry had asked her, earlier.

"My God, Joie! What happened to you?"

 *Chapter 11*

"*F*ood poisoning, I think," Joie responded.

She looked terrible. Her face was drawn, and her skin had taken on a sickly green. She looked worse for wear than the poor lizard that Li-Po had dropped at Carley's feet as a gift the previous week.

"When did it happen? What did you eat?" Carley asked, shutting the door while Joie dragged herself back to bed.

"It started yesterday, around two o'clock. I went to the Yellow Dragon after church services, and had a delicious Moo Goo Gai Pan. It's never affected me this way before."

"Well then, could it have been a dessert? Did you stop and buy an éclair later, or something else that might have been spoiled?"

Joie hesitated, as if she didn't want to be questioned further. "Whatever it was, I feel much better this morning."

"Well enough to ride back to Mobile?"

"If you do the driving."

In less than an hour, Carley showered, went downstairs to pay the bill, and then brought the car to the front entrance, where a weak Joie was sitting in a chair.

Agatha was quite solicitous as they left. "I hope your bad experience won't keep you from coming back."

"Oh, no," Carley replied. "And you were grand to see to Joie while I was away. Thank you."

Because food was rather low on Joie's priority list, Carley

scuttled her plan to stop off for another leisurely lunch on the way home. But having missed breakfast, Carley ordered a to-go chicken sandwich and coffee for herself, and a cup of hot tea and crackers for Joie. They paused again only long enough for a pit stop for Joie and gasoline for Gran's gas-guzzler.

Joie was interested in what had happened on Horn Island. As much to keep her mind off her unsettled stomach as anything else, Carley told her the entire story, being careful to make it sound like an adventure, rather than the potential disaster it could have been.

The return trip from Ocean Springs seemed much shorter than their initial trip, and the Cadillac gave a much smoother ride than the truck would have. For Joie's sake, Carley was glad.

In record time, they pulled into the driveway. Carley drove on to the old carriage house and then helped Joie up the stairs to her apartment.

"Now, you're sure that you'll be all right?"she asked, turning on the air conditioner.

"I'm sure, Carley. The worst is over."

"Just call me if you need something. And I'm still sorry that you got sick."

"It wasn't your fault."

Carley hurried to the house to attend to the cats. They greeted her with great displeasure. Cho-Cho, in particular. She completely ignored Carley and kept cleaning her paws in a studied manner.

Carley checked the water bowl. It was full because of the constant fill-up of the new contraption that Gran had purchased at the pet store—a feline water cooler. But the food bowls were empty.

It seemed to be the day for apologizing. "Guys, I'm sorry," she said, opening two cans of cat food as quickly as she could. While they began eating, Carley left the kitchen and walked toward her bedroom.

In her absence, the cats had paid her back for leaving

them alone. Face powder was scattered everywhere, with cat's paw prints decorating the carpet, like a Matisse masterpiece. Lip-glosses were scattered over the room, and the scent of musk overwhelmed her. A decanter of perfume that she had never used was slowly dripping onto the small, white flokati rug adjacent to the dressing table.

Carley quickly righted the antique decanter and replaced the crystal stopper. Next time, when she left the cats for the day, she would make sure that the bedroom door was closed firmly. She should have remembered that Maltese cats, or Russian Blues, had a penchant for opening doors not securely fastened.

A few minutes later, when Carley checked in her office, she saw that the answering machine light was blinking. She stared down at the message counter—eight messages. But she didn't bother to listen to them. She had worn the same clothes for three days straight and even slept in them the previous night, so other matters seemed much more important. Besides, she didn't want to face any bad news until she felt ready to cope.

Much later that afternoon, she took some soup to Joie. Then, she finally listened to the waiting messages. Jake had called to let her know that he had finished signing up workers for the landscape crew. Only one call needed to be returned—that of Lizzie, the chairman of a Tricentennial committee, reminding her of her part in the next citywide event.

While her divorce had been pending, Carley had kept busy, working with the Festival of Flowers and the refurbishing of the Botanical Gardens. But after Gran's death, she had opted out of the July 4th celebration with the tall ships and fireworks in the Salute to the Sea, as well as several other important events that had kept residents busy since January.

Now, it was imperative for her to appear at the final black tie, fundraising party for the d'Iberville statue, which was to be erected at Mobile Landing in November—a replica of the original bronze facing the old seawall in Havana. Gran would expect her to go, especially since the statue had been one of her interests. Her main problem, though, was that she did not have an escort.

Bob was certain to be there with Sherrie. So what was she going to do? Hire a gigolo from the Madame in New Orleans? Ask Boris Cavanaugh, the notorious bachelor? Or go with one of Gran's poker buddies?

Carley decided to worry about that later, since she had so many other things to keep her occupied.

On poker playing night, Goose took the problem out of her hands. He arrived at the house earlier than the other two. After he took a seat in the den, he said, "Carley, if you haven't already asked someone, I have an escort for you for the party."

Carley should have been pleased, but it was not the best feeling to realize that it was so obvious that her social life was in shambles.

"Oh, Goose. I know you mean well, but I'm not Gran's little girl anymore. You don't have to feel responsible for me."

"I recognize that," Goose admitted. "And I certainly don't want to do anything to offend you. But I know how difficult it is socially, after...after losing a partner."

Carley could see the hurt in his eyes. She realized that he was only trying to be helpful, so she backed down. "It's true that I need an escort. I've been rattling my brain, trying to come up with an eligible man."

"Then, rattle no more, my dear. Let me be a matchmaker for one night."

"Who is he?"

"A businessman in town for several weeks to close on a hush-hush commercial deal."

"His name?"

"Evian Whitstone."

"Like the spring water?"

Goose laughed. "He has distant connections with that area of France—yes. And he's quite suitable for you in both age and looks."

The doorbell rang, and the conversation ended.

"Edward. Henry. Do come in. Goose is already here."

Henry was once again wearing his toupee. His gray eyes twinkled when he greeted Carley, but he said nothing about their last encounter. The discussion centered on the party and auction that coming Saturday night.

"Do you think that your wife will feel well enough to go, Edward?" Carley asked.

"Perhaps. We'll just have to wait until the last minute to see."

Jorja, his wife, had once been a wonderfully witty woman, but now, she was in an extended care facility, with worsening Alzheimer's disease. He had kept her at home with a nurse, until she began disappearing at night and he could no longer manage. There were still days, however, when she appeared quite lucid. Perhaps Saturday might be one of those better days.

"Goose, are you taking Miss Agnes?" Henry asked.

"Yes. She's looking forward to it."

Goose had been a confirmed bachelor, when a young divorcée swept into town, knocking him off his feet. They had been married only a few years when she just as suddenly swept out of town again, leaving Goose to deal with the broken relationship. He had never remarried. Agnes, his longtime assistant, had stepped into the breach when he needed someone on his arm. But it was a platonic friendship—at least as far as Goose was concerned. Agnes was still mute about her feelings in the matter.

Carley could not contain her curiosity any longer. "What about Lucinda Bledsoe?" she asked. "Do you think she will be coming, too?"

For a moment, there was complete silence. "Since her ancestor was one of the founding fathers, it would be rather pointed, if she didn't," Goose replied.

No one else spoke until Henry asked, "And with whom will you be going, Carley?"

"I have a blind date, thanks to Goose."

That was when Goose waded into the conversation again. "His name is Evian Whitstone. A very interesting fellow. I think Carley will like him."

"What does he do?" Edward asked.

Carley looked at Goose to answer. "He's an entrepreneur. Owns some international conglomerates. He's in town for a month or so. I thought it would be a good idea if he got to know some of the people here, since he'll probably be coming back and forth from time to time."

"I'm glad you have a date, Carley," Henry commented. "Otherwise, I might have offered to take you, myself."

"And I probably would have a much better time with *you*, Henry."

"Let's play poker," Edward intervened.

Carley filled the beer steins and put the snacks on the table. Soon, they were all involved in trying to win the kitty that had climbed to a grand sum of fifteen dollars.

The poker game did not last as long as usual, since the three insisted on leaving well before midnight. "Tomorrow is your first day on the job, Carley," Edward reminded her. "So you'll need plenty of rest tonight."

"Yes. We'll be going along now," Henry piped up. "Good luck, tomorrow."

"If there's anything that you need..." The men were like three chivalric knights, ready to come to her aid. She was really touched by their friendship.

"Thanks, but I think I have everything under control."

Later, after the lights had been turned off and Carley and the cats were getting ready to settle down for the night, she realized that she wasn't at all sleepy. She wasn't nervous about the next day. It was the prospective blind date that unnerved her.

Saturday night would be the first time that she had gone out with a man since the divorce. And as usual, she didn't have a thing to wear for such a formal event. With the new job, she didn't even have time to go to New Orleans to buy something really chic. And it was important to her bruised ego that Bob, seeing her for the first time after their split, would realize what a mistake he had made in choosing Sherrie over her.

If only Morgan were back, with all her wonderful clothes. Carley suddenly switched on the light, climbed out of bed, and walked barefooted up the steps to Morgan's bedroom. She usually left clothes scattered from house to house and continent to continent, because of the hassle in getting through airport security. Maybe she had left something in the closet that might do for her. After all, they were still the same size.

Carley turned on the upstairs lights, including those in the large walk-in closet that had been remodeled as part of Morgan's birthday one year. Immediately, she saw that there were a number of zippered bags to choose from.

After spending at least a half-hour looking through the clothes, Carley finally pulled out several evening and cocktail dresses and draped them over the bed. In examining them, Carley realized that they were much too flamboyant for her. She didn't have the nerve to wear a single one.

Dejectedly, she hung the dresses back in the closet, turned out the lights, and went downstairs to bed.

Chapter 12

On Thursday morning, several hours before the trek of artists was to begin, Carley, Barnie, Jake, and the rest of the gardening crew arrived at Boris Cavanaugh's property, Cavallegria.

Following in the procession were the two port-a-potties to be unloaded and the food truck containing the day's supply of water and food for the workers. Carley had always found that the extra money spent on the physical needs of the crew resulted in a much better landscape job. Two large dumpsters also followed, to hold the debris of the renovation.

With all the activity and noise, Boris stuck his head out the front door.

"Good morning, Mr. Cavanaugh," Carley greeted him.

He nodded, closed the door, and she didn't see him again for the rest of the day.

Carley's first priority was to clear the vines and underbrush immediately surrounding the house. Jake always used a machete, which was a rather awesome weapon upon the landscape and demanded a lot of respect from the other workers.

One of the reasons that Carley had chosen that area to work on first was her determination to stay away from the water and avoid the possibility of bumping into her ex-husband as long as she could.

Within a few minutes, Barnie had unloaded the tractor

and driven it to the rear of the house. There he began the chore of digging up the broken tile of the patio.

Carley had divided the various work sites and given copies of the master plat to Jake, so that they could stay on schedule. She had designed seven gardens, or retreats, that would be loosely connected by walkways or paths. Each garden reflected some aspect of the coastal flora, from a sea garden to a native wildflower garden, to another that would recall the heritage of the aboriginal people of early days. The last one, to be left as primitive and wild as possible, was the one she and Wingate had selected in which to plant his bis pole.

With the crew dispersed in various directions, Carley and Jake began tagging trees to be kept in each area.

By necessity, she was finally forced to go nearer the bay. Then, hearing a different kind of noise, she looked through an opening in the screen of trees to see a boat making its landing at the old dock. A large supply of lumber and other building materials was visible on deck.

Hoping that her ex-husband had not arrived by the waterway, she was relieved to see Martin Pemberton, one of the architectural firm's favorie contractors, as he jumped onto the old pier that was due to be demolished. Satisfied, Carley resumed her own chores with Jake.

Taking into consideration the humidity along the coastal areas of the Gulf, with July and August the worst of the scorching season, Carley was forced to make a number of adjustments to insure a healthy new landscape.

She had seen so many viable plants transported in open trucks, assuring that they would be completely dried out by the wind before they reached their destination. So one of the reasons that she liked to deal with Artie was that he always protected them and sprayed them with a moisture retentive substance for the trip. Combined with well-prepared soil, that gave the plants a much better chance for survival.

Unlike some landscape architects she knew who merely

drew up the plans and advised off and on during the course of a project, Carley was a hands-on type of person. Consequently, by mid-morning, she was equally as hot and sweaty as the crew.

Aware that her extremely delicate skin did not fare well in all the heat, she was determined to protect it as best she could, especially since the important black-tie event was only two days away.

She didn't care what she looked like on the job, since it certainly wasn't a social occasion. But despite the sunscreen, the zinc cream slashed across her nose, and the pith helmet, she had still turned a bright pink. The heat splotches were only temporary, though, and would disappear with a nice cool shower later.

She had just walked up to the food wagon for a bottle of cold water, when a voice behind her said, "Hello, Carley."

She recognized the voice immediately — the very one she had hoped never to hear again. It took a lot of courage for her to turn around.

"Hello, Bob," she said as nonchalantly as she could, while she unscrewed the cap from her water bottle.

He was dressed in a pristine white knit shirt and charcoal slacks. With his designer sunglasses and his excellent suntan, he looked as if he might have stepped out of GQ magazine.

He seemed surprised to see her on the job. Taking off his sunglasses, he stared at her. "God, you look awful, Carley."

"How gallant of you to notice."

He grimaced in a familiar, irritating way. "From the tone of your voice, I see that I put my foot in it again."

He did not sound apologetic.

Carley merely shrugged and began walking away. He didn't deserve any further conversation. Besides, she wasn't sure how much longer she could control her temper.

A short distance away, Jake was waiting for her. He wore a scowl on his face, and he was tightly clutching his machete. "Is he bothering you?"

"Not really. I was bound to bump into him at some point."

Jake returned his machete to its sheath and fell into step with Carley.

She knew that she had lied to Jake. Although she'd had visions of meeting her ex-husband under much better circumstances, and her pride had been wounded by his unflattering comment, it was Jake's expression that had alarmed her most. Joie had been vague about the reason for Jake's leaving the firm's employ so suddenly. She would have to question Joie about that later.

Not long after lunch, the sand-graveled road became clogged with vehicles—motorcycles, vans, foreign-made cars, and one limousine. The various occupants, both male and female, emerged and swarmed into the dining hall/meeting room, where Wingate had set up registration for the artists.

Carley was particularly interested in the person who had arrived in a black limousine with such fanfare. She was a tall woman with flaming red hair. Despite her size, she appeared graceful and elegant, with an air about her that indicated she was used to being noticed.

Surprisingly, her luggage was taken directly into Boris's house. Later, Carley saw the limousine parked in front of one of the shotgun houses, while the muscular chauffeur, who resembled a bodyguard, sunned himself on the small deck. At the time, Carley wondered if he, also, would be staying the entire session. But perhaps he was merely spending the night, to depart the following morning.

The day progressed much as she had planned. There were a few hitches caused by the traffic and the artists swarming over the compound. Carley could hear some very vocal complaints about their activities, but by late afternoon, she and the crew were all ready to quit and leave the artists to their own pursuits.

When she reached home, Joie was waiting for her in the

kitchen, with the cats content in their hammocks. She had seen to them that day, making sure that they were petted and groomed.

"Would you like something to drink?" Joie asked.

"How about the two of us having a nice cold beer? But let me take a shower, first."

Carley went into the mudroom, peeled off her dirty outside clothes and, with only her underwear on, she hurried into the downstairs bedroom.

It had been Gran's room for so long that Carley knew it would take quite awhile before she would feel entirely comfortable in calling it her own. Sometimes, she could feel Gran's presence, as if she were in the same room. Joie had told her that many people felt that way when a loved one departed.

A few minutes later, with her old cotton robe wrapped around her, she returned to the kitchen. The cool shower had revived both her tired body and her spirits. It had also taken away the unbecoming heat flush of her face.

As she sat down and poured the ice-cold beer into a pilsner, Carley was still thinking about Jake and his reaction to Bob. Before she had a chance to question Joie, the former housekeeper surprised her by bringing up another subject.

"Carley, I have something most unpleasant to tell you."

"What is it, Joie?"

"I've been doing some detective work since our trip to Ocean Springs. You know the saltwater taffy that was left on your bed?"

"The box I gave to you?"

"Yes. That Sunday, it was shortly after I'd eaten a piece of *your* taffy that I suddenly became ill."

"You didn't mention that earlier. Do you think something was wrong with it?"

"I not only think it, but I *know* it. You see, I brought the rest home to have it analyzed. The results came back today. It was deliberately adulterated."

"Oh, Joie, I'm so sorry. Will you be all right?"

"Yes. It didn't have any lasting effects. I'm more worried about you, though. When I asked the maid about the taffy, she said she hadn't left it. So someone with a master key must have put it on your bed while we were out to dinner — someone who was determined to keep you from your trip to Horn Island."

"How could they have known which bed was mine? And why not poison both boxes?"

"If we'd both become sick, then we would have suspected something immediately and looked for the source." Joie added, "It wasn't hard to decipher which bed was yours. You seem to have a habit of leaving personal items on your bed."

She became serious again. "You must be careful at every turn, Carley. Take care of yourself while you're on this project."

"Don't you think that the danger is over, now that I *am* on the project? All this seemed to be about preventing me from starting."

"You might be right. But you should still be careful."

The two women sat and finished their beers. Carley did not have the heart to bring up anything else controversial. Instead, she told Joie about the interesting artists who had arrived at Cavallegria. On the next day, though, she would see for herself, since Joie would be spending part of the day at the compound, as they began on Boris's private garden together.

 *Chapter 13*

The next morning, as the sun began its rise over the bay, Carley and Joie started out to Fairhope. They had left the house earlier than usual, so that they could beat the slow traffic over the causeway.

All along Mobile Bay, the heavy morning fog forced everyone to drive with headlights on. Still, a few stubborn drivers had refused to obey any safety rules, and Carley happened to get behind one of them. Since the car blended in with the fog, and there was no possibility that she could get around it, Carley became extra vigilant.

Joie, sensing her extreme concentration, elected to remain silent for the first part of the trip. Once they got off the bridge and onto land again, both relaxed.

"I hear that a tropical storm is churning up in the Caribbean," Joie said.

"Well, I hope it dissipates before reaching land. A violent wind could be devastating right now, even though we could use some rain."

Joie agreed, while she watched a few dark storm clouds gather. A sudden splat on the windshield startled both women.

Carley laughed as she turned on the wipers to get rid of the moisture. "Do you know what Gran used to tell Morgan and me when this happened?"

"What?"

"That a giant living on another planet just won a spitting contest."

Joie smiled. "Sounds like her."

The traffic became less congested, and by the time they reached the gates at Cavallegria, they had left behind most of the early morning fog, and the landscape had begun to reassume its familiar shape.

They arrived in the compound just as the artists had evidently finished breakfast. They swarmed out of the dining hall and dispersed in myriad directions.

One male artist with a small, pointed beard — unmindful of anything except his conversation — stepped directly into the path of Carley's truck.

She slammed on the brakes to keep from making contact with him, and he glared at her in an angry, hostile manner. He acted as if she were the culprit for invading his space.

"Heck! I bet I've upset his creative juices ."

"You're probably right," Joie agreed. "It might be interesting to see what color he uses today."

"Red. Decidedly red." Carley turned off the engine, and she and Joie emerged from the truck and walked to the rear of the house.

That morning, the noise level from several areas was quite prominent. The ping and pounding sounds coming from the waterside indicated that the construction of the new boathouse and dock had begun.

Behind the house, where the patio had once stood, stone masons were erecting the garden wall, with its moon gate. In another direction, rogue trees and saplings were being felled by Jake and some of his crew, while in still another direction, tractor-like hums from the Bobcat erupted.

Those multiple sounds, which were pleasant music to Carley's ears, could easily have been a dissonant, annoying experience to people waiting for the Muse to whisper her gems of inspiration. But after all, wasn't that what Boris had wanted?

At least, she and Joie were quieter as they marked the

placement of boulders, the bridge, the dry sand stream, and the exact plant sites for Boris's Zen garden. Carley and Joie had incorporated other features, as well, such as the meditation bench. It was not strictly the *kari-sansui* type that Zen Buddhists had favored — especially in the famous monastery garden at Kyoto.

Regardless, the oriental garden design had received Joie's blessing. Boris might not realize it, but he had been thoroughly *feng-shui*-ed by an expert. Whether it would make any difference in his paintings, Carley would have to wait and see. It would be interesting to take a peek at his next work-in-progress, to discover if he had become more harmonious with nature.

By early afternoon, with Joie's work finished, Carley took her into Fairhope. There were a number of shops in the tourist town, and Joie enjoyed browsing in them. So they made plans to meet at the Target store on the outskirts of town at six o'clock, after Carley had finished for the day.

When she returned, Barnie was waiting for her. "You need to see something, Carley." He looked around to make sure that he had not been overheard.

"What is it, Barnie?"

"Just come with me."

They walked in the direction of the site where the obelisk was going to be erected near the water. Evidently, there had been some hitch to his digging the foundation, and he obviously didn't want anyone else to know about it.

All sorts of things entered Carley's mind. She was praying that it would be nothing major. She had already cut her expenses as much as possible, and she didn't need some problem that would cause a delay or more outlay of money.

"I covered it up again, so no one would see it," Barnie said, as soon as they reached the site.

He began to unearth a large metal box that had been buried heaven knows how long. It was too large to be a French dowry box. It looked more like a pirate's chest. A rusted chain and lock showed the ravages of nature.

Clearly, Carley was in a dilemma. All the talk with Ed, the surveyor, came back to her. "If this is an early archaeological site, we'll have to stop work here," she commented.

"You think we should open the chest first, to make sure?"

"How hard would it be to break the lock?"

"Not hard at all. A few hits with a chisel ought to do it."

Carley quickly made a decision. "Then, go get one."

"I got one right here. Borrowed it from Jake's truck."

Carley knew how careful Jake was about lending his tools to others. But since Barnie already had it in hand, she said nothing.

The striking of the chisel blended in with the noise from the boathouse construction. After several hard hits, the lock fell open. Barnie removed the rusted chain surrounding the chest and then used the chisel to pry open the metal-riveted lid.

Once the chest was wide open, Carley knelt beside Barnie and watched while he pulled aside the raffia covering the top and poked around with the chisel.

When the grotesque contents came into view, Carley didn't know which was the more startled.

"Holy shit!" Barnie said. "They look like shrunken heads." Then, realizing what he had said, he apologized.

Carley was too stunned to be offended by his language. She immediately thought of Wingate and the conversation on the day she met him. So he *was* planning to use a shrunken head on his aboriginal bis pole, even though he had been noncommittal about it.

"Cover it up, Barnie. Don't say anything about this discovery to anyone."

"But—"

"The chest belongs to one of the artists. He'll come for it soon. So just leave the digging for a day or so and concentrate for now on the walk to the seashore garden."

"If you say so."

Carley took the chisel from Barnie to return to Jake. As she began to walk away, she felt both angry and sick at the same time. It was a horrible sight—those little heads with their long black strands of hair. How could anyone in modern civilization think of them as artistic ornaments?

The discovery of the chest and its contents certainly put a pall on her afternoon. But once the truck delivering the solar lights for the pathways arrived, Carley's mind turned to the boxes. Wondering where she might store them until needed, she knocked on the large cypress front door to confer with Boris.

When a sullen Wingate appeared instead, Carley became tongue-tied. Finally, she was able to tell him what she needed. After a minute or so, he came back to the door with a key to one of the cottages.

"The Warhol cottage is vacant for this session," he announced. "You can use that one for storage."

"Which cottage is that?"

"The last one on the right as you head toward the gates. It's next to the Hockney cottage."

"Thanks!" That was about all that Carley could manage to say as she took the key.

With Jake's help, she loaded the boxes into the back of her truck, and he rode with her to the cottage to help unload them.

"I guess all the cottages are named for artists," Carley said. Her voice still didn't sound too steady.

"Is everything all right with you, Carley?"

"Sure." She quickly changed the subject. "How's the job going? Anything that I should know about?"

"I had to let one of the guys go this morning. He started celebrating the weekend a little too early. He protested a good bit. Other than that, we're still on schedule."

"Good. I hope we can say the same thing on Monday."

Both were aware of the notorious number of Monday no-shows on the job when they'd both worked for Regan,

Barnes, and O'Reilly.

While they were still busy transferring the boxes, a silver Lexus approached from the direction of the entrance gates. Two people were inside—Bob and his new wife, Sherrie. Carley recognized them immediately, but said nothing to Jake. Instead, she carried another box to the porch of the Warhol cottage.

When they had finished and all the boxes had been taken inside, Carley opened the last box to make sure that the lights were what she had ordered.

One time before, on an expensive landscape job, she hadn't checked, and a wrong order had been shipped. It delayed the finish of the project an extra week. Carley couldn't afford for that to happen again.

"Everything seems to be all right," she said, examining one of the lights. With Jake following her out the door, she took the key and locked the cottage.

As they started toward the truck, Jake stopped. "I can walk back, Carley. It's late, so why don't you call it quits for the day and go on home?"

"You don't mind?"

"Nope. Need the exercise—to get the kink out of my back."

"Well, I do have to pick up Joie on the way out of town. And I've got lots to do at home before a big black-tie affair tomorrow night."

Jake grinned. "You got a date for that?"

"Yep. See you on Monday, Jake."

"Wear something extra sexy," he yelled as she pulled her truck onto the road.

She laughed. Jake didn't know the meaning of harassment in the workplace. In his own Cajun way, he was merely wishing Carley the best for her first night out after the divorce. She needed all the good wishes she could get.

 *Chapter 14*

When Carley arrived at home, her message light was blinking. The first three messages did not require an answer, but the fourth one did. It was her blind date, Evian Whitstone, making contact before the next night's party.

Three times, she listened to his deep, polished, cultured voice that had a slight accent—not quite foreign, yet not quite homegrown, either.

"All right, Carley," she said to herself. "You'll have to call him back." Then, another voice inside her head reasoned, "But not now. Wait until after dinner."

She took a nice, cool shower and then slipped into her sweats. Instead of going for a run, she went to the kitchen, where she took her time preparing a bacon and scallion frittata, cutting a nice, fresh piece of cantaloupe, and then opening a package of pink lemonade mix. It was not exactly a gourmet meal, but it was life sustaining and probably a lot healthier than the barbeque and fries that she had eaten for lunch.

All the time that she was eating, she was thinking of Jake's comments about wearing something sexy for the party. She didn't have a clue as to what it could be. Not only that, but as she stared down at her hands and saw the results of the past few days of landscape work, despite the gloves, she realized that they needed major attention.

Carley had already made a Saturday morning appointment for a shampoo and hair styling, so she began to hope that the manicurist could work her into her schedule at the same time. It was too bad that she couldn't get an entire makeover, but it was much too late for that.

Finally, when she had finished eating, had put the dishes into the dishwasher, had taken the cats out for their daily chasing of butterflies in the garden and a soulful glance at the koi in the small pond, where she had thrown in a mosquito dunk to keep the mosquito larvae from hatching, she knew that she could no longer put off the telephone call to the mystery man.

At eight o'clock, she dialed the number he had left. It rang quite a few times and, just as she was getting ready to hang up, a voice answered. "Whitstone, here."

She hesitated for a split second. Should she call him *Whitstone* or *Evian*?

"Evian?"

"Yes?"

"This is Carley Burnside, returning your call."

"Oh, yes, Carley. Thank you. I wanted to confirm our date for tomorrow night. Goose has already given me directions to your house. Will it be convenient for me to come by for you at seven?"

"Seven will be fine."

"Good. I'm looking forward to meeting you in person."

"Then, I'll see you tomorrow night."

"My pleasure."

"Good-bye."

"For now."

As Carley hung up the phone on the rather stilted conversation, she was sorry that she didn't have Morgan's flair for provocative comments. "Weren't you on that dangerous safari to Africa?" always started up an interesting exchange. Or "I think I was at the same roulette table in Monte Carlo last winter. How much money did you *actually* lose that night?"

Carley had always been fascinated by Morgan's stretch-

Ing of the truth. Even if she hadn't bothered to go to Monte Carlo that winter, or was even aware of a life-threatening safari, she could always open up a stimulating conversation that would last for hours.

It was too bad that Carley had to stick to the truth, making her repartee much more mundane. She had never really envied that questionable ability of Morgan's until now. What on earth was she going to talk about to a total stranger, this Evian Whitstone, who sounded so cosmopolitan? She was sure that he wouldn't be interested in her local landscape endeavors. From Goose's comments, he was evidently a big player in the international scene. Perhaps, she could just listen. Carley was really good at listening.

The telephone rang. It was Joie. "Have you decided on what you're going to wear tomorrow night?"

Carley immediately became defensive. "Why?"

"Because I have two spectacular necklaces I brought back from Ella's. I'd like for you to wear one of them, but I would need to see your dress, first."

"That's quite kind of you, but so far, I haven't decided on a dress."

"I'll be right over with the necklaces."

"But—" Joie had hung up.

Carley was usually quite stubborn about making her own decisions. It was one of her failings, as Bob had pointed out a number of times. But Joie had a way of insinuating herself into Carley's life, and even more so, now that only a garden separated the two living quarters.

When Joie arrived, they immediately went upstairs.

"Okay. Let's see your choices," the woman insisted.

They were in Morgan's old room, and Carley had pulled out the same garment bags that she had rejected earlier.

"There's no question about it. You must wear this turquoise dress."

"But just look at it, Joie. The top has so little material, there's only one sleeve, and the back is too low-cut."

"Put it on."

Reluctantly, Carley did so. Once it was zipped up, and she had put on the matching sandals, Joie smiled.

"Perfect. It has just enough glitter to be elegant, and the skirt is *made* for dancing."

Joie reached into one of the velvet boxes and fastened the necklace around Carley's neck "Now, look in the mirror."

Carley had never seen such a beautiful necklace. Of jade, pearls, and gold, it was encrusted with the Chinese symbols of health and happiness. Its patina proclaimed its vast age, perhaps as ancient as the terra cotta soldiers buried for a thousand years, or a treasure taken from some sarcophagus in Egypt.

"Oh, Joie, I could never wear anything so valuable."

"It's only a reproduction."

She did not tell her until much later that this reproduction was still quite old and of museum quality.

From that episode on, Carley's life took on the elements of a whirlwind. The hours on Saturday flew by. At that, she managed to get in a long, early morning run to relieve some of her anxiety, before proceeding with the beauty regimen.

At the salon, Wendy was able to squeeze her in for a manicure. Her hair was duly styled in a more sophisticated coiffure. The noise of the blow dryer was a good excuse for Carley not to get involved in the gossip spreading throughout the salon, as to who was going with whom to the black-tie event.

Back at home, Carley even managed a nice afternoon nap, with two Pond's cucumber patches over her eyes. It had been a long time since she had paid this much attention to her appearance.

Feeling like someone whose coach might turn into a pumpkin long before midnight, she finally dressed in the newly pressed turquoise cocktail dress, and by six-forty, she was ready. With ten minutes to spare, she practiced, "Didn't

I see you at..." She soon gave that up. She would just have to wing it.

At precisely seven o'clock, a large black limousine pulled into the circular driveway of her English Tudor house. With unashamed interest, she watched from the upstairs window, as a liveried chauffeur got out and opened the door for his passenger.

The man was tall, well built, and dressed in beautifully tailored evening clothes. Carley could not see his face well from her vantage point behind the sheer under drapery, without risking being seen, herself.

She descended the stairs and was almost in the hallway, when the doorbell rang. Less than thirty seconds later, she opened the door to the stranger.

If Boris Cavanaugh had made her feel as if she had been examined through the lens of a powerful telescope, his inspection was nothing compared to the scrutiny of this man's Prussian blue eyes. He stood there for what seemed like ages, taking in Carley's dress, the necklace around her neck, and seemingly everything about her.

Finally, Evian Whitstone smiled, showing his perfect white teeth. "Hello, my beautiful Carley."

Alarmed and in typical Morgan fashion, she blurted out, "Weren't you in Ocean Springs last week?"

 *Chapter 15*

*E*vian Whitstone laughed. "Guilty, as charged." Then, dismissing that opening salvo, he said, "Are you ready to leave?"

Carley hesitated. "Perhaps I'd better bring my cell phone."

"You won't need it. There's one in the limo."

Carley actually didn't have room in her small evening purse, anyway. She had taken off her house key from the oversized key ring, but even then, she barely had enough space for her compact, lip-gloss, comb, and one credit card.

"Then, I guess I'm ready."

Just as she started to lock the door, the man said, "Here, let me." Like one accustomed to taking over any situation, he reached for the key. When their hands connected, a static spark erupted. The electric shock caused both to jump, and the key fell onto the doormat.

"I'm sorry," Carley apologized. "I seem to be electrically charged tonight."

"I'm glad that I've been duly warned," her date said in an amused tone. He retrieved the key and locked the door. "If you don't mind, I'll give the key to you later." He then put it into his own pocket.

Carley didn't know why that should make her uneasy. She could understand, though, that he might not want to get shocked again. So she said nothing and walked with him to the limousine, where the chauffeur was standing by the opened door. He looked vaguely familiar, but that was to be expected, since the same ones drove for numerous social events all over the city.

Once they pulled out of the driveway, Carley cleared her throat and said, "Do people usually call you *Evian*?"

"Only business associates. My friends call me *Whit*. Your given name is *Carleton*, isn't it?"

"Yes. Sometimes it causes confusion, since its sounds so masculine. But it's a Burnside tradition to give family surnames to daughters."

"Goose tells me that you have a twin sister."

"Yes. Morgan. She's in France at the moment. What about your family? Do you have brothers and sisters?"

"A sister. No brothers."

He did not elaborate. Carley waited for him to continue, but he seemed deep in thought. She was never one for making conversation just to fill up a lull. A certain amount of silence was usually welcomed, especially if she felt comfortable with a person. But she didn't feel comfortable with this man. There was something about him that disturbed her. She was hesitant about bringing up Ocean Springs again, although she was curious. Evidently, he didn't intend returning to that subject either, and she was at a loss to initiate another subject.

Finally, a loud crack of thunder unblocked the conversation. "Do you think that we might be in for a major storm tonight?" he asked.

"I certainly hope not. Isidore has just been sitting in the Caribbean for days. Of course, it could change directions in a split second. Tropical depressions are hard to predict."

"If it reaches land, how much damage is it apt to do to your present landscape project?"

"I wasn't aware that you knew anything about my work."

"Goose showed me your plans for Cavanaugh while I was in his office. I hope you don't mind. "

Within a few seconds, Whit had opened a deluge of conversation. His interest, seemingly so genuine at the time, helped to allay Carley's annoyance at Goose for discussing her project with a stranger.

They had a long drive to the Grand Hotel at Point Clear, where the party was taking place. By the time they passed through Daphne and Fairhope, Carley relaxed. A glass of Merlot from the well-stocked limousine, and the latest Josh Grogan CD playing softly in the background, put Carley in a much mellower mood.

Then, the fledgling feeling of camaraderie came to a crashing thud. "Did you and your housekeeper enjoy the lunch at *Giverny's* last week?" he asked.

Carley scrambled for an answer. She distinctly remembered him from the *Sea Horse*. "And did you enjoy your dinner at the *Sea Horse*?"

"Touché. So you remember me from there, and not *Giverny's*."

"Were you there, too? Were you the stranger who paid for our lunch?"

"No. That must have been another admirer. But I was there, also—waiting in the bar area for a colleague, when you arrived."

Carley began to feel threatened. "I hope that this is a mere coincidence, our being together tonight."

"Not exactly. But it took a little longer to find out your name, since you were in your grandmother's car. Does it bother you that I initiated this date, when I was in Goose's office?"

"Only if you're a certified stalker."

He laughed. "It's true that I used the same methods. But I had the best of intentions."

Carley glanced at the stranger beside her. Torn between flattery and annoyance, she began to wonder what else she was going to find out about him, besides his ability to track down women. Surely, he had nothing to do with invading the bed and breakfast and leaving the saltwater taffy. Yet, for all she knew, she was being abducted by a psychopath. Maybe they weren't even going to the Grand Hotel.

That fear, at least, was soon alleviated when Carley recognized the approach to the hotel that had been a landmark for years, but had been purchased by a major hotel chain and renovated. It had been a long time since Gran had first brought Morgan and her to a Sunday brunch at the hotel. Those earlier visits had been quite pleasant, but Carley wasn't so sure that it would be equally enjoyable this time. She needed to talk with Goose.

When they entered the lobby, it was already crowded, with dozens of people milling around. Waiters in white gloves circulated throughout the group, with silver trays holding an assortment of canapés and stems of champagne.

"Morgan, I didn't know you were back in town," one of the older grande dames said, greeting her with a smile.

"No, Mrs. Eldrin. I'm Carley." Then she whispered in her ear, "I borrowed one of her dresses for tonight."

"Very becoming," the woman answered and waited to be presented to Carley's escort. "Mrs. Eldrin, may I present Evian Whitstone." She turned to Whit. "Mrs. Eldrin is a former queen of Mardi Gras."

In Mobile, that was an honor that followed one to the grave, and it always pleased Mabel Eldrin to be introduced as such to any stranger.

"How handsome you are, young man," she said, holding out her hand as if she expected a princely kiss. "Whitstone. Are you related to the Whitstones of Metairie?"

"Only distantly," he replied. "What one in the South would call 'shirt-tail cousins.' "

Mabel laughed heartily. "Mr. Whitstone, I shall expect you to dance with me later tonight. I'm seated at Table 12."

"It will be my pleasure."

"Oh, there you are, Carley." Goose came into view, with Agnes at his side. "We're at Table 6."

Agnes was wearing an apricot cocktail dress, blending in with her strawberry blonde coiffure. She had lost a few more pounds, due no doubt to her yoga exercises. Agnes collected antique jewelry, so she immediately noticed Joie's necklace. "What an exquisite piece," she said, putting on her glasses to see it better.

Carley gave Joie the credit. After a brief conversation, the four crossed the lobby into the main ballroom. Knowing that her first venture out with a date would be duly noticed, Carley was nervous. She suddenly put her hand on Whit's arm and leaned toward him. "You certainly made a big hit with Mabel Eldrin."

He tucked her hand into his. "I have an aunt who resembles her. She enjoys attention, too."

"Don't we all. The right kind, of course."

"I suspect you'll get more than your share tonight, judging from the people staring at you. Especially the man to your left. Your ex-husband, I believe?"

Carley looked in that direction. Bob and Sherrie were standing together, but his attention was not on Sherrie. He was staring straight at Carley. She averted her eyes before he could acknowledge her.

Once again, she was uneasy at how much Whit knew about her life. Yet, now that she was inside the Grand Hotel, she felt safe. Surrounded by friends and acquaintances, she was determined to enjoy the evening. Regardless of any reservations that she had about the stranger beside her, she was thankful, at least, that she had not been forced to come alone.

"Lucinda, how nice to see you again." At Whit's greeting, Carley swallowed hard. Lucinda Bledsoe, her bosom draped extravagantly with her famous diamonds and pearls, had just arrived at Table 6, with her jailbird husband, Rudy Markowitz.

Oh, God, Carley thought. Lucinda had not only come to the party, but as one of Goose's clients, she was going to be seated at the same table.

Lucinda smiled at Whit and then, with a wave of her

hand, she said, "Everyone, this is my husband Rudy."

He was certainly handsome, that was for sure. He resembled a certain book cover model, except that his hair, also too long, was dark. Lucinda, with her snow-white hair, looked more like his mother. It took a lot of chutzpah on her part, Carley decided, to appear among the very people who had shunned her.

Within a short time, others had arrived and taken their places at Goose's table.

Edward had brought his fragile-looking wife, Jorja, who cradled a moth-eaten teddy bear in her arms. She turned to her husband and asked, "What day is this?" He told her that it was Saturday, and as soon as he had seated her, she turned to him again and asked the same question. A gentle, patient Edward answered her each time.

Goose had invited Gaddi, of the prosperity handkerchief fame, to sit next to Henry. Her favorite topic of conversation was her volunteer prison ministry, but with Rudy at the table, Carley doubted that anyone would encourage her. So, with Goose and Agnes, Edward and Jorja, Lucinda and Rudy, Gaddi and Henry, and Whit and Carley, the ten made up probably the most unusual table at the party.

Just as Carley was feeling extremely self-conscious, all the attention suddenly shifted to another group, who had arrived. Carley hardly recognized Boris Cavanaugh, since he had abandoned his apostolic robes for a black tuxedo.

She was not surprised to see him, since one of his paintings was being auctioned. She had expected him to be seated at Goose's table, instead of the adjacent one. But he had brought his own entourage — Wingate, and some of the other artists from the compound, including Consuelo Tolliver, the interesting flame-haired woman, who had appeared on that first day of the landscape project.

Boris and Wingate were the only ones in conservative dress. The others looked as if they might be auditioning for the *Cirque du Soleil* cast. Carley recognized the artist that she had almost run over, but she was hoping that he would not recognize her. Slung over his black polo shirt and black jeans, he was wearing a black evening cape with a red lining, and he was brandishing a long cigarette holder, with an unlit cigarette. It would certainly have to be a prop, since no smoking was allowed at this event. Carley had not seen a costume like that since visiting the FDR museum at the Little White House in Warm Springs.

"An interesting mix, don't you agree?" Whit confided.

"Almost as interesting as our table."

At another table, where the firm of Regan, Barnes, and O'Reilly were seated, along with their wives, Sherrie was absolutely furious. Rocky Donovan had been totally inept. She had warned him that if something didn't happen soon, he was going to be out of a job.

Why, she could do better, herself. On the way to the hotel, she had suggested to Bob that he needed to enlarge the boat ramp space at Cavallegria to include the area nearby. It was one of the sites that Carley had chosen for an extra special garden, with its native plants. Of course, she didn't mention any of that to Bob.

Now that she knew how to manipulate his ego, Sherrie had found it quite easy to use him to get back at Carley. She finally relaxed and smiled at him lovingly, as she unobtrusively put her hand under the table and rubbed his inner thigh. She could feel him beginning to harden at her touch.

Lizzie, the chairwoman of the night, garnered everyone's attention long enough for a few announcements and grace pronounced by the Right Reverend Stockton, who was related, on his mother's side, to an early Mobile settler.

As soon as he had finished, noise erupted again in the ballroom, in a cacophony of clinking glasses, clattering plates, and high decibel conversation that almost drowned out the soft orchestral music playing in the background. While everyone was busy eating, the dance floor was empty.

When the plates were being taken away from the first course, Lucinda's husband Rudy said, "Carley, would you care to dance?"

She almost choked on her last bite of salmon mousse. Before she could answer, Whit intervened. "I believe Carley has promised the first dance to me. Shall we?"

How grateful she was to Whit. In her rush to get up, she almost upended her chair. But she realized that Whit had only delayed the inevitable. She would be expected, as a matter of courtesy, to dance with each man at Table 6 before the evening was over.

 *Chapter 16*

On the way to the dance floor, Carley and Whit had to pass by the table reserved by Regan, Barnes, and O'Reilly. If it had been one year earlier, she would have been at that table too, with the other wives — Mimi, June, and Rhonda.

It took quite an effort on her part to smile as she passed by. Only Rhonda returned her smile. The others merely stared. Whether deliberate or not, Bob and Sherrie soon left the table and began to dance only a few feet away from Whit and Carley.

With only two couples on the parquet dance floor, the room grew unusually quiet. Carley felt as if all eyes were on them. It made her most uncomfortable.

"Whit—"

He drew her close and said, "Pay no attention to anyone but me."

That grew increasingly easy to do. With her backless dress, Carley was aware of his warm touch on her skin. The lyrics of the song were so appropriate for the occasion:

Dance with me, and seem entranced with me...
...For he's in the room and watching me,
With the girl he's chosen over me....

The mood was soon broken as the orchestra segued into another song.

Lizzie had deliberately chosen an orchestra that catered

more to slow dancing, fox trots, and cha-chas than to funky music because of the median age of the crowd.

Carley wasn't surprised when Goose and Agnes sailed by, and then were followed by a number of other couples. Even Henry was maneuvering Gaddi around the dance floor.

"That's better," Whit said. "You're relaxing."

"I don't feel such a spectacle, now that the dance floor is getting crowded."

The orchestra leader had the music well timed. Fox trots and waltzes ended just as waiters served the next course. In between courses, Carley managed to dance with Henry, Edward, and Goose.

During the main course of Cornish hen, stuffed with plums and wild rice, Carley discovered that Lucinda was selling some prime commercial property to Whit, and that was how the two had met. Goose was brokering the deal for Lucinda.

The moment Whit and Carley had arrived at the hotel, a downpour of rain had started. Now, as waiters were removing empty plates from the various tables, a rapid, staccato noise on the roof indicated that the rain had intensified. A loud crack of thunder announced the worsening of the tropical storm.

A door somewhere in the hotel blew shut with a loud noise, indicating that the wind had also risen. Except for the waiters coming in and out of the ballroom, few paid any attention to what was going on outside. Too much was happening at each table.

Carley was surprised that Rudy seemed to fit in so well at Table 6. She could see that the matronly Lucinda clearly doted on him. Joining in the conversation, he sounded much more educated than an ordinary handyman. Perhaps, though, after his incarceration, he had found it extremely difficult to find a job.

There *was* an awkward moment when Gaddi mentioned the Tutweiler prison outside Montgomery and the work she

108 • Frances Patton Statham

was doing there. Rudy took it in stride, saying, "Too bad you weren't in Louisiana. I would have enjoyed your programs."

"He was framed, you know."

"Now, 'Cin, darling, there's no need to go into that," Rudy chided.

Goose quickly changed the subject. "Carley, what are you auctioning off tonight?"

"A free landscape design—either commercial or residential."

Agnes said, "I understand that Boris is donating one of his surreal paintings. I do hope it's something that *someone* would like to purchase."

"A museum in Amsterdam bought one of his canvases, recently," Whit informed her. "For quite a hefty sum."

"Well, museums are different," Agnes responded. "Folks around here enjoy *pretty* things. So I hope Boris took that into consideration for this homegrown crowd."

Carley was amused at Agnes's response. She sounded so much like Joie—that it was far better to surround oneself with beauty, rather than with a painting of a lopsided blue face, three eyes, and a fragmented nose.

"How much money has already been raised for the statue?" Lucinda asked.

It was then, when Goose and Lucinda were in a deep discussion that Rudy stood up and held out his hand for Carley. She could not refuse for the second time to dance with him. That would be too ungracious.

The orchestra leader, noting a younger crowd on the dance floor, pepped up the music, diving into a retro-World War II boogie-woogie that had just come back into style along the coast. Rudy's eyes lit up, and Carley found herself at his mercy.

Twisting, turning, being thrown out, and even lifted, she was powerless to stop him while the rhythm grew even more frantic and her full skirt swirled around her legs. In all the activity, Carley was fearful for Joie's fragile necklace.

Soon, the rest of the dancers moved to the sidelines and watched, while the two—the jailbird husband and the jilted wife—performed. Carley knew that this was her penance for borrowing one of Morgan's dresses. She would never live down this night if she lived to be a hundred and three.

Then, mercifully, Peter, the orchestra leader, took pity and the music stopped. Carley closed her ears to the applause and rushed, not to Table 6, but to the nearest exit for the ladies' room.

Fifteen minutes later, Agnes came looking for her. She laughed at Carley's embarrassment. "Half the people think you're Morgan. You remember, of course, when you used to switch places, and even Lydia was confused. I think your former husband is confused, too. So just come back and enjoy yourself."

"You mean I'm not completely ostracized?"

"By no means. Goose is still laughing at how good a sport you've been. It was quite awkward for Lucinda tonight. You've really helped her."

The door opened and Gaddi came in with Jorja, who was still clutching her teddy bear.

"Now, who are you?" Jorja asked, looking at Carley.

"I'm Carley. Carley Burnside."

"Oh, I thought you must be Morgan."

Sometimes, Jorja was more lucid than people gave her credit for being.

By the time Carley returned to her table, the ice cream had melted on her luscious Grand Marnier dessert. She didn't mind. She attacked it with vigor, while Whit watched her. She couldn't tell what he was thinking, but she had given up on that. After tonight, she probably would never see the man again.

She had no more than finished her dessert, when Boris suddenly appeared at her elbow. "May I have this dance, Ms. Burnside?"

"Of course."

Whit immediately stood, helped Carley with her chair,

and then walked to Boris's table. He held out his hand for Consuelo Tolliver, and the two joined Boris and Carley in a slow rhumba.

Visions of Beauty and the Beast ran through her mind — not that she considered herself a beauty — the entire time that she was dancing with this huge, overpowering man with the white beard.

At least, she would have something to write about to Cristina to cheer her up. She was still unhappy with her mother's final decision to send her to boarding school.

When Carley happened to glance at Whit and Consuelo, she saw how well suited these two tall, elegant people were to dance with each other. It was almost as if they had practiced together, they moved with such grace.

"Have you heard the latest weather forecast?" Boris inquired, forcing Carley's attention back to him.

"No. Do you think the storm is getting worse?"

"Wingate went to find a TV a short time ago. The news is not good. If it keeps up, the storm might affect the roads and causeway."

"Then, perhaps we'd better ask Lizzie to begin the auction soon, or a number of us will be stranded."

Other people had the same idea. Within a few minutes, after Whit had done his duty in dancing with Mabel Eldrin, the orchestra gave way to Lizzie and the professional auctioneer.

Carley, who was on the committee, began to distribute the numbered paddles, corresponding to the place cards at each table. Then, she took her place in her assigned section to serve as a spotter.

Sherrie had been assigned, with several others, to the table at the rear to record each sale and receive the money. Henry, still a director of the bank where he had served as CEO, had arranged for credit card payments, as well.

It had been awkward for Carley to serve on the same committee as Sherrie, but the assignments had been set up long before the divorce.

At the very back of the ballroom, three representatives from the auction company manned telephones for bids that might be made by absentee buyers.

The lights flickered several times, and there was a spreading uneasiness throughout the ballroom. But once the bidding began, Isidore, the tropical storm that was churning in the Gulf, was temporarily forgotten.

The auctioneer started out with a number of smaller items. When Carley saw an unusual red lacquered box, she decided to bid, herself. It would go quite well with Gran's red phoenix screen in her office. She was pleased when she won the bid, although she paid more for it than she'd intended.

Shortly after the first grouping had been disposed of, a second one, including her own offering, came up for bids.

"The next item, Number 24 in your catalogue," announced Lizzie, "is a complete landscape design of the property of your choice by the award-winning landscape architect, Carley Burnside." She added, "Her garden designs are even more spectacular than her dancing."

The crowd laughed, to Carley's chagrin, while the auctioneer took over. Except for Lucinda, who kept up a steady bidding, Carley couldn't see the others. She was pleased, nevertheless, when one of the men at the back table started talking on the telephone, indicating an absentee bidder.

After a suitable interval, the auctioneer wrapped it up. With Lucinda's paddle in the air a number of times, Carley assumed that she would be landscaping her new property in Point Clear, after all. But then, the auctioneer announced that the design had been won by an absentee buyer.

Wondering who that bidder might be, Carley suddenly smiled. This was something so typical of Morgan—to engage her services for her own gardens at Milly-la-Forêt, while at the same time contributing to Mobile's fundraising efforts.

The auction continued, with many more items—Persian rugs, a Caribbean cruise, a week in London, a year's worth of gourmet foods, all donated by various businesses and corporations.

These were interspersed with family heirlooms donated by private citizens—ormolu clocks, jade figurines, rare coins—all to raise as much money as possible.

There was a constant movement to the payment table, where Sherrie sat. Carley was not looking forward to that awkward moment when she would be forced to go to that same table to pay for her red lacquered box.

Finally, Boris's large painting came on the block. It was quite modern, with vivid colors. The people nearest to the front reacted immediately with oohs and aahs. Some, who were seated farther away, got up from their seats for a closer inspection.

From where Carley was positioned, she was relieved to see that the painting bore no resemblance to the one Boris had been working on the day she'd met him. It was recognizable as a landscape, but unlike anything that Mother Nature had created. Beyond the purple trees, the shadowy figure of a woman disintegrated into smoke, to be resurrected into a garden sculpture in the distance. Death and rebirth? Carley wasn't sure of the theme, since she couldn't really make out the details from that distance.

The auctioneer was in no hurry to start the bidding on this last item in the catalogue. He waited until all the viewers had returned to their seats. Even then, he took his time, building the momentum until he called for the first bid.

The telephones became busy. The people in the ballroom responded, also. With all the bidding going on, Carley struggled just to point out the bidders in her own portion of the ballroom. It continued for quite a time, with the bidding going into the thousands. As the calls began to wind down, the auctioneer finally struck his gavel and announced, "Sold." The final bidder had been connected by telephone.

"Who bought it?" someone whispered near Carley.

"I haven't the foggiest," her table companion replied.

It couldn't be Morgan again, Carley decided. She

wouldn't spend that amount of money on a painting. Realizing that, Carley began to wonder if she had been wrong in thinking that her twin was the one who had purchased her own landscape design.

What a rush of activity at the end of the evening! Boris and his *Cirque du Soleil* entourage vanished, along with many others who were eager to leave. With being so busy to help wind things up, Carley didn't even get to say good-bye to Goose and the others at her table. They had vanished quickly, also.

Before the committee finished tallying the success of the evening, Lizzie decided to dismiss everyone. A few, like Sherrie, had already gone. "I've reserved a room here at the hotel for the night," she announced. "So I'll stay and finish. The rest of you need to get home."

"Let me pay for my lacquered box, first," Carley said.

Lizzie looked at the register. "Your date paid for it, Carley, and took it with him."

When Carley reached the lobby, she spied a frowning Whit standing near the door. He no longer had any packages, so Carley assumed that they were already in the limousine.

"I'm so sorry that you were forced to wait," she apologized. "But I'm ready to leave now."

"Good. Then, let's dash out."

The wind turned over a trash can outside and sent it rolling along the covered walkway in the opposite direction, while the slanting rain beat against the lighted shrubbery lining the walk. Only one car was visible under the sheltered entrance.

"Oh, but I don't see the limousine."

Over the noise of the storm, Whit shouted, "I'm taking you home in Goose's car."

They made a frantic rush for the waiting vehicle. By the time the car doors closed, both the doorman and Carley were soaked. Immediately, she turned to Whit, who had also been targeted by the rain. "Where are Goose and the others?"

"He was anxious about driving at night in such bad weather. So I sent them ahead in the limousine."

Why that should alarm her, she didn't know. The same uneasiness that she'd felt earlier returned, as they left the hotel driveway and emerged onto the main road.

Carley remained silent, straining to see the pavement ahead, as if to help the stranger at the wheel to get them both safely home.

The car moved along at a tortoise pace, but it was impossible to go any faster. Storm debris had already scattered across the road at various intervals, and Whit was forced to be vigilant.

They had traveled for some distance when Carley shouted, "Watch out. There's a ladder in the road."

Whit swerved, barely missing the long, metal stepladder that could have ruined the tires or caused a wreck. At that moment, Carley regretted ever leaving the hotel. She should have done like Lizzie and reserved a room for the night. Then, instead of being in a wet dress and wondering what the blue lights ahead meant, she could have been safely in bed.

Whit slowed and then stopped the car, as a policeman in a neon-coated poncho waved them down with his flashlight.

Once Whit found the right button to press in the unfamiliar car, he rolled down the window. "What is it, Officer?"

"The causeway over the bay has just been closed, and the road ahead is flooded. You folks need to turn back and find shelter as quickly as possible."

The police officer indicated the turn-around area. When Whit had proceeded only several hundred yards south, he said, "All right, Carleton Burnside. You're the native here. Any suggestions?"

# Chapter 17

Carley did not answer immediately. What she really wanted to do was to return to the hotel. Yet, she wasn't sure that they could make it that far. Water was already lapping at the car wheels.

"Carley?"

"Several miles back, we passed the road that leads to Boris's property," she finally responded. "We can find shelter there."

"Then, let's head for it."

Straining against the seat belt, she edged forward, trying to get her bearings so that she could direct him. Driving on such a pitch-black road, with no streetlights to guide them, it was extremely difficult.

The total darkness spurred an uneasy memory of another time when she had been caught in such a situation. It had been on an island off the coast of Georgia, where she had attended a conference. Arriving early, so that she could visit with a friend on an adjacent island, connected by a causeway, she had gotten horribly lost while trying to return to the conference hotel. Even worse, her gas tank had been extremely low.

That same terrible silence surrounded her then, with the tall, sentinel oaks with their beards of moss monitoring her uncertain progress. No lights shone from any house; no service station marquee beckoned. It was as if everyone had left the island, or even the entire world, and had neglected to tell her. Finally, she had found her way back, after retracing her route several times. Carley shivered with that unwelcomed remembrance.

Coupled with that remembrance was the additional uneasiness of being marooned in a storm with the man beside her. If the puzzling events of the past few weeks had not occurred, perhaps she would have been able to treat this night with a greater sense of equanimity.

"Do you see the turnoff?" Whit inquired.

"Not yet. But it shouldn't be much farther."

The wind bombarded the car, causing it to shift toward the edge of the pavement. Whit gradually returned to center, at the same time trying to keep the car from hydroplaning.

The windshield wipers were locked in rapid mode, but even then, there were times when they did little good because of the sheer volume of rain bombarding the windshield.

With water also obscuring the division between road and landscape, Carley couldn't be absolutely sure when they had reached the turnoff, but she thought she recognized the shrubbery at the side of the road.

"I think this is it," she said. "Turn left."

"I don't see any road," Whit answered. "Are you sure?"

"I recognize the shrubs," she said, with more certainty. "Just drive between them."

Brief glimpses of the hard-packed ribbon of sand and gravel affirmed that they were on course. At times, Whit was guided only by the crunch of tires on the gravel beneath the water. When the car leaned too far to the right, or too far to the left, Whit corrected the steering so as to remain on the roadbed and not slip into the ditch.

When they approached the closed gates. Carley felt relief. Safety now seemed to be within reach. "I'll get out and press the code. Then, you drive on and wait for me on the other side."

"Are you sure you don't want me to get out? You'll be soaked even worse."

"No. I can press the code with my eyes closed. It's better for you to drive through, since the gate closes quite rapidly."

With the car's headlights offering the only illumination, Carley sloshed her way to the intercom and pressed the code. Nothing happened. The gate remained closed. She pressed again and waited. Still, nothing happened. It was then that Carley realized that the electrical system must have been taken out by the storm. That meant that they would either have to remain in the car all night, or abandon it and go the rest of the way on foot. For Carley, there was only one option.

"The gates won't open," she called out. "And there's no other area where a car can get through. We'll have to walk the rest of the way in."

Carley wondered how much Morgan's designer dress had cost. By the time she and Whit had found a breach in the scrub trees and shrubs, it would be completely ruined — not to mention the shoes.

"Get back in the car, Carley," Whit said, "until I see what Goose has in his trunk. I hope he has an emergency kit."

Dripping wet, she climbed into the passenger side and waited, while Whit rummaged around in the trunk.

"I found one," he said, slamming the trunk closed.

"What?"

"A flashlight. At least we won't have to stumble around in complete darkness. That is, if the batteries are still good."

A meager light indicated that the flashlight worked. "I found something else, too," he added, opening the passenger door. "Here, put these on." He thrust a pair of galoshes toward Carley. "They'll keep you from breaking your neck in the dark."

While she removed the high-heeled sandals and replaced them with Goose's oversized galoshes, Whit walked to the driver's side and switched off the car's headlights. Once they were both out of the car, he locked the doors.

Before Carley's eyes had become adjusted to the sudden change in light, Whit was back again, taking off his tuxedo jacket. "Put this on, too," he ordered.

"Thanks, but my dress is already soaked, so you might as well keep it."

He ignored her protest. Forcing her bare arms into the sleeves, he then put his arm around her waist, holding her with an iron grip. "All right, Girl Scout. I guess you know the direction. So lead the way to civilization."

She resented this sudden intimacy. "I was never a Girl Scout," she commented petulantly. "But I was once a card-carrying *Boy Scout*."

"My God. Are you trying to tell me something?"

"It's a long story. I'll tell you after we reach the house."

She knew that Boris would take them in and make some type of sleeping arrangements for them—apart, of course. Even the dining room/conference center would be adequate to wait out the storm.

At the next burst of near hurricane force wind, Carley was grateful for Whit's steadying arm. Without it, she would have been blown along with the storm's debris. But being so close to him, she was aware of the odor of wet wool and a fleeting fragrance of his after-shave.

His tight grip, however, did not keep her from stumbling on a submerged log. When she had recovered her footing, she said, "It's too bad that Goose didn't have some night goggles in the trunk, too."

"He had something else almost as good."

"What?"

"Two granola bars."

She smiled at his attempt to defuse the seriousness of the moment.

"Did you bring them?"

"Yes. They're in the pocket of my jacket."

There was something else in his jacket, too—something hard and cold in an inside pocket. She could feel it through the silk lining. A gun? Why was Whit carrying a concealed weapon, especially on what was to have been a smashing gala evening?

Carley suddenly stopped, throwing off the rhythm of their walking together.

"What's wrong?"

She certainly was not going to accuse him of having a gun in such a deserted, wooded area. "My galoshes are waterlogged," she quickly responded. "Can't you hear the squeaking?"

He shone the flashlight down at her feet. "Do you want to stop and pour out the water?"

"No. Let's keep going."

Their progress was slow, since they were in the full thrust of the storm. The long, meandering drive, covered by water, was invisible, while the woods were illuminated off and on with sudden flashes of lightning, followed by loud reverberations of thunder. Then, just as quickly, the surroundings reverted to almost total, rain-filled darkness.

The next flash of lightning hit far too close, with a deafening boom. Carley saw a tall pine tree in the distance split and send missiles of wood in all directions.

Despite the wetness of the wood, the top of the damaged tree caught fire. The strange odor of ozone, mixed with resinous sap, was overwhelming.

The dangerous display of pyrotechnics and her wish to stay alive made her forget her initial plan of walking all the way to the main house. Grabbing onto Whit's hand, she immediately changed direction.

"I don't think we can make it to the main buildings."

"Then—"

"The Warhol cottage is much nearer. Boris gave me the key to it on Friday."

A few minutes later, another flash of lightning pointed the way to the small cottage, hidden among the trees. When they finally reached the diminutive porch, where the water level had already risen past the first step, she suddenly realized that the key to the cottage was on her large key ring, which she'd left at home.

"I'm afraid I don't have the key with me."

"That's no problem. Here, hold the flashlight while I pop the lock."

She did as she was told, trying to hold the flashlight with a steady hand. She didn't know which to blame—her realization of yet another disturbing facet to this man's character, or being soaked through and through, but she was not successful. Her hand shook so badly that Whit took the flashlight from her.

True to his avowal, Whit had the door open in record time. A burglar could have done no better. While she removed Goose's waterlogged galoshes, Whit stepped over the threshold of the cottage to lead the way.

"Be careful," Carley warned. "My boxes are stacked just inside the door." She didn't want him to stumble and break the two solar lights that she had taken out of the box and left lying on top.

"What the...?"

Seeing the twin glow that greeted them from floor level, Carley laughed. "My solar lights. They must have absorbed enough sun since Friday to come on when it got dark."

"Great. I thought a raccoon had gotten inside."

"Well, I'm glad that you didn't try to shoot my lights with your gun."

"So you found it, did you?"

He was certainly cavalier about it, acting as though perfectly normal people carried weapons in their tuxedo jackets.

Torn between keeping on the wet coat or returning it to Whit, she decided on the latter and swapped one worry for another.

All the way through the woods, she had been afraid that the gun would go off and shoot her in the foot. She was gratified that he immediately hung the coat on a wooden peg in the hallway.

Whit used the flashlight for a quick perusal of the cottage. Carley followed, carrying one of the solar lights. When Whit saw the fireplace, laden with logs, probably from the previous winter, he said, "Let's see if we can get a fire going."

Even though it was high summer, the wind and rain had served to cause a chill. "While you're doing that, I think I'll go and see what I can find in the way of something dry."

"Some dry wine might be nice."

"Ha! You won't find anything like that in this cottage. We'll be lucky to find a sheet or blanket to wrap around us."

"Then, take the flashlight," he said, swapping it for the less brilliant solar light.

The cottage seemed to be trembling on its foundation as she walked down the main hallway that divided the four rooms, two on each side. Was the construction sturdy enough to withstand the wind? Or would it be like the flimsy trailer parks, where mobile homes were lifted from their foundations and tossed into the air like confetti?

She located the bath, where a small cupboard held only one towel. Boris evidently had not stocked it well, since the cottage had not been assigned to any artist for the session.

Taking the towel with her, she walked cautiously down the hall to one of the bedrooms. There she found at the foot of the unmade bed two folded sheets, a pillowcase, and a thin, thermal blanket. She scooped them up and retraced her steps to the main room, where Whit was kneeling on the hearth with his back to her and coaxing the small flame he had started.

He had taken off his wet shirt. There was something very primitive about this well-muscled man, whose skin still glistened with the effects of the rain. For a brief moment, in the fire glow, he resembled a rugged caveman, who had just returned to the hearth from the hunt.

Carley blinked her eyes several times to rid herself of the disturbing image that she had created. Even more disturbing was the realization of how much she had missed being in a man's arms these past months.

"I found some bed linens," she announced, trying to sound matter-of-fact. "We can wrap them around us to alleviate some of the dampness."

Whit turned to face her. "It might be better for you to take off your dress, first."

She stammered a little in answering him. "If I stand before the fire, it won't take long to get dry."

"Suit yourself. But I don't plan to remain in these wet clothes for the rest of the night."

 *Chapter 18*

With a sheet wrapped around him in toga fashion, Whit sat in one of the rocking chairs. Carley remained standing by the fire, twisting and turning from front to back, as if being roasted on a spit.

"You might as well give up, Carley. You'll never get dry that way. Especially with the logs burning down."

"You didn't see any others stacked anywhere?"

"Only outside. They're so wet, they'd never catch fire, even if I brought them in. You'd be much more comfortable hanging up your dress and wrapping yourself in the other sheet."

When she seemed to ignore him, he teased, "Or are you afraid that I'll discover that you actually *are* a Boy Scout?"

Carley did not take the bait. Instead, she switched off the flashlight and placed it on the mantel. She then proceeded to sit down in the adjacent rocking chair and retorted, "There was nothing remarkable about my experience as a Boy Scout. I was the sponsor of a teen Explorer group, under the aegis of the symphony. That automatically made me a member."

"So that explains it," he said. "I presume then these scouts had an interest in music?"

"Yes."

"Too bad we don't have a little music tonight, ourselves." He held out a granola bar. "Would you like a midnight snack, instead?"

"Rather late for that. It's already two o'clock."

"Well, it has to be midnight *somewhere* in the world."

Despite herself, Carley laughed and accepted the granola bar. Surprised that she was hungry, she finished it in record time and threw the empty wrapper into the dying fire.

The back door blew open and a gust of wind swept down the central hall, from back to front. The two jumped up at the same time. Whit grabbed the flashlight from the mantel and they hurried down the hall.

Looking for something to shore up the door, Carley and Whit shoved the rustic, Mission-style kitchen table against the back door and, for good measure, piled on the two matching chairs. Then Carley groped for a kitchen towel to mop up the water that had come in with the wind.

From that time on, the sniping with each other subsided, and they settled down to becoming a team to ride out the storm together.

"I'm sorry, Carley, to have gotten you into this mess."

"It's not your fault, Whit. When you saw how bad the weather was getting, you should have gone on and left me at the hotel."

"Do you actually think that I would have done such a thing?" he asked, in a voice that sounded a little angry. "Then, you don't know me very well."

"No. I guess we're still strangers." Carley yawned. "Very tired strangers." But she was determined to remain vigilant for the rest of the night.

Early the next morning, Carley heard a persistent knocking, followed by voices. She opened her eyes and looked around. She was no longer in the rocking chair by the fireplace. Instead, she was in bed, with the thermal blanket thrown over her. The sound of a steady rain pelting the cottage roof indicated the residue of the tropical storm, Isidore.

Within moments, Whit, who was already dressed in his tuxedo, walked into the bedroom.

"It's time to get up,Carley. We have a ride waiting."

"Is Goose outside?"

"No. The chauffeur is here with the limousine. He says that the causeway is open again."

It did not take long for Carley to pull herself together. As they left the cottage and climbed into the limousine, Carley realized that neither she nor Whit bore any resemblance to the well-dressed couple of the previous evening.

Whit's tuxedo was damp and wrinkled, and he sported more than a five o'clock shadow. As for herself, the brief glimpse in the bathroom mirror indicated that she was equally disheveled. She hoped she might get home without being seen by her churchgoing neighbors.

Dresnick, the chauffeur, handed them two Starbucks coffees, and Carley was grateful.

"Thank you," she said.

The chauffeur nodded, started up the motor, and headed for the gate.

"I don't understand," Carley whispered to Whit. "How did he know where we were?"

"He saw Goose's car."

"But it isn't visible from the road."

"Drink your coffee, darling, and stop being so nosy."

How could one man be so irritating and evasive, and still so charming at the same time?

When they reached the gate, it was wide open. Had the electricity come back on, or had the chauffeur found some way to open it manually?

The limousine slowed and Whit turned to Carley. "I'm getting out here, to follow you in Goose's car. So I'll say goodbye for now." His eyes twinkled as he added, "Carley Burnside, I don't know when I've enjoyed a one night stand more."

Not waiting for her bristling retort, he closed the door while Carley took another gulp of hot coffee. Dresnick idled the motor until Goose's car started. He carefully maneuvered the limo along the ravaged sand and gravel road, while checking to make sure that Goose's car was in sight. Seeing it, he pulled onto the highway and headed back to Mobile.

Halfway home, Carley remembered where she had seen this burley chauffeur named Dresnick. He was the same one who had brought Consuelo Tolliver to the artists' compound on that first day.

Something didn't add up. Was there a connection between Evian Whitstone and Consuelo? Or was it just coincidence? The nagging question vanished as Carley suddenly realized that Whit had her house key in his pocket.

"Dresnick!"

"Ma'am?"

"Mr. Whitstone has my key. I'll need it to get back into my house."

The chauffeur pressed the limo speakerphone and dialed a number. Only a sound responded, almost like a signal from an outdated fax machine. "My passenger needs her house key, when we arrive."

There was no vocal response, but Dresnick seemed satisfied. He disconnected and kept driving, while Carley became more puzzled than ever.

When Carley was only a block from her house, the limousine pulled to the curb and stopped, with Whit directly behind. Dresnick got out, retrieved her key, and then continued on his way.

"You can pull down the driveway," Carley suggested. "I'll go in the side entrance."

Dresnick did as she asked. Without waiting for him to open the door, she jumped out of the limousine. "Thanks for the ride," she said and, with her key in hand, she hurried to unlock the entrance that was sheltered from the street.

Within moments, she was safely inside the house. Touching the jade necklace, she hoped that Joie had not seen her. She didn't feel like explaining anything to anybody — least of all, Joie.

The cats were gone, and so were their water and food

bowls. The note propped against the vase of bamboo shoots on the kitchen table said, "I'm taking the cats to the carriage house for the night, since they're afraid of the storm. I suppose you'll have to stay at the hotel because of the roads. Let me know when you get home. Joie." She added a postscript. "The telephone lines are down, so just knock on my door."

Carley wasn't eager for Joie to see her in Morgan's ruined dress. She decided to take a bath and wash her hair, first. Unfortunately, the water was luke warm.

Later, after she had put on her jogging suit, she dashed through the garden, with the box containing Joie's necklace. She walked up the carriage house steps and knocked. "Joie, it's me."

The door opened immediately. Usually so placid in expression, Joie showed a visible relief. "I've decided to get a cell phone," she announced. "If I'd had one, you could have called me last night to let me know you were all right."

Carley didn't tell her that the satellite was probably knocked out, too. "I'm sorry that you were worried. But as you can see, I'm fine."

"Have you had breakfast?"

"Only coffee."

"It's a good thing that your grandmother put in a gas stove in my little kitchen. So just sit down, while I make us a cheese and tomato omelet. You can tell me about the party while I'm cooking."

Li-Po and Cho-Cho had come to greet Carley. So while she scratched their ears, she chatted with Joie.

"Your necklace was a big hit. Thanks for letting me borrow it. Agnes was most impressed."

"I presume she was there with Mr. Goosens?"

"Yes."

With Joie's prodding about the party and the auction, Carley told her about Table 6, about Lucinda and her husband, and the success of the bidding. But when it came to Carley's blind date, she was noticeably silent. Having a feeling that Joie was waiting for her to bring up the subject, she finally said, "Evian Whitstone is quite an interesting guy."

Joie smiled. "So, are you seeing him again?"

"I have no idea."

"What do you mean? Did he not say that he would call you?"

"I'm not sure that I want to go out with him again."

"And why not?" Joie seemed disappointed.

"I think he's a little too..." Carley searched for the right word. "...too *dangerous* for me."

Joie gave her one of her classic looks, peering over her glasses and waiting for her to explain.

"Joie, he had a gun in an inside pocket. I felt it while we were..." She hesitated. "...dancing. With everything else that has been going on, it made me quite uneasy."

"Are you sure it was a gun? Maybe it was his wallet."

"No. I'm sure."

"Well, there could be a number of reasons why he carries a weapon."

"There're just too many unanswered questions. And I don't think I want to know the answers. I even wondered if he might not be who he says he is."

"Maybe he's in the witness protection program."

Carley laughed at her suggestion, which was exactly what Joie intended. "Or a spy," Carley proposed.

"Or the CIA."

They had almost finished breakfast when the lights came back on. Carley didn't linger. She thanked Joie for taking care of Li-Po and Cho-Cho, and with the cats following , she made her way back to the main house.

With all the activity of the previous night, she felt quite lethargic. Finally, she gave up doing anything strenuous and climbed into bed for a nap.

Shortly before she went to sleep, she remembered thinking how boring Bob had been for their entire marriage, in comparison to one night spent with Evian Whitstone

 *Chapter 19*

Carley awoke to the sound of a telephone ringing. She'd slept so deeply that, momentarily, she had no idea of the hour, the day of the week, or even where she was. By the time she was functional, the phone had stopped ringing.

She glanced at her watch. Five o'clock. She couldn't believe that she had slept so long. But at least, the phone lines were working again.

When she walked to her office, to see if someone had left a message, the red light was blinking.

"Carley, I'm so glad that you stayed at the hotel, rather than trying to make it home last night." She recognized Agnes's voice. "It was really quite dangerous on the road. We barely managed to get over the causeway before it closed down. Do call me when you have a moment."

Who had told Agnes that she had stayed at the hotel? Should she just let it go? But Goose was sure to know what had happened, with Whit's returning his car nearly twelve hours later.

Carley dialed Agnes's number. She answered on the second ring. "It's me—Carley. I just picked up your message."

"It's good to hear your voice. I understand that the chauffeur went back for you after the causeway reopened."

"Yes, he did."

"I particularly wanted to tell you what a great sport you

were last night. Goose was in a rather uncomfortable position, with Lucinda and all."

The *all* being her husband Rudy, Carley thought. "I was surprised that the evening went as well as it did. I was glad to help."

In Mobile, as in so many other Southern cities, there is an unwritten social ritual that calls for a few polite exchanges at the beginning of any conversation before the meat of the matter is dealt with.

Now that Agnes had the fluff out of the way, Carley waited for her to broach the real reason for the call.

"I also have a favor to ask of you," she finally said. "Actually, it's Goose who wants the favor, but he was rather hesitant to approach you on the subject."

"I don't see why."

"Maybe you will, when I tell you."

Carley's alarm antenna spiraled upward. "What is it?"

"Last night, one of the members of the architectural firm cornered Goose. They've decided to reconfigure the boat dock at Boris's, and it necessitates taking away some space from one of your gardens.

"Carley, are you still there?"

It took her a moment to find her voice. "You're speaking of Bob, aren't you?"

"Well, yes."

"So, what does *he* want?"

"Your aboriginal garden space."

"But that's where some of the most beautiful native plants are located. It would be a crime to destroy them."

"Is there any way that you could, say, transplant them to another location?"

"I couldn't guarantee that they would live, Agnes. The storm has already made me lose a day. Tomorrow, I'm sure, will be spent entirely in assessing the damage to the property, and then starting on the cleanup."

"Goose realizes this, and he's prepared to set aside more money, if you need to pay your workers an extra amount.

Why don't you think about it and then call me back?"

"When do you need to know?"

"Within the next day or two."

"All right, Agnes. I'll see what I can salvage and then call you."

"Thank you, Carley. You've no idea how upset Goose is, over this situation."

Carley certainly didn't want her favorite poker buddy to be caught in the middle. It wasn't his fault that Bob was the way he was. But what had she done to irritate her ex-husband sufficiently for him to try to sabotage her landscape project for a second time?

She sat down at her desk and pulled up the plans to the wild, aboriginal space, to reacquaint herself with it and try to find some other suitable venue for the garden and Wingate's bis pole. But she had too much on her mind to tackle the problem.

Finally turning off the computer, she stared at Gran's red phoenix screen, instead. What was the matter with her? She had not only forgotten her house key that morning, but also the red lacquered box from the auction. That wasn't like her. She was usually so responsible.

Now, she would have to claim the box and reimburse Whit for it. She had originally planned to put it on a credit card, since her cash was getting low.

Knowing that she was playing with fire and in danger of being burned, she, nevertheless, began making plans to contact Evian Whitstone — one last time.

Just then, the doorbell rang. With the cats racing her to the door, she walked to the front hallway and looked through the viewfinder. She saw Dresnick, the chauffeur, standing on the steps.

"Your box, ma'am."

How disappointed she was. "Wait. I need to write a check for Mr. Whitstone."

"He didn't say anything about that," the chauffeur insisted, walking back to the limousine and leaving Carley standing at the door.

She took the box into her office to find a suitable place for it. After trying several different locations, she decided on a small table adjacent to the screen. Then, since the mid-morning omelet was only a memory, she went into the kitchen to prepare supper.

On Monday morning, with the sky still looking rather dreary, Carley started out for Fairhope. All along the way, signs of the storm were apparent, from downed trees with their shallow roots pointing upward, to water-filled ditches along the roads.

When she arrived in the compound — the gate was still open — Jake had already started on the job of cleaning up the aftermath of the storm. As the rest of the crew filtered in, they too set to work.

The storm seemed to have been the catalyst for all the artists. So many of them were painting *al fresco*, recording on their canvases the damage that Mother Nature had done to the environment.

The black-clad fellow of the past Saturday night, Maxim Tourkay, protested strenuously when Jake attempted to haul away a dismal looking specimen. "I haven't finished painting that log," he said. "Please put it back where it belongs."

Jake looked at Carley, and when she nodded, he reluctantly put it back. With such glaring between the two of them, Carley decided that it would be the propitious time to get Jake's opinion on the sudden change in plans.

As they walked toward the water, Carley waved at Consuelo, who was also painting outdoors. She smiled briefly and then went back to her easel.

Along the way to the original site of the aboriginal garden, Carley tried to explain the problem to Jake in an unbiased manner. But when they reached the site and saw several stakes had already been driven into the ground, and a number of plants had been trampled on, Jake's temper flared. He took his machete and whacked the wooden stakes to ground level.

"Jake, this isn't going to help matters," she cautioned.

"He had no business doing this to you."

"I know. But we'll have to live with it. So let's take a look at the plants and decide how many we can move to another location."

They tagged far fewer than Carley wished, but most were too fragile to survive, even with the utmost care. They were in an ecosystem of their own, and any other place would be alien.

Standing there, looking at the site, Carley was struck by the fleeting, limited partnership between land and landscape designer. The paintings and canvases of artists, once finished, remained the same. They hung for years in their assigned frames and spaces. But land was a living thing and constantly changing.

After walking over several different areas, Carley and Jake finally decided on a possible new site. It was farther from the water, but equally as wild. In fact, the approach was so well hidden that a more *inauspicious* site, as Joie suggested, could not be found.

While a few of the crew began digging up the plants to be moved, Carley decided it was time to consult Wingate. She didn't know how upset he would be over the change, but surely Boris had already spoken to him about it.

She also wondered how she might approach him diplomatically, to dig up his treasure chest, without his discovering that she and Barnie were aware of its grotesque contents. Of course, finding the lock broken, he would know that something was wrong.

A few minutes later, she saw Wingate coming from the dining hall. Waylaying him, she said, "We need to talk."

His expression was sour. "I don't have time today."

"That's too bad. We're getting ready to pour the foundation for the artists' obelisk, but something appears to be buried in that very spot."

Her comment got his attention. "Maybe I can make time. How about ten minutes from now? I'll meet you in the small conference room."

"Fine. By the way, how is your pole coming along? Almost ready to put in the ground?"

"Another day or so, and it will be finished."

He rushed on to the house, and Carley continued toward the food wagon to get a bottle of water.

In the conference room, while she waited for Wingate, Carley unrolled the master plat that she had drawn and spread it on the table. Although she had used the computer for much of the work, she had also used her draftsman's skills to complete the design.

Thinking back to her first drafting class in college, she remembered how glad she was to have another woman, Gerda Blixen, in the classroom amid all the male students. She and Gerda had bonded immediately, but after graduation, she had returned to Switzerland, to the little town of Gruyere, the fairy tale village where the famous cheese factory was located. They had kept in touch for several years, but then even the exchange of Christmas cards had ceased.

If she were going to be spending some time at Milly-la-Forêt, redesigning Morgan's garden, then perhaps she might try to locate her. After all this time, it would be nice to see her again.

When Carley heard Wingate's footsteps, her mind returned to the present as she geared up for the confrontation to come.

 *Chapter 20*

Wingate's temper exploded.

"I know how you feel," Carley said, attempting to salvage the conversation that had started so ineptly on her part. "But I don't have a choice, either. The garden was taken from me. So together, we'll just have to find another spot."

"I never liked the idea of the boathouse anyway. It makes it too convenient for other people to dock here."

"But Wingate, Cavallegria needs another approach to it beyond the narrow road. The storm this past weekend certainly proved that."

Carley couldn't believe that she was defending the boathouse and its expanded dock.

"I have two possible sites to show you. You can choose which one you prefer."

His mind seemed to be elsewhere. "When are you going to start on the obelisk?"

"Probably by Wednesday." That should give him enough time to retrieve the buried chest.

He seemed to relax a bit. "Then, let's go now and select the new place for my sculpture."

Carley always sensed a different ambiance after a storm. Like people, plants and trees seemed to be divided between those that bend and survive, and those that remain rigid and suffer. Yet, she couldn't help but admire aged old trees, arthritic and misshapen, still battling against their enemies of time, wind, and drought.

As she and Wingate tramped over the tender earth and left a pooling trail of foot casts behind, she took note of a few of these ravaged behemoths, their limbs dressed in tattered moss.

Some of these specimens would not survive this latest attack, and it made her sad, realizing that all living things eventually die. She supposed that she was feeling particularly sad that day, because it was Gran's birthday.

Carley suddenly wanted to turn back, to buy Gran's favorite flowers—purple fuchsias—and to sit and talk with her at the mausoleum, as was the custom of the early French settlers, who communed with their dead as easily as they did with the living.

Instead, she continued on, until she and Wingate arrived at the first wild site.

He looked around, lifting his head and sniffing the wind, almost as if he were some thin, feral hound, determining danger. After a few minutes, he said, "I don't know. Let me see the other one, before I decide."

She guided him into a denser bower of green, where the sun was a stranger to much of the day—the site that she and Jake had discussed.

"This is the second one on the plat," she said, and then remained silent, neither trying to persuade nor dissuade Wingate in his decision.

Finally he said, grudgingly, "Well, I'm not happy with either one. But if I have to choose, I'll take this one."

Carley nodded, to confirm his decision. "It will be a spectacular garden, Wingate, but a secret one."

A slight smile indicated his reaction to her comment— only the second time he'd smiled since she'd met him.

* * *

By Wednesday night, Goose, Henry, Edward, and Carley were back to playing poker. A tacit agreement seemed to have been struck, with no one bringing up the subject of the previous Saturday night or the tropical storm. Yet, the silence spoke louder than any conversation, as if a stray word, an intemperate response might open up the Pandora's box that no one wanted to explore.

To Carley, the uneasiness was as evident as the morning's vapor trail in the sky that predicted an imminent rain.

For the first time, they seemed to be walking on eggshells with each other. It pained Carley to see what was happening to their well-knit little group.

Was she fooling herself? Had they become tired of this Wednesday night ritual, yet were too gentlemanly to tell her? When had it occurred, this gradual shift, this realization that she needed the shared camaraderie as much as they did?

"All right, guys. Out with it. What's bothering you? The fact that I was forced to spend the night with my blind date? Or that you've had enough of the investment club, but don't want to hurt my feelings."

"Gosh, Carley," Henry said. "You know how much we enjoy coming to this house and playing poker. It's not that, at all."

"Then, what is it? Friends need to be honest with each other." She looked at Edward, at Henry, and then her eyes rested on Goose.

He cleared his throat. "We all feel as if we've let you down, my dear. Lydia, as well. You see, we've done a sorry job of watching over you. Take Saturday night, for instance. That was a dangerous situation."

"Horse...trough!" she interrupted. "You had nothing to do with the storm. And you certainly can't oversee my virtue. But for your information, Evian Whitstone was a gentleman." Carley laughed. "Even if he *did* say how much he enjoyed our one night stand."

The three laughed, too, and visibly relaxed.

"I have only one question. He's not a stalker, is he?"

"Oh, my, no!" Goose replied. "It's just that he's quite adept at getting what he wants."

Carley left it at that, and the poker game resumed.

Early the next morning, the landscaping resumed, as well.

The obelisk foundation had been laid the day before, and with the concrete being given a chance to harden, there was no further delay in the erection of the classical garden structure. Disguised by mandevilla vines and white wisteria, the obelisk became an integral part of the landscape.

Carley stood at the top and surveyed the bay through the trellised slats. She was rewarded with the sight of two wild ducks skimming the water and then silently drifting with the current—a picture waiting to be captured on canvas.

A pattern of soft solar lights along scenic pathways also took shape, hinting, in the midst of the wildness of the estate, garden mysteries slightly beyond view, with geometric designs and less formal ones suddenly appearing, to give pleasure to the eye .

The consummation of each garden was accompanied by the sounds of the boathouse construction. But Bob seemed to have lost interest in his own design. He seldom arrived to view the work in progress. When he did, Carley made herself scarce at that first flash of silver along the sandy drive.

As soon as Jake and the crew finished with one garden, a number of artists with their easels appeared—vying for prime space, to capture the filtering of light and shade, the unusual chiaroscuro effect giving interest and depth to what nature had created.

A huge shell fountain became the centerpiece of the shell garden, with an encrusted tabby floor indicating a bygone day along the coast. It was not nearly so spectacular as the shell garden she had visited at St. Aubin's in the Channel Islands, the largest in the world. No moon shell, no Jersey ormer. Carley had used only the native shells that washed upon the sands of the Gulf, giving the garden an intriguing uniqueness of its own.

By Friday, the time came for the planting of the sculpture that Wingate had carved, a labor of six months or more; yet, years in the planning. The concrete base, with aboriginal markings, was ready to receive it; the exact dimensions tortuously acquired beforehand from Wingate.

For this out-of-the-way garden with his carved sculpture as centerpiece, the man wanted no fanfare. He had deliberately chosen the time when the other artists would be getting ready for dinner and Boris's seminar to follow. So Carley, with Jake and Barnie, remained behind, later than usual, to attend to the mounting of the pole after the other workers had left for the weekend.

On that first morning, when she and Boris had walked over his property, Carley had inquired about a ramshackle barn-like structure at the northern boundary of his property. He had informed her that it was off limits and did not figure in the overall restoration of the landscape.

So in the survey, Carley had used the small, meandering creek bank with its stand of willows as a ha-ha, separating the outer perimeter of the plans to the more natural meadows in the distance, as in many of the old English gardens.

Now, with Barnie and Jake in the back, and Wingate seated beside her in the red Toyota truck, Carley started over the rough terrain in the direction of the deserted barn.

Was that where Wingate had stored his imported mangrove roots, and where he had been working all along on his sculpture?

If so, why had he not stored his chest of shrunken heads in the same place? Perhaps, though, he was afraid the barn might burn down. The poles could be replaced, but the heads were probably contraband, by now.

Once they arrived at the edge of the stream, they left the truck to go the rest of the way on foot, using the rickety small bridge to make the crossing.

Wingate seemed torn between secrecy and the need for help in getting his masterpiece out of the barn and set in its proper place. "Wait here," he ordered, unlocking the combination lock on the door. He guarded the numbers as if the crew were potential thieves at an ATM machine.

The three looked at each other, but said nothing. Then, when Wingate was out of sight, Barnie leaned over and whispered, "I think we're dealing with a lunatic, here."

Jake started to say something, as well, but seeing Wingate's head suddenly reappearing at the door, he coughed, instead.

"All right. You can come in now."

Carley was extremely curious to see this aboriginal art form, but when they entered, the sculpture was shrouded in a gray tarpaulin.

With the four dispersed along the length of the pole, they hoisted the carving, tarpaulin and all, and turned it to point toward the open door. Cautiously, they walked over the footbridge with it, and then slid it onto the padded bed of the truck, while the end of the pole stuck out beyond the confines of the truck.

Wingate retraced his steps to the barn, shut the door, padlocked it, and then climbed into the back of the truck with Jake. Barnie rode up front with Carley.

When they arrived at the sculpture site, Carley wondered whether New Guinea warrior-head hunters had a special ritual for dedication or celebration of an ancestral pole, and whether Wingate intended having one, too. But it was getting late, and since it had been a long, tiring day, Carley merely wanted to get the pole into its base, anchor it sufficiently, and then head for home. The landscaping around it could wait until Monday.

Wingate slowly removed the canvas tarpaulin. Although she was curious, Carley was far too busy with the mechanics to view it properly until it came to rest in its base. Then, she stepped back and viewed it in all its awful splendor.

Words have a way of being translated differently by those who hear them. The quiet, non-threatening description at the luncheon table had nothing to do with this carved mangrove root, with each curve, each decoration caressed by the chisel of a master sculptor.

Carley took little note of the grace of the canoe, or the void where a shrunken head belonged. Her eyes were glued to the giant *asmat*, the phallic symbol that rose straight in the air, its erogenous tip shamelessly touched by the rays of the slanting sun.

 *Chapter 21*

*I*t had been a week since the fundraising party, and in that time, Carley had not heard a word from Evian Whitstone. She realized that she had ambivalent feelings concerning this silence. On the one hand, she was relieved, but on the other, she felt a sense of disappointment. No woman, particularly one picking up the pieces of her life, wants to think that she is not desirable enough for a second date.

On her way home from Fairhope, Carley began thinking of the weekend. The prospect of a dull two days at home with only Li-Po and Cho-Cho as companions seemed quite unappealing.

The idea of driving down to visit the Bellingrath Gardens at Theodore immediately came to mind. She had not been there in awhile, and since the gardens were constantly changing, it would be nice to see the renovations that had been done in the last few years. But she did not want to go alone. Neither did she want to rely on Joie as a companion, since she had a life of her own. Perhaps she could ask Eleanor, who had also served on Lizzie's committee.

Although they were friendly, Carley had never really gotten to know her while she was married to Bob. Now that she was single again, she needed to reach out to other singles.

The trip back and forth to Fairhope five days a week had become so automatic, that Carley pulled into her driveway before she realized the trip had ended. She had made only one stop—at the local butcher's shop on the corner. She knew that the cats would be glad to see her, if not for herself, then for their special Friday treats.

Li-Po and Cho-Cho were waiting for her. She lavished them with praise for having left the bamboo shoots alone, but they were interested only in the chicken livers, not in her enthusiasm for their good behavior in her absence.

The moment she stepped inside the house, the telephone had started ringing. She let the answering machine pick up. But just in case a friend had called, she went to her office to check the messages.

Buried in offers to replace her windows, refinance her house, and give her a fabulous deal on a new car, a personal message brought an immediate smile.

"Carley, this is Whit. I've just gotten back into town. I'd love to see you this weekend, if you can manage it at this late date. Dinner tomorrow night? Call me when you get in."

Her heart began a little dance, much to her chagrin. She quickly dialed the number Whit had left. After a few rings, his answering machine cut in. Disappointed, she hesitated before speaking. "Hi, this is Carley. I just got your message, so am returning..."

"Carley?" He picked up in the middle of her sentence.

"Whit?"

After a few polite exchanges, he said, "What are your plans for the weekend, Carley? Would you be free for a dinner cruise tomorrow night?"

She did not want to appear too eager. "Actually, I was planning to visit Bellingrath Gardens in the afternoon." Then she lost her resolve and hastened to add, "But a dinner cruise originates from their marina at seven. If you haven't already made reservations elsewhere, I could meet you at the gardens then. They're quite lovely this time of year."

"So where is this place?"

"About twenty miles south of here, at Theodore."

"Will anyone else be with you?"

"Actually...not."

"Well, then, what if I picked you up earlier, so that we can stroll together, or whatever one does in a garden—before the cruise?"

"You wouldn't mind?"

"Not at all."

Once more, Carley dug into Morgan's wardrobe, to find something suitable to wear for the afternoon and into the evening on the boat. She finally decided on an enormous, floppy hat for the sun and wind, a coral chiffon top with sailor's white slacks, and white, rope-soled shoes. This time, she didn't feel half the guilt of borrowing from Morgan's designer closet. In fact, it could easily become a habit, if she didn't repent soon.

When the doorbell rang around half past three the next day, Carley looked out to see a red Ferrari sitting in her circular drive. She opened the door and a smiling Whit stood on the steps.

"Come in," she invited, trying hard not to stare at this big, gorgeous, dangerous man, dressed in casual clothes, with a dark blazer slung over his shoulder.

"I'm a little early," he apologized.

"Then, how about a Bloody Mary before we go?"

"Sounds good."

Whit followed her to the kitchen, helping to mix the drinks while she attended to the celery. She also opened a little tub of spinach Florentine, put it in a crystal dish, and placed it on a tray with cheddar butterfly crackers.

They had no more than sat down in the den when the doorbell rang again. Then, the door opened, and a voice called, "Carley?"

She froze. It was her ex-husband Bob, walking into the unlocked house as if he were still welcomed. "In the den," she called out.

"That's a great looking car in the drive... Oh, I see that you have company."

"Whit, this is my...my former husband, Bob Dickerson. Bob—Evian Whitstone."

Whit had stood up and Bob walked across the room to shake hands. Seeing Carley's reaction, Whit smoothly took over. "We were just having Bloody Marys. Would you care for one?"

"No thanks," Bob replied, with a slight frown. "I just stopped by to leave a check."

He sat down in an adjacent chair, pulled out his checkbook, and began writing. When he finished, he said, "The auctioneer sold the bedroom suite. So Carley, this is your half of the money from the sale."

He stood up, handed her the check, and then said, "I owe Joie a check, too. Is she in?"

"I have no idea. But you know the way to the carriage house."

"It was good to meet you, Whit," he said, as he left the den and then vanished through the side door.

Li-Po, resting in his kitchen hammock, acknowledged Bob's presence with a hiss. Gran's cats had never taken to Bob.

Whit's blue eyes were twinkling. "Does he come here often?"

"This is the first time since the divorce."

He laughed. "Well, it was bound to happen—his seeing you in this house with another man."

Carley forced a smile. "I'll make sure to lock the doors from now on."

They leisurely finished their drinks and Carley went to get her handbag. She had assumed that, after seeing Joie, Bob had walked down the driveway to his car. But as she returned to the den, she saw that he had come back through the house. He shook hands with Whit again and walked out the front door, closing it behind him.

Oh, God. How embarrassing. I may not make it through the day, Carley thought.

"Ready, Carley?" Whit asked.

"Just as soon as I double lock the side door."

It was a beautiful afternoon, with soft, pillowed clouds forming the most amazing sky menagerie, or so Carley imagined. Shapes formed, changed, drifted, and then vanished behind the sun.

With the convertible top down and the mild wind blowing, she was thankful for Morgan's floppy hat. It was tied securely to her head, with its brilliant coral and lime green scarf trailing behind like the tails of a kite.

"Too much wind for you?" Whit asked.

"No, I'm fine. But if my hat flies off, we'll have to go back for it. It's borrowed," she confessed.

"Like Goose's galoshes."

"I hope the hat's more becoming than those size twelve's."

"Decidedly so."

That was how the trip started—with a light touch. Carley tried to forget the embarrassing episode with her former husband, but his actions still nagged at her. Why had he not put the check in the mail, instead of delivering it in person? That awkward situation certainly put the kibosh on her mentioning the lacquered box to Whit. She decided that she would do what Bob should have done—say nothing and drop the check in the mail with a thank-you note.

After a few miles, they left I-10 and turned south on US-90. Soon they were on Bellingrath Road, with the entrance of the Museum House directly in front of them. The wide, jeweled green expanse of lawn was impressive, encircled as it was by lush borders of brilliant annuals. The azaleas had finished blooming, but Carley knew that the roses would be magnificent.

After Whit had purchased tickets, they began their garden tour. From the bayou boardwalk to Mirror Lake, to the Rockery and the Rose Garden, each was a busman's holiday for Carley. The widest response from Whit came as he viewed the famous sculpture of the mermaid with two tails.

"I'm impressed," he said. "Maybe she should be called the Paul Revere mermaid. One by land and two if by sea. Or was it the other way around?"

Carley laughed. It was such fun being with Whit. After a brief respite for something cool to drink, they eventually made their way to the marina. Already the passengers were boarding the *Southern Belle* for the dinner cruise.

Carley was ready to get in line, but then Whit put his hand on her arm. "We're not taking this cruise. I've reserved a private one—just for the two of us."

 *Chapter 22*

*T*he first person that Carley saw on board their private cruise was Dresnick. He gave a brief nod of recognition and then moved on quietly and efficiently with his duties. Carley's questioning look toward Whit elicited a bland expression, and she hesitated in saying anything within Dresnick's hearing.

His appearance on the boat, however, puzzled her. Was Dresnick a hired chauffeur, or did he assume a much greater importance to Whit, such as a bodyguard? That brought up another question. Why would he need one? Then, there was the matter of Consuelo Tolliver, who also seemed to have a connection with Dresnick. Were all three linked together? The possibility was unsettling.

She didn't want to feel suspicious that night. Carley wanted to enjoy the lazy drifting down the river, to see the lights from the vast estates in the distance, and to delight in the intimacy of dinner alone with the man beside her.

It was a fantasy, she knew—the kind that she had never experienced before. All her life she had been the practical one. But with Evian Whitstone suddenly appearing in her life, she realized how much she had missed.

Now, she felt a great need to be cherished and, in Gran's old-fashioned vocabulary, to be wooed, to partake of all those unfulfilled dreams; yet knowing at the same time that they were the very things that made a woman vulnerable—

especially one on the rebound.

As they stood at the railing with their hands barely touching, Carley was quite aware of Whit, even as she was aware of the coves and inlets they passed, and the great live oaks, swaying in silhouette against the river banks.

Dresnick brought pre-dinner drinks to them, and then disappeared.

"I hope you like this wine I've selected," Whit said.

Unlike Morgan, Carley had never been a connoisseur of wine. An occasional beer with the guys and a Bloody Mary with her former Sunday brunch friends were the extent of her repertoire.

"What is it?" she asked, holding up the stem to view its golden contents, sparkling through the prism of the sun's fading rays.

"It's a little known wine I picked up in Strasbourg awhile back. I liked its bouquet, so I invested in the vineyard."

Carley coughed as the first sip went down the wrong way. She made a quick recovery. "It's quite smooth. And the name?"

"Longchamp's *Sans Merci.*"

"Like *la belle dame sans...*"

"So you know your Keats."

"Better than I know my wine. But is the wine *actually* without mercy?"

"Only for those who drink too much of it."

"And you? What about you — in your business dealings?"

"Absolutely ruthless — especially when I see something that I want."

Carley felt a shiver up her spine. Below the surface of this supposedly lighthearted conversation was a strong undercurrent — sexual and intimate. Looking at each other, they were both aware of it.

She didn't know which went to her head first, the wine

or Whit's intimation that he usually got what he went after. From the moment she'd met him, Carley sensed that he was a dangerous man.

In view of what happened later, she should have pulled back. Instead, she savored every moment that they were together.

At the disappearance of the sun past the horizon, the dining experience commenced and continued on through the unveiling of the night sky, with the brilliant, twinkling stars surrounding the moon that had not yet reached its fullness.

The dinner began with artichokes, peeled and dipped in a fragrant orange and aioli sauce. That was followed by a cup of lobster-sherry bisque, a salad of blanched spinach and arugula, all in moderate proportions and eaten slowly, as if to prolong the special bond that was blossoming between them.

Everything seemed to be in perfect rhythm—the gentle swell of the boat in the water, the mild breeze that rippled the awning overhead.

They talked, but later, Carley had no conscious memory of the dinner conversation. The words were unimportant. Only the senses, the feelings, the longings, seemed reshaped into something new.

Off and on, Dresnick reappeared, removed plates and, between courses, brought small silver cups of sorbet, designed to refresh the palate for the next taste experience.

Each course was more spectacular than the previous one in its presentation. Then came the *piéce de resistance*—Duck á *la Russe*. It arrived amid a flaming comet of vodka that lit up the deck and then subsided a few moments after it reached the table.

Carley applauded in delight and Dresnick, briefly noting her enthusiasm, returned his attention to serving the plates.

At last, when Carley felt that she couldn't possibly eat more, Dresnick removed the plates and substituted a tray of frosted grapes and cheese.

"Would you like an after dinner coffee?' Whit asked.

"Yes, please." Carley was hoping that strong coffee would help combat the wine that she had consumed with each course, and would bring her back to some semblance of reality.

Whit nodded to Dresnick and, within a few minutes, the coffee arrived, pungent in its aroma.

Carefully orchestrated to last a major part of the evening, the entire meal had been satisfying without being overly filling. It should have sated both her body and her blood. Instead, in the rhythmic setting of wilderness and water, it had served to heighten another appetite that had been malnourished for the past six months.

"That was lovely," she commented to Whit, as they rose from the dinner table to return to their deck chairs with their coffee. "What a delightful evening it's been. Thank you."

"It isn't over yet, Carley. I still have something to show you."

Wondering what was next, she slowly drank her thimble-sized cup of strong Turkish coffee as Whit disappeared.

Almost immediately, she felt the boat's abrupt change of course. Realizing that the cruise was coming to a close and they were now returning to the marina, she felt a twinge of regret that this magical night had to end.

But when Whit returned, empty-handed, as if he had forgotten his promise, he sat down in the deck chair and propped his feet on the railing.

"You said that you have something to show me," she prompted.

"Yes. But it will take a few more minutes for the captain to reach our next destination."

"Are we not going back to the marina?"

"No. There's no need to do so, since this boat didn't originate there."

"But the car is parked..."

"Dresnick will pick it up later."

Sensing her uneasiness, he added, "I want you to see some property, and it's best viewed from the water."

However independent, Carley had always had the handicap of manners, of not appearing too abrasive, even at her own peril. So she didn't question Whit further about their destination.

Instead, they listened to the music along the banks, of frogs and katydids, and in that natural atmosphere, Carley relaxed. The boat continued on its steady course, leaving the river and then sailing in the direction of Dauphin Island.

Suddenly, Whit took her hand and caressed it, finally bringing it to his lips. "Carley, what do you want in life?" he asked.

She hesitated. How could she answer him intelligently, when she could hardly breathe from his closeness? She stood to break the spell, and then walked to the railing.

Whit followed and took his place beside her.

"To be successful, of course."

"No. I wasn't speaking of your work, even though that's important. I want to know your dreams, your innermost desires."

He was demanding more than she wanted to reveal, but there was something that compelled her to reply, "I suppose...I suppose that it's to get over this awful sense of loss and to feel loved again. Gran's death came at such a difficult time in my life. I miss her loyalty and support."

Before she knew how it happened, she was in Whit's arms. The kiss, long anticipated from the moment they walked in the gardens, came to fruition. Carley didn't know which one appeared more startled at the emotional fireworks; for once ignited, the passion fed on its own flame, until she finally pulled away to preserve her sanity.

"I've wanted to do that from the first moment I saw you," he confessed. "And you have no idea how much danger you were in, on that ridiculous night we spent together."

Before she could respond, the boat demanded their

attention as it came about, heading for shore.

In the darkness beyond the pier, a security light shone. "This is what I wanted to show you," Whit announced.

Forcing her voice to remain steady, she said, "Is this the property you're buying from Lucinda?"

"It's a done deal," he said. "It's mine, now."

A few minutes later, with a lantern by their side, Whit and Carley walked along the path to the tremendous house in the distance. He located a hidden set of keys and unlocked the massive doors that faced the water.

As they stepped inside, into the semi-darkness, Whit whispered, "Stay with me tonight, Carley."

She forgot everything that she had ever resolved, the short time they had known each other, and the consequences of such folly.

She only remembered the fire of his kiss and the promise of being loved as never before.

 Chapter 23

The lantern swinging back and forth was soon answered by flashing lights from the boat. Shortly thereafter, Carley heard the engines start up, and the boat departed. She had made her decision, however unwise, and now she and Whit were completely alone. There was no turning back.

Upon his return from the lanai, Whit switched on more lights. "Would you like to see the house?" he asked.

To forestall the inevitable, she nodded.

"I haven't had time to furnish it completely. That will have to come later."

They started the tour at the very top of the house, in a third-story office, which Whit called his aerie. The surrounding windows gave a 360-degree view, with a large, powerful telescope aimed directly at the channel, where the ships bound for Mobile Bay passed.

As Carley stood at the window and looked out toward the water, a foghorn sounded in the distance. Whit came up behind her and kissed the nape of her neck with a gentle, teasing touch, before wrapping his arms around her waist and drawing her to him.

In that intimacy, they stood in complete silence, each seemingly unwilling to break the spell. But Carley knew that she would never see the rest of the house unless she resisted.

"May I see the other rooms?" she inquired.

"If you like."

There were two ways to get to the third story—by the

stairs, which they had climbed, and by a small elevator, its shaft hidden from view by a cherry-paneled door. On the way down, they used the elevator, bypassing the second floor, to the main one.

They went from room to room—from the dark wooded library, void of anything except a few books, to the well-furnished kitchen, the sparse living and dining rooms.

"It's a beautiful house," Carley commented. "But somehow, I thought you were buying prime commercial property from Lucinda."

"That, too. But if I'm going to be coming back and forth to Mobile on business, I prefer staying in a house, rather than a hotel."

After a brief time, they climbed the stairs to the second floor, walked along a bridge over the open den, passed several doors, and came to a stop at the end of the hallway.

Carley paused at the entrance to a massive room of muted beige. It took up the entire east wing of the house. When Whit pressed a button on the wall, Carley heard a whirring and sliding sound. As she looked up, she saw part of the vaulted ceiling open to the sky, leaving only a mesh screen for protection. The winds from the bay suddenly swept through the room, cooling it with a natural breeze that smelled of salt and tropical essence.

A large frieze of a powerful horse, a white stallion, hung over the Carrara marble fireplace. Flanked by two large chairs, also of muted beige, the fireplace spoke of intimate winter nights. The largest piece of furniture was the carved Italian bed, impossible to ignore.

They were in the master bedroom, and the tour had come to an end.

Love denied for a time has its own retribution. All at once, Carley felt like a shy, thirty-one-year-old virgin, who had never experienced the act of love. But she was a willing participant in Whit's elegant seduction.

Within moments, the chiffon blouse, the sailor's slacks had been tossed to the floor—companions to his own outer wear—and they were locked in each other's arms.

"Carley," he whispered. "My beautiful, vulnerable Carley."

He traced the curves of her body, lingering on the most responsive places. Attuned to the sudden inhalation of breath, the tightening of muscle and tautness of flesh, Whit seemed in no hurry to end the exploration of touch and seduction.

Then, as if she were a floating wisp of down, Whit lifted her and carried her to the bed, which had distinctly been made for a man who treasured comfort.

Lying at Carley's side, Whit covered her mouth with his own, demanding while giving, bringing her gradually along the path of fevered intensity, and then regressing, to postpone completeness. Back and forth, like the ebb and flow of tides, he gave and then took away, until her body became equally demanding.

She forgot all restraint, all decorum, and became a wanton, seeking that exquisite fulfillment when one body becomes part of another; the two, inseparable by flesh and fire. Only when she could no longer deny her own ecstasy did Whit finally begin to seek his own, giving her double pleasure.

It was a night for love. They slept, then found each other again in the middle of the night, with an even greater intensity.

By morning, when they awoke to the sound of sea gulls overhead, they were still hungry for each other.

Something primitive had been unleashed, and Carley feared that she would never be the same again. That part of her that had escaped the bonds of propriety refused to be bound again.

Leaving the bedroom, she headed for the bath that she had used the previous night. In the suite, two separate baths were angled off the master bedroom. Earlier, her mind had not been on the elaborate contents. But that morning, in a more rational frame of mind, Carley noticed a large assortment of personal items—the toiletries, soaps, perfumes, the hairdryer—almost anything that a woman might need. She viewed the luxury in a new light and realized that she had stepped into a setting made for assignation.

Was she the first, or one among many?

When Carley looked in the mirror, she suddenly smiled. Morgan seemed to be staring back at her with a quizzical expression. With three husbands, she'd had so much more experience than Carley. But she could guarantee that her twin had never been loved any better than she had in these past twelve hours. The glow of her skin proved that.

Carley showered and dressed and, smelling coffee, she walked downstairs, where Whit was preparing breakfast.

"Good morning, sweetheart," he greeted her. "Hungry?"

"Ravenous."

He smiled and began pouring two cups of coffee. "I thought we might have our coffee out on the lanai."

"That would be pleasant."

Whit was dressed in casual sweats, but had not bothered to put on shoes. His dark hair was still wet from the shower and, as he handed Carley a cup, he leaned over and gave her a playful kiss on the lips.

"I have important things to learn about you," he said. "Like, do you take sugar and cream?"

"Always. And you?"

"Black."

Carley was determined not to show what an earthshaking milestone the night had been for her. Whit was only the second man she had been intimate with her entire life. The first had been her former husband Bob.

Joie's phrase echoed in her head: *You don't want to act as if you've just fallen off the turnip truck.* That had been her way of advising Carley to go slow in any new love interest, but her heart had not taken Joie's advice.

"This won't be a gourmet breakfast," Whit apologized later, bringing out a box of cereal from the cabinet. "Spending the night here wasn't something that I planned in advance. Otherwise, I'd have stocked the kitchen with more than cereal and frozen pancakes."

What was he telling her? That he had been just as precipitate as she had been?

"The breakfast is fine," she assured him. "I'm always happy with anything sweet or anything chocolate."

"I wish we could stay for the rest of the day," Whit said. "But I have an afternoon flight out of New Orleans."

"And I have work to do before tomorrow," Carley responded with a sigh.

"How much longer will it take for you to finish at Cavallegria?"

"One more week. Then Boris is going to open the estate for an art exhibition of his students and a tour of the gardens." She hesitated. "Will you be back in Mobile by then?"

"I'll do my best."

After breakfast, Carley put the dishes in the cupboard, while Whit went upstairs to dress. It was not long after that when she heard a car approaching from the land side.

"That must be our ride," Whit said, coming back down the stairs.

This time there was no Dresnick to rescue them. Instead, a yellow taxi waited to take them back. On the way they did not touch hands, and their conversation could have been the same mundane conversation exchanged over a hundred breakfast tables that morning. Whit's eyes, however, spoke another language.

When they arrived in Carley's driveway, there, on the discreet side of the English Tudor house, sat Whit's red Ferrari. Dresnick had evidently done his duty and rescued it from the parking lot at Bellingrath.

The flowers in the window boxes below the mullioned windows at the front were slightly droopy from the heat. The water in the irrigation tubes in the bottom of the window boxes must have gone dry, so Carley made a mental note to replenish the water in the system that afternoon.

Whit paid the taxi driver, then began to walk to the side door with Carley. "Will you come in?" she asked.

"As much as I'd like to, Carley, I'd better not. I might be tempted to remain with you and miss my flight."

Lying across the threshold of the door was a florist's white box. Surprised, Carley stooped to retrieve it.

"Looks as if you have another admirer," Whit said, frowning.

"Perhaps they're from Wingate," she quickly responded. "After a great deal of trouble, I finally anchored his bis pole in the landscape on Friday."

"You mean that strange man at Cavallegria?"

"The very one. But how do you know him?"

"I met him at the party. Remember, he was at Boris's table."

Whit's manner had softened immediately at the mention of Wingate, who was obviously no threat. Yet, Carley didn't know whether to be flattered or alarmed by his initial reaction.

Whit leaned over, kissed her, and said, "I'll call you when I get back."

"Have a good trip," Carley said, and with that exchange, the man she knew as Evian Whitstone walked out of her life on that sunny Sunday afternoon in August.

 *Chapter 24*

*T*hat is not to say that the man disappeared from Carley's life for good. He returned, only under a different guise — not as entrepreneur, not as lover, but something else entirely. In the end, she wasn't even sure of Whit's real name.

That afternoon, when she opened the florist's box, she found a dozen lush pink, out-of-season peonies. They had always been among her favorites, but she'd never had any luck in growing them, since Mobile was much too far south. Only someone who knew her well would go to the trouble of finding them.

Curious to discover who the sender might be, Carley opened the enclosed envelope. There was only one word on the white card — Bob.

What on earth was her ex-husband doing, sending her flowers? She shook her head at his audacity, but she found a vase for them anyway. They were much too beautiful to throw in the trash.

So many things needed to be done that Sunday afternoon, since she had neglected the house while working steadily at Cavallegria.

As soon as she changed her blouse and slacks for her sweats, Carley attended to the window boxes. Within a short time, she could see the flowers begin to perk up their heads.

While she went on to various other chores, Joie's words of the previous week nagged at her. "You will never have anything new come into your life until you have made room for it. And the house will never truly be yours until you realize that your grandmother is gone."

In a gentle manner, she had made Carley see that Gran had no further need of the personal items scattered throughout the house.

She went into the kitchen and made a tuna salad sandwich for lunch. As she ate it and then munched on her favorite orange-chocolate cookies from Baker's Dozen, Inc., she kept thinking of her reluctance in dealing with Joie's advice.

She intensely disliked the word *closure*, as if one could perform a ritual that would suddenly end one's grief and sadness. That was a process that might take years. Even then, the loss would remain as a scar upon the heart.

Carley had done nothing to start the process toward healing and had deliberately avoided the upstairs bedroom where Joie had moved Gran's things. She still wasn't ready emotionally to go through her clothes and separate the ones to give to charity or the Junior League thrift shop.

Perhaps she could begin in the cluttered attic, filled with dusty old trunks, discarded furniture, and broken toys. That would be much easier to deal with.

Like so many of the houses built eons ago, the space under the eaves had been used as a vast repository of the past. But that repository represented a distinct fire hazard to the fine old English Tudor house. So taking her glass of lemonade with her, Carley climbed the stairs to the third floor to determine what needed to be done.

Turning on the wall switch, she was relieved that the overhead light bulbs were still good. The heat, however, was sweltering, trapped as it was in the eaves. Carley went back to the hallway and turned on the attic fan. It groaned into service, stirring the dust from the rafters. She coughed from the dust devils swirling about the room. It had been a long time since anyone had braved the narrow steps to the attic.

Carley was overwhelmed at the amount of junk piled in

every corner. The sheer volume was enough to question her starting, and she had to confess that she was tempted to walk back downstairs again.

Yet, she knew that she needed to keep her mind busy, instead of lingering on the previous night; for like an imprint on the flesh, a remembrance of passion filled her being.

Cho-Cho and Li-Po meowed at the open door and walked into the attic. They seemed to be extremely interested in their surroundings. Carley wondered if they might have picked up the scent of a mouse, or perhaps a squirrel, since they also made no move to return downstairs, where it was cooler.

While they explored the nooks and crannies, and became quite dirty, Carley began her own exploration. Noting all the pieces of furniture stacked in so many directions, Carley decided that task was too daunting without help. She redirected her attention to cleaning out the old trunks before disposing of them, also.

As teenagers, she and Morgan had investigated the contents of several of them. Finding some vintage retro clothes of Gran's that they had worn to a few of the debutante theme parties, Carley knew that others contained former Mardi Gras costumes. If they were in reasonably good condition, perhaps she could donate them to the museum.

The trunk that had been the object of the most speculation back then had been locked, with Gran never willing to share its contents. They had decided that it contained old love letters from someone other than their grandfather. But like typical teenagers involved with their own lives, they had, just as suddenly, lost interest.

Now, that curiosity returned. For the first time since Joie had seen to moving Gran's things upstairs, Carley decided to go to her room and search for the key. Shortly before the funeral, Carley had seen several keys in her handkerchief drawer. Perhaps one of them would fit the lock on the trunk.

Walking into her former bedroom, Carley hesitated.

There was a different ambiance, an air of neglect, as if the room had never been occupied — which was a strange feeling. It was not at all like the closeness she felt to Gran in the downstairs master bedroom. This bedroom seemed to belong only to the house and was empty of any individual's presence. Perhaps it was that feeling that gave her the courage to open the drawer and look for the key.

Gran was always the neat one, so Carley expected to find things arranged exactly as she had left them. Only, the little box containing the keys was not in its original place. Of course, Joie had taken out the contents when the furniture was moved. Perhaps she had not put everything back in the same order.

Carley found the little box in another drawer. Not knowing whether any of the keys would fit the trunk, she took them all to the attic, where the cats were still exploring.

After trying several of the keys, Carley eventually found the right one. The lock was rusty and it didn't open willingly. She didn't want to force it and risk breaking off the key, so she worked with it gently, until it finally opened.

At first glance, there seemed to be nothing of value in the top bin of the trunk. No love letters or anything earthshaking caught her eye — only old tickets from airlines and cruise ships, and old passports that had long since expired. They were just faded memories of the past.

Yet, that afternoon, Carley developed a new insight into how the sudden arrival of twin granddaughters had impacted Gran's personal life. She must have curtailed her travels almost overnight. At the time, it would not have occurred to two twelve-year-olds that she had another life besides that of grandmother. Children are like that, Carley thought — especially ones who are consumed with the sudden loss of their own parents.

Picking up an old passport, she was eager to read all the destinations stamped in it, and to find the last time that she might have gone to her house in Milly-la-Forêt. She started from the end, for the most recent dates of entrance and exit visas. She saw those for France, Germany, Switzerland, the Netherlands, Singapore, Cuba, and a host of other countries. Evidently, Gran had not traveled back to France since their own college days. But she had gone to other places, taking short trips without mentioning them in any later conversation.

Finally, Carley reached the inside front page of the passport. As she gazed at a picture of Gran, she became confused. The name beneath the picture was not Lydia Garson Burnside.

She turned to another old passport. There was Gran's picture again, but with another name, another country of birth. With each expired passport she examined, not one had her grandmother's true name listed.

Tremendously disturbed at these findings, Carley closed the trunk, switched off the lights and the attic fan, and fled downstairs, with Li-Po and Cho-Cho behind her.

If she had wanted to take her mind off the events of the past twenty-four hours, she had succeeded beyond belief.

Carley's attention turned to the cats, dirty from their own exploration of the attic. Like most cats, Li-Po and Cho-Cho hated water, except to drink. So it took a long time to convince them that she merely wanted to give them a bath, before they ruined the damask comforter on her bed.

Carley was also in need of a bath and shampoo. By the time she finished with those chores, fixed a steak and salad for dinner, it was evening.

When the phone rang, Carley, hoping that it was Whit, picked up immediately. Instead, it was Mabel Eldrin, inviting her to a dinner party at her home on the coming Friday evening.

"And do bring that nice young man you were with last Saturday night."

"I may not be able to do that," Carley apologized. "He flew out of town this afternoon, and probably won't get back in time."

"Well, I want you to come, regardless. You know that I always have a few extra men around."

Since she had once given a spectacular debutante party for her and for Morgan in her beautiful garden, Carley felt obligated to go. When Mabel Eldrin issued an invitation, the people around Mobile considered it a command performance.

From the telephone call to the hour she went to bed, Carley gave herself no time for introspection. She'd desperately wanted to talk with Morgan about her discovery in the attic, but the chimes of the old grandfather clock told her that, although it was still evening in Mobile, it was 4:00 A.M. in France.

Once the lights were out, it took Carley a long time to go to sleep. Her romantic tryst on Dauphin Island now seemed only a dream. Harsh reality had greeted her upon her return trip home. And it was that reality that now demanded her attention.

 *Chapter 25*

On Monday morning, Carley backed her truck onto the street and began her usual morning trip to Fairhope. She had a mere five days left to complete the landscape design and put everything into place before Boris opened his estate to an "invitations only" public.

In this double celebration of his artists' works and the restoration of the Cavallegria gardens, Carley realized that the success of her career as an independent landscape architect depended upon no mistakes being made before Saturday's event.

While she dealt with the traffic across the bay, Carley felt a sense of restlessness. So many things were crowding in, forcing her to rethink her life—from past to present to future. It had never occurred to her that things might not be what they appeared to be on the surface. Yet, surprises were bombarding her from every side.

Who would have thought that her sweet, socially conscious grandmother had once led a double life? In Carley's mind, she had been the typical woman of a certain generation, inwardly strong as steel, with an outward gentility, a lover of the arts. But yesterday, she realized that she didn't know her grandmother at all.

Carley tried to recall their conversation when Gran had come home with the two Maltese kittens and named them.

"I recognize *Cho-Cho*," she'd commented—" the Cio-Cio from Madame Butterfly. But where did you get the name, *Li-Po*?"

Sadness seemed to fill Gran's eyes. "Don't you remember the ancient Chinese poet? *I will weave a little message into the hem of his garment and, reading it, perhaps he will remember me.* The young woman was sending a new robe to her lover, who had failed to return to her."

As soon as she said it, Gran laughed that wonderful, throaty laugh of hers and hugged the kittens, instantly dispelling the air of sadness.

That two-year-old conversation with Gran prompted Carley to think of her own lover—Evian Whitstone—and his sudden arrival in her life. Would he also disappear and leave her with only a lingering heartache? Was that what had happened to Gran? Well, one thing for sure, Carley couldn't mope and pine while she waited for Whit's return.

She felt a great need to finish her current project and then to move on. But where? A place where she wouldn't forever be looking over her shoulder, she decided. Although nothing untoward had happened since Ocean Springs, she was still wary. And until Lizzie got back in touch, giving her the name of the winning bidder of her gratis landscape design, Carley felt that she couldn't make any long range plans, such as a nice, lengthy visit to Morgan.

Adding to her sense of restlessness was the morning news that she had listened to at breakfast, giving her a case of indigestion. She was particularly disturbed over the flagrant erosion of laws to protect the natural resources, especially this latest one of allowing strip mining in the Okefenokee Swamp. That was the sort of thing that had caused arguments with Bob during their marriage.

In working together, she'd had to fight for every inch of green space to be included in his architectural plans. If he'd had his way, he would have concreted the world.

She had never been political in the usual sense, but Carley cared passionately about the wetlands, the trees in the National Forests, the streams and mountaintops that kept vanishing every day. She didn't think it was a woman thing, as opposed to a man thing.

Carley supposed that she had the same philosophy as the tribes of Indians who'd inhabited the coast—that we should show respect for the nursery and lungs of Mother Earth. But those same tribes had also been destroyed in the name of immediate financial gain.

Driving into the compound, Carley tried to forget all the negative things that had bothered her that morning. Instead, she turned an eagle eye on the extended approach to the house, looking for aspects that might be improved.

Directly behind her came Jake in his truck, followed by Barnie. The three parked side by side along the sandy strip of road that they had left untouched until the last day of the project.

While they worked in the aboriginal garden, with its mangrove root sculpture in the center, Carley tried to keep her eyes off it, as the workers laid long, rectangular pavers fanning out from the center in a wheel-like pattern. She didn't know who was more embarrassed, the crew or herself.

Once the pavers had gone in, they were packed down, with wild thyme planted between the spaces. Jake uncovered the native plants that they had rescued from the original site and dropped them into a casual circle surrounding the base of the sculpture.

As the garden itself took shape, with twisted vines, mammoth-sized ferns, and the last of the Love-Lies-Bleeding, Carley saw that the sculpture began to fit in better and did not seem nearly so stark as it had looked several days previously. Nevertheless, she was glad to leave the aboriginal garden to the watering crew.

Unlike the other six gardens, this one had a disturbing element to it, which couldn't be blamed entirely on Wingate's bis pole. Even the air had a faintly malodorous scent to it.

The only one who had looked on with any enjoyment was Wingate, who had hidden in the adjacent thicket, to watch. Carley did not acknowledge his presence, since he'd seemed so reluctant to come out into the open.

Before starting on the next phase that day, Carley, Jake, and Barnie took a break. The three wound up at the food wagon, where they stood around, drinking bottled water, nibbling on their mid-morning snacks, and discussing the final plans for the week.

"Remember, I'll have to turn in all the equipment tomorrow, Carley," Barnie reminded her.

"You don't think that you can get an extension for another day or so?"

"No. Everybody's nose seems to be out of joint at Hings and Popple. They've already told me that I've been taken off their rental list."

"Oh, Barnie, I'm so sorry. I didn't mean for you to get caught in this turf war."

Carley Burnside had nothing to do with his being blackballed. He decided, though, that it would be to his advantage to let her think so. He suddenly smiled. "But I've lined up a piece of equipment that we can use to finish. The heavy work is almost done, anyway."

"Then, let's get on with it," Carley said, placing her empty bottle in the recycle bin.

Carley had selected an old orchard with gnarled fruit trees for the wildflower garden. In the meadow, the flowers could easily reseed themselves from year to year. Like the grassy strips along the highways in Texas, where bluebonnets thrived, to the red poppies planted along the sides of the Carolina expressways, the wildflowers would be a source of beauty for years to come.

Perennials, biennials, and annuals were loaded into the back of her truck, as well as numerous bags of wildflower seeds. With visitors coming so soon, Carley wanted to have the bare bones in place. The seeds would germinate rapidly in the humid, tropical weather, and would be quite spectacular in their own good time.

But *time* was what Carley was running out of. At the arrival of Barnie in the Bobcat and Jake in his truck, with another load of flowers, she left the planting to the crew and returned to the house, where Boris had set up a luncheon meeting to discuss Saturday's events.

It was not often that Carley brought a change of clothes to work, but today was special. She could not walk into Boris's house in grimy shirt, slacks, and pith helmet. Yet, changing clothes in the confines of a port-a-potty was challenging. She was sorry that she had returned the key to the Warhol cottage. Rather than getting the dust and grime off her skin with baby wipes, she could have taken a nice, cool shower.

Bob Dickerson, driving to Cavallegria for the luncheon meeting, felt sick with apprehension. He had really screwed up his life, but it wasn't until he'd seen Carley with another man that he'd realized it. That was only the beginning. Somehow, Rocky Donovan's bill had been sent to the office, and had mistakenly been put in his IN box that morning, rather than in Sherrie's.

There was no doubt about it. His wife was crazy. Bob was so alarmed that he'd resealed the envelope and put it in Sherrie's box, as if he had never seen it. It would be better for him to pretend ignorance, until he decided what to do. He also began to wonder if all the things Sherrie had said about Carley and Jake these past two years had been lies.

Still, there was something very exciting about Sherrie. She made him feel important, and heaven knows, she was certainly a wildcat in bed. But most important of all was the family connection with Regan, one of the senior partners. If he tried to divorce her, that might damage his bid to become another senior partner in the firm. Everything was so complicated.

By the time he arrived, the others on the celebration

committee, with the exception of Carley, were already there. He joined them around the bar.

When Carley walked into Boris's house, she followed the noise level emanating from the dining room. Wingate and Maxim Tourkay, the artist she had almost run over on that first day, were chatting in an animated manner.

Since she had seen them every day, Carley had learned to cope with their eccentricities. So she was not worried about working with them, to help set up their canvases and to place their varied works in appropriate spots in the gardens. With flags flying and tents for refreshments and shelter, in case of rain, it would resemble a renaissance fair — a spectacular event of the summer season.

"Hello, Carley. What would you like to drink?" Boris, the host greeted her.

She looked over the bar display of wines and mixes. "How about a diet drink?" she said. "I have to work this afternoon," she added, with a laugh.

Boris became the genial host, mixing drinks as easily as he mixed pigments on his palette.

As the participants stood around, waiting for lunch to be put on the buffet in the more formal dining room, Bob walked over to Carley. He had been debating as to whether to say anything about the flowers, but since she had given no indication of thanking him, he said, "I hope you're enjoying the peonies."

"Very much, although I have no idea why you sent them."

"Perhaps for a peace offering? For not making such a fuss over the garden space I needed." That was as good a reason as any other, he supposed, although he still wasn't absolutely sure why he had done such a thing. If Sherrie ever found out, it would be hell to pay.

Bob walked on, speaking to others, while Carley became engaged in conversation with Angela, one of the few women artists.

The luncheon was catered, so Wingate did not play the

role of server, as he had on that day when Carley had come to Cavallegria for an interview. He was the resident sculptor, with an important place on the organizing committee.

While Carley was serving her plate, Maxim, dressed in his usual black, turned to her and said, "I like the obelisk, Ms. Burnside. It's a great place to hide and watch the goings on at the boathouse."

"That's an advantage I hadn't thought about. But surely, while you were up there, you painted something wild and wonderful on the water."

"Not the feathered variety," he confessed.

Carley moved on and found a place at the table beside Consuelo. "And what are you showing this coming Saturday?" she asked, expecting a description of her works.

"Oh, I'm not really a professional artist," she answered. "Just a dilettante. I don't plan to exhibit."

Her frank reply surprised Carley. She knew that the session, even with subsidies, was quite expensive, and Boris only allowed the most talented to come to Cavallegria.

Everyone seemed to be talking at once, and the noise decibel level was high in the wooden beamed dining room. So once the luncheon was over, they traipsed to the dining hall/seminar building for the meeting and, for Carley, the first view of the selected art to be exhibited.

"This is mine," Maxim said over Carley's shoulder, while she stared at the painting. The two figures he had captured on canvas at the boathouse were unmistakable — the flaming-haired Consuelo and Evian Whitstone.

"Rather good of you, don't you agree, Consuelo?" Maxim said as the woman joined Carley. "Must have been a helluva night."

Carley didn't know which of the two women was more dismayed at the obvious intimacy of the painting.

 *Chapter 26*

"*It*'s not what it looks like, Carley," Consuelo hastened to assure her.

If she ever needed a poker face, it was at that moment. But what a struggle it was, not to show how the picture of the two together had affected her. Carley looked away from the canvas and, as nonchalantly as she could manage, she said, "Well, I hardly know the man. Our being together at the fundraising party was arranged by my grandmother's attorney."

Carley left it at that and walked on, pretending to be interested in the other canvases about the room.

She really didn't know how she got through the next hour. Inside, she felt betrayed. But she could only blame herself for what had happened. Carley vowed that she would never be so naive again.

Forced to keep her attention on the work at hand, she made suggestions as to the placement of the art in the various gardens, pairing the styles from traditional to avant-garde, from canvases reminiscent of the works of Frida Kahlo, to the surreal world of Boris Cavanaugh. Some were splashed with vivid colors, while others were monochromatic.

With all the colors of nature surrounding these artists, Carley was amazed at the sparsity of tints and hues in some of the works. Yet, several were quite beautiful in their frugality. Had she not done the same thing at times — using a white garden or a blue garden to set a specific mood?

Carley thought of the mood rings that little Cristina was so fond of wearing. "See, Carley? My ring says that I'm happy today." She was thankful that she wore no ring to target how she felt, for it would surely have turned black.

An even blacker mood had developed in the offices of the Regan, Barnes, and O'Reilly architectural firm, due to the summer intern's mix-up of incoming mail — especially for the two Dickerson boxes.

Sherrie sat at her desk and rapidly tapped her drawing pencil, while waiting for her anger to subside enough for her to think straight. She had opened the florist's bill, to discover that Bob had sent Carley Burnside a dozen pink peonies. What did this mean? That Bob was having second thoughts about their marriage? God forbid! So what was she going to do about it?

Sherrie put down her pencil and closed her eyes. She began to visualize a calm blue sea, the exercise that Dr. DeSahle had recommended when she'd become overwrought in the past.

Reasonably calm again, Sherrie smiled as she began making plans. She knew that she could deal with her husband, but it would take Rocky's help in stopping that bitch, Carley. If flowers were what she expected, then flowers she would get.

Not trusting the privacy of her office, she walked out into the secluded courtyard and used her cell phone to call Rocky. With this next move, he would finally earn his pay.

A few minutes later, Sherrie walked into Bob's office. "Oh, by the way, darling. I think this little bill belongs to you." She tossed the florist's bill on to his desk and then went back to her own office.

Seeing the opened envelope, Bob froze. He realized that he had made a terrible mistake, and Sherrie would certainly exact due recompense.

On Tuesday morning, the major cleanup at Cavallegria began with the removal of the two large dumpsters containing debris. The diesel smell of the rigs permeated the landscape as the hydraulic systems lifted the dumpsters onto the truck beds.

It was a delicate operation, carefully monitored by Barnie, Jake, and Carley, since they wanted as little damage done to the landscape as possible. Any remaining debris for the rest of the week could be hauled away in the trucks.

On that Tuesday, the slight drizzle of rain, soft and steady, was a boon to the plants, if not to the artists. They were forced to paint indoors, while the weather worked to Carley's advantage. The team did not have to work around the artists, but had the outdoors to themselves.

Carley was still subdued on that day. Although she kept it to herself, she was still troubled by Whit's perfidy and Gran's secret life. She didn't know which of the two discoveries bothered her more.

So, at the end of the day, Carley stopped off at the deli and loaded up on comfort food, including a quart of chocolate mint ice cream. Since it was her turn to provide refreshments for the next night's poker game, she also purchased cheese and pretzels, nuts, beer, and the trail mix that Edward seemed to prefer.

When Carley arrived home late on that Tuesday afternoon, she stopped at the mailbox to pick up her mail.

She was pleased to see that she had received a letter from Cristina. The postmark said *Lausanne*, so Carley surmised that her niece was already settled at her boarding school in Switzerland.

Carley drove on, stopping her truck halfway down the drive. Juggling her purchases, she walked to the side door.

Once again, a florist's box had been left on the threshold. She frowned. Was this another one of Bob's peace offerings? She was tempted to throw this one in the garbage can. But what if it were from Whit, instead? Thinking of him, Carley was even more inclined to toss the box into the trash.

She stepped over the obstacle, to unlock the door and put down her first load of groceries. As she went back to her truck for the second load, she stepped over it again, this time giving the box a slight kick as she went.

All at once, a rustling sound came from inside the box. Curious, Carley thought — flowers didn't rustle and rattle.

She took her cell phone from her pocket and dialed Joie. Within moments, Joie appeared. "What's the matter, Carley?"

"I don't know. I must be paranoid, but I have a feeling that something's wrong with this florist's box."

"Why do you think that?"

"Listen. Do you hear anything?"

A few seconds later, Joie said, "I don't think you should open it."

"Then, what am I going to do? I'd look awfully silly if I called the Fire Department, only to find a bunch of roses."

"Carley, in view of what has been going on, you can't afford to be careless. Go ahead and call them."

What an embarrassment when, ten minutes later, a fire truck with sirens screaming, drew up to the house. "Where's the emergency, Lady?"

"There, on the steps."

"The flower box?" one of the men asked, incredulously, seeing a long, white box, with an extravagant yellow ribbon tied around it.

Joie spoke up. "Officer, this woman has been the victim of some cruel jokes, lately. We think there might be something harmful inside."

"Then, maybe you need the bomb squad," the second fireman said, with a grin.

Just then, the Fire Chief's car drove up. "What's the trouble?" the captain asked, coming to join the group.

"I think we have some poisonous flowers, Sir. But we're not sure."

In disgust, Carley stooped over to untie the ribbon. She would open the box herself, since no one was taking her seriously.

"Just a moment," the captain cautioned. "Is there a ticking sound?"

"No. More a rustling," Carley replied.

"You have enemies?"

"Yes. Only I have no idea who they are."

"And you weren't expecting flowers from anyone?"

"No."

A small crowd had gathered down the street to watch, and Carley felt embarrassed at all the to-do. It grew even worse, when another car drove up, and a police officer with his K-9 dog got out.

The dog immediately began to growl at the box. "Easy, Bugler," the man called.

"There must be something alive in the box," the dog handler pronounced.

"Shall we see what it is?"

Carley and Joie were ordered to stand back. With prodding, the men removed part of the lid, and out slithered a giant snake—a timber rattler.

"My God, look at the size," one of the men said, while another chopped the snake in two with an expert throw of his ax. "Enough venom to kill a horse."

"My apologies, ma'am. I should have believed you," the first fireman said.

"It's a good thing that you didn't take the box inside your house," the fire chief added. "You would have been bitten for sure."

An hour later, Carley was still shaken. The police had been careful to remove all evidence, even dusting for footprints. But Carley did not expect them to solve the case anytime soon.

So, for the next few days, she would have to be extremely careful. Saturday couldn't come soon enough for her. With the success of that day, then it would be too late to sabotage her garden restoration. And that was the only thing that she could think of to precipitate such malice.

Later that night, Carley remembered Cristina's letter. As she opened it, a picture fell onto the floor, and Carley had to retrieve it quickly before the cats pounced on it.

The picture had been taken from the garden side of the property. Carley felt an immediate affinity for the restored millhouse, with its two-hundred-year-old linden tree casting long shadows on the old quarried terrace. Cristina, looking so small, sat on a bench in the background of the picture

Dear Carley, How are you? I am fine. I hope you like my picture. This is our new house. Mommy brought me to school yesterday. Write me.

Your homesick niece, Cristina.

At first, Carley was alarmed. She felt sorry for the child so far away from home. Yet, Carley remembered using almost the same homesick phrase, herself, when she had gone to camp one summer. By parents' day, she would have kicked and screamed at the suggestion of leaving. Although she would have preferred having her niece for the school year in Mobile, Carley knew that Cristina was resilient and made friends easily. Thinking of her own experience at that age, she felt better.

She went to her office and wrote a reply to the letter. Then, she taped the box of presents that she had accumulated to send her, now that she had her school address. She could easily stop off at the UPS office to mail the package on her way to work.

Because of that decision, Carley was a little late in getting to Fairhope the next morning. When she arrived at Cavallegria, the entire compound was abuzz. Wingate had finally completed his sculpture, wedging a shrunken head into the empty space in the mangrove carving. Since she had already seen the grotesque artifact, Carley was not nearly so scandalized as some of the others, who were viewing it for the first time.

"I hear that the fire department killed a poisonous snake

at your door," Jake commented, standing beside her in the aboriginal garden.

"Bad news certainly travels fast," Carley replied. "How did you hear about that?"

"It was on this morning's radio crime report."

Carley hesitated. "Did the reporter go into detail?"

"No. Didn't give your name, either. Just the address, which I recognized."

"Well, there must be precious few happenings in Mobile this week, for that little incident to be highlighted." Carley was deliberately low key, and no one else mentioned it during the rest of the day.

By that evening, Edward, Henry, Goose, and Carley were back to playing poker. The radio report must have slipped by them, too, else one of them would have said something about it.

At that point, Carley was much more interested in talking about Gran's past. She decided to pry a little. If anyone had an inkling about her double life, then these three poker buddies were the ones more apt to know.

"I was cleaning out some trunks in the attic last Sunday," Carley began, "and came across some old passports. I didn't know that Gran had traveled so much."

It was as if a shutter had come down. "Well, not in years," Henry responded. "Until we all went to Cuba together as part of the U.S.-Cuba Sister Cities committee."

"You were in Amsterdam at the time, Carley," Goose commented, "working on that playground, if I remember correctly."

The three then began to bombard her with their thoughts on the embargo, and their hopes for the day when it would be lifted, effectively changing the subject from Gran's earlier travels.

"Castro can't last too much longer," Edward insisted.

"Lydia always regretted that the long, close relationship between Havana and Mobile had to be ruined by that man," Henry said.

"She always looked forward to the time when diplomatic relations could be resumed."

"Did she ever tell you about the man who tried to speak to her at the San Cristobal burial site of d'Iberville, but was quickly hustled off by one of the brown shirts?" Edward asked.

"No, she didn't mention the trip at all."

"That bothered her no end. I think she recognized him from years past," Goose added.

Carley had never seen three men so talkative about things in which she had no interest. But they seemed determined to bore her with all the facts of the long relationship between the two cities, until she was more than ready to return to the poker game and stop asking questions.

For the next two days, a frenzied pace at Cavallegria meant that Carley had little time for even taking a break or eating. The small tractor that Barnie had rented for the final days was put into service, smoothing and leveling the sandy driveway all the way to the gates.

Carley had borrowed two massive olive jars, filled with greenery, to place at the gates, and with flags flying, the guests were assured of finding their way.

So by Friday, everything that needed attention had been done. The refreshment tent had been set up; the pedestals along the driveway and the easels in each garden had been anchored in place—all except in the aboriginal garden, where the bis pole would have no competition.

Now, there only remained for the committee to place the art on Saturday morning, before the guests arrived.

All the last minute activities had taken a toll on Carley. Her back ached; her feet hurt, and she longed for a nice, soaking bath at home, before getting ready for Mabel Eldrin's dinner party that evening.

Just as she was ready to leave, however, Boris decided that he wanted to walk over the property with her, to survey each garden. She could not refuse, so they began their trek to view all seven gardens. Boris said little. He just nodded his head and moved on, with his long strides setting the pace.

Finally, when they returned to the house, Boris said, "By the way, I've had a request to show another painting at the festivities tomorrow."

Carley's heart sank. Adding a painting at this late date would ruin the entire setup and printed program. Evidently reading her expression, he said, "Don't worry. It won't change any of the present arrangements. But I do want you to take a good look at it before you go."

"Where is it?"

"In my studio."

"Then, let me meet you at the back patio. I'll remove my shoes there." Carley wasn't about to relive the ritual of the terry cloth slippers in the foyer.

They met at the back door near his studio.

Carley walked inside, in her sports socks.

"It's the auction painting," he announced. "I wanted you to see it before tomorrow, since I don't think you saw it up close on auction night."

"That's true. Too many people were crowding around it."

Carley walked toward the huge canvas. She came face to face with her own image. *She* was the woman in the garden, amid the purple trees. And *she* was the one who had vanished into a cloud of smoke and reemerged as the statue.

"I'm quite surprised," Carley commented. "I had no idea."

"You make a very good subject," Boris said. "I'm sorry to see you go."

That was the first compliment she had received from him. He'd made no mention of the seven gardens or her hard work. Only her suitability as his model received his praise. Trying not to show that resentment, she asked, "Where will the painting be exhibited tomorrow?"

"On the terrace in front of the house. I'll place it there

myself tomorrow morning."

"Well, thank you for letting me view it."

Trying not to sound ungracious, she added, "I'll see you tomorrow.

"Aren't you going to Mabel's dinner party tonight?"

"Why, yes, I am."

"Then, I'll see you there."

That was an even more surprising revelation—that Mabel had been able to persuade Boris, the semi-recluse, to attend.

Then, in a hurry to beat the traffic, Carley slipped on her shoes before heading for home.

That evening, Carley swapped her Toyota truck for Gran's black Cadillac. She drove to the Patillo house, where she picked up Gaddi. Alva had ceased going to social functions since her health was not good, so Mabel had asked Carley to stop by for Gaddi.

It was a rather long ride, for Mabel lived in an antebellum plantation house near the bridge to Pascagoula.

"I wonder who will be there tonight," Gaddi ventured, getting into the car.

"Probably the usual crowd."

"Mabel told me that a few extra men will be in attendance, too. That sounded interesting."

"I wouldn't get excited about any of them," Carley cautioned. In her coterie of friends were two confirmed bachelors, and another of uncertain sexual persuasion. But Bruce was always quite witty and had a propensity for ferreting out the latest gossip. So like the troubadours of old, who went from village to village, Bruce always had a prominent seat by the fire, so to speak.

When they arrived, Carley saw that lights had been strung through the great live oaks, giving the place a festive air. A crowd had already gathered around a drinks table set up on the lawn. After Carley parked the car in the meadow beyond the drive, she and Gaddi gravitated toward the table, where a bartender and a waitress offered immediate refreshments.

Mabel was a lover of birds and all aspects of her house showed it in a number of ways. She was quite proud of her two large collections—of Boehm birds and prints by Athos Menaboni, the Italian/American Audubon, whose works lined the walls in her dining room. Even her favorite china pattern by Wedgwood showed the famous Fabergé egg of the Romanov era.

"Hello, Carley. Gaddi. So glad you could come," Lucinda Bledsoe greeted them. "Isn't this sweet of Mabel to give a party in my honor?"

That was the first that Carley had heard of it. "Very nice," she managed to say. As she looked up, Rudy was walking toward them, with two drinks in hand.

"Here you are, 'Cin,'" he said to Lucinda, handing her one of the stems of wine. Then he turned to Carley and Gaddi. "What can I get for you at the bar, lovely ladies?"

 *Chapter 27*

Carley would never forget that evening, in view of what happened later. It started out wrong and kept getting worse. By the time all the guests left, almost no one was speaking to the next person. If it had not been that Gaddi would have been stranded, Carley would have left early, with no hesitation in turning her back on the entire assemblage.

Lucinda and Mabel had been friends for years, but sometimes friends can do the greatest damage in the name of trying to do a good deed.

After Carley encountered Rudy and Lucinda, the next indication that her evening might run into difficulty came with the arrival of Sherrie and Bob. It seemed that Mabel was intent on repairing more than the relationship of her friend Lucinda.

Since most of the guests present traveled in the same social milieu, Carley supposed that Mabel had taken it upon herself to fix all the cracks and crevices at one time. But not even Venetian plaster could have done the job that night.

Carley had finally declared Morgan's closet off-limits and had reverted to her own wardrobe, choosing a black cocktail dress. Around her neck she wore the silver wire collar laced with small Hawaiian pearls that had been a Christmas present from Gran.

The dress, itself, was not new. In fact, she had worn it on a number of occasions in the past. But Carley figured that one basic black dress was as good as another.

Sherrie, seeing Carley in apparently good health, could not disguise her hostility. Sherrie was not often thwarted in her plans, but Carley had survived even her latest efforts, and now it was too late. The gardens at Cavallegria were finished. Still, she could not help but hurl a few choice words at her.

"Well, I see that you've finally come to your senses—and gone back to your own wardrobe."

Carley's smile was taut. "I have no idea what you're talking about, Sherrie."

"That dress, of course. I'm sure it was never one of Morgan's castoffs."

"Speaking of castoffs, how are you and Bob getting along?"

"Wonderfully well. We're headed to Jamaica next week for a long-delayed honeymoon."

"Well, I do hope that Bob has recovered from his, er, disability. Or has he started taking Viagra?"

Carley walked away, realizing that she needed to keep her mouth shut. It had never been in her makeup to be so catty. And it didn't make her feel good.

Gaddi had found a friend in Maxim, who had come with Boris as an extra man. Carley was rather glad that he had not brought Consuelo with him. Her presence would only add to the tension that seemed to be spreading over Carley like the fog rising from the river.

In an attempt to foil this miasma, and with a second glass of wine to help the process, Carley began to flirt outrageously with Bruce, who egged her on.

"I love your tan," he commented. "It looks great with your sun-streaked hair. You must have just come back from Monte Carlo."

"No. I've been residing at Cavallegria for the past several weeks."

"What? You and Boris? How fascinating." He leaned over and in an intimate voice said, "Let me know when you've gotten tired of him, and I'll take you off to my little love nest in Tuscany."

"Is Monday suitable with you?" Carley batted her eyes at him in an exaggerated manner.

"Be careful, darling. I just may give up Claude for you." He tucked her hand into his and led her off toward another small group under the trees.

Bruce was a member of one of the Krewes, and he had friends and acquaintances all along the coast. As a designer, he was quite knowledgeable about costumes, and had worked with the museum to save some of the more elaborate Mardi Gras costumes of the past. Because of that, Carley thought she might consult him about the costumes in the attic.

Evidently, Mabel had paired them as dinner partners. Carley felt safe with Bruce. Despite his tendency to be a little treacherous, he was always good for a laugh or two. Carley saw Bob glancing in her direction, as if he disapproved of the fun that she and Bruce were generating.

As soon as Bruce started back to the drinks table, Bob suddenly appeared at her shoulder. "Carley, I must speak with you."

"What about?"

"Us."

"There *is* no us. It's just you and Sherrie."

"I think I've made a mistake."

Carley raised her eyebrow and waited for him to explain.

"It's not working—my marriage to Sherrie."

"I'm not your psychotherapist, Bob. If you two are having problems, I'm the last one you should consult."

"But I miss you, and I'd like for us at least to be friends again."

"Not in this lifetime," Carley managed to say, walking away to meet Bruce who was coming in her direction.

So was that what the peonies were all about? An attempt

to soften her for this revelation? Had he suddenly become jealous, seeing her with Whit at the party and again the past Saturday at her house? Did he think that she would remain grief-stricken forever?

Bob didn't know it, but the new relationship with Whit was over, nipped before it had a chance to blossom fully. Carley was a one-man woman, and she refused to care for someone who was intimate with others while pretending that she was so important in his life. As much as she regretted it, Evian Whitstone was no longer welcome in her life. And neither was Bob.

"Oh, I think that's wonderful," Gaddi said, smiling at Rudy as Carley walked by. Gaddi reached out and grabbed her arm. "Rudy is going to start coming to my motivational classes. It's to help people who have been..." She hesitated and then finished "...out of circulation for a while, to reenter society."

Carley immediately felt sorry for Alva. The last time Gaddi had invited a motley group into her home, Alva had been robbed of her diamond ring, five place settings of silver, and an heirloom mantel clock.

Would Gaddi never learn? She needed to have the meetings at the local YMCA or the police station. But what could she say in front of Rudy? "That's nice," she finally responded.

Later, Maxim seemed to be particularly interested in talking with Rudy. They disappeared together toward the pier on the water, leaving Gaddi and Lucinda to fend for themselves.

Mabel always had a trophy guest to entice the rest, but in looking over the crowd on the lawn, Carley didn't see anyone who might qualify for that position. She knew that Mabel didn't tolerate certain types of people — particularly politicians and religious zealots, unless they were Mobile's own politicians and zealots. Then, they were forgiven.

Shortly after Maxim and Rudy had vanished, a black

limousine approached the drive. As if they had become a Brigadoon tableau frozen on the spot, the crowd waited to see who might emerge.

Holding her breath to see if Whit might be the one to claim an exalted position in Mabel's table plans, Carley relaxed when a complete stranger became visible under the lights.

He was tall, as ramrod straight as a toreador, and slightly older than Whit, with a glimpse of gray at his temples. His elegant dark silk suit spoke of money and custom tailoring.

Mabel immediately walked forward to greet him. He kissed her on both cheeks. Within moments, someone had put a drink in his hand, and as hostess, Mabel led him from one small group to another, introducing him.

"Carley, may I present Luis Delgado from Barcelona. His conglomerate is thinking of purchasing a large chunk of Biloxi's coast for development." Mabel turned to him and announced Carley's full name. "Carleton LeMoyne Burnside."

"How do you do?"

He smiled at Carley and said," Do you have a twin?"

"As a matter of fact, I do. Her name is Morgan."

"How singular. We must speak later," he commented, walking on with Mabel and leaving Carley quite puzzled. Had he met Morgan in Europe?

Soon, Bascom, Mabel's longtime butler, announced dinner, and they all went inside to the dining room, where a huge wicker fan stirred the air above the long, polished mahogany table, covered by damask.

The old house had never had air conditioning installed. The breeze from the water, the shade of the live oaks, and the cross ventilation had been sufficient for four generations. And so it was that night in the dining room, where magnolia blossoms and porcelain birds were aligned down the center of the table, with one tall silver, five-branched candelabrum in the middle.

With sixteen places at the table, it took Carley a few

moments before finding her place card. Mabel had seated Bruce on her right and Rudy on her left. His place remained empty, until he and Maxim, appearing angry from their private talk, walked in. Carley noticed that Lucinda visibly relaxed as Rudy belatedly took his chair.

Sometimes to his hostesses' dismay, Bruce had a penchant for switching place cards at the last minute. Carley was sorry that he had not had time to do so at this gathering. He would have made certain that she would not have been forced to stare at her ex-husband, whom Mabel had seated directly across the table from her.

At one end of the antique table, Mabel, dressed in an elegant ecru lace dress, presided, while her brother-in-law, Edgar, occupied the chair at the opposite end. He and his wife, Rhett, who was Mabel's sister, had driven over from New Orleans for the dinner party. Mabel had placed Luis to her right, while at the end of the table, Lucinda occupied the place of honor at Edgar's right.

Carley looked around at all the familiar faces. Absent was Will Longstreet, a doctor, long divorced and on every hostess's list as an eligible man. He must have been on call, Carley decided, and that was why Maxim, an outsider, had joined the group. Also conspicuously absent was Goose, who almost never missed one of Mabel's soirees.

"Mr. Delgado, are you going to allow gambling in your new development?" Gaddi inquired.

"Gaddi, for Pete's sake..." Bruce interrupted. But the damage had been done.

"That will be left up to my partners," Luis answered in a rather cold voice.

Soon, there was a rush of conversation, with various ones eager to erase the awkward moment. Boris stepped in, engaging Luis. From what Carley could hear of their exchange, it was evident that they were already acquainted with each other.

But with Rudy's nudging of her knee under the table and Bruce filling her ear with the latest gossip, while Bob watched her like a hawk, Carley missed the subtleties going on around her. Until Bruce called it to her attention, she had not noticed Mabel's trophy guest casting his glance a number of times in her direction

"The *Señor* seems to be taken with you, Carley."

"He's just remembering my sister. I think they must have met somewhere in Europe, and I remind him of her."

"You'd better be careful," he cautioned. "You might wind up on another dinner cruise."

"What are you suggesting, Bruce?"

"It's all right. I can keep your little secret."

Carley seriously doubted it, for Bruce was a rapacious purveyor of secrets, which he spread liberally wherever he went. She desperately hoped that he was not aware of anything beyond the cruise; else the entire city of Mobile would soon know every detail of her indiscretion.

The various courses were served in a leisurely manner, but by the time dessert came, Carley had little appetite left. She toyed with the dessert, a particularly rich pecan pie, with a dollop of ice cream on top. She was glad when a suitable time elapsed, and it was whisked away.

Mabel always served after dinner coffee with a little liqueur in the double parlor, allowing only enough time for female guests to freshen their lipstick before coming together again. Having been a widow for a number of years, she enjoyed the company of men. She also enjoyed holding court as in former days. It was understood that no cigars and brandy waited for her male guests in another room. Instead, they were expected to be charming and entertaining for the entire evening in the company of women, whether at a game of bridge or in conversation.

"I have not had a chance to speak with you," Luis said, signaling for Carley to sit beside him on the blue velvet sofa.

The sofa had a history as rich as its owners. In Civil War days, soldiers had slashed its original fabric, looking for hidden silver or family heirlooms, as they marched through Alabama. Mabel's great-grandmother had never forgiven them for this sacrilege. So, from that time on, not just anyone was allowed to sit on this hallowed sofa. But Carley supposed that it was all right for Luis that night, since he was an honored guest.

Almost as soon as Carley sat down, Mabel announced that three tables were being set up for bridge, and one set aside for poker. Any talk between Luis and Carley would have to be postponed, as a matter of courtesy.

"What game are you going to play?" Luis asked.

"Poker."

There was a glint of amusement in his dark eyes, at Carley's answer.

"Then, so will I."

Chapter 28

*T*he choice of poker sealed Carley's fate for the rest of the evening. In the company of Luis, Rudy, and Boris, she was the only woman. But unlike the camaraderie with Gran's poker buddies, Carley felt no such cohesiveness. It was as if something unsettling had been unleashed, and she was powerless to stop it. Even worse, each one seemed to expect something from her, and she appeared to be the only one who had no idea what it might be.

Coupled with a few hostile glances from the bridge tables, she also realized that she was being blamed for keeping Luis from circulating with the other guests, as the bridge game progressed.

Her only reason for choosing one game over the other was to avoid Bob and Sherrie, who were avid bridge players.

In the course of the first hand, during a small lull, Boris said, "Does anyone know which king in the deck is missing a mustache?"

Carley laughed. "This isn't *Go Fish*, Boris. You're not going to catch anybody on that one."

Realizing that his bluff hadn't worked, Boris grinned and answered his own question. "The king of hearts."

During the next hour, little conversation interrupted the game, except during the dealing of cards. They were all playing to win, but what the prize would be, no one had any idea. Mabel was the one who would replace the winning chips with her own unique prizes at the end of the evening.

Off and on, Bascom came around, taking orders for drinks or snacks. Since Carley had drunk her limit of wine earlier, she stuck to water. Unfortunately, it was Evian water, and that made her think of Whit.

"Have you ever visited Barcelona, Carley?" Luis inquired as she took a sip of water.

"No, I haven't. I've been to towns along the Costa del Sol and to Granada. But I missed Barcelona."

"Then we must see to correcting that oversight. There're many beautiful gardens in Spain that you would enjoy."

Not aware of any conversation at the dinner table concerning her love for landscape architecture, Carley held out her hands and examined them. "Is it that obvious? I tried to wash off the garden dirt before coming tonight. I thought I was successful."

"And so you were," Luis hastened to assure her. "But I've been invited to Boris's tomorrow, and I look forward to seeing your garden designs."

"When you were in Granada, Carley," Rudy cut in, "you must have enjoyed the Alhambra's *Court of the Myrtles*."

"Yes," she answered in surprise. "Sounds as if you've been to Spain, yourself."

He smiled. "That's where I met Lucinda. Not at the Alhambra, but in a sherry shop in Jerez."

"How interesting."

Boris, not to be outdone, said, "Rosinôl painted a rather good canvas of *The Court of the Myrtles*. Are you familiar with it, Luis?"

"Yes. Rosinôl was also a Catalan."

Carley noticed Luis's slight withdrawal, as if he refused to be drawn into this strange conversation that had to do with male egos vying for attention. It was as if he were intimating that he could afford to wait for whatever he was seeking.

What was interesting to Carley that night was Rudy's

194 • Frances Patton Statham

obvious European experience. A handyman was not apt to be a world traveler. So what had he been before incarceration? Remembering his flirtation at the dinner table, Carley wondered if he had been an international con artist, looking for a rich woman to support him.

By midnight, Carley was yawning. The poker game had grown stale. Mabel finally took pity and announced that the games were over. Now, it was beads and moon pie time, when the prizes would be meted out to the winners.

When the guests reassembled, Carley made sure to sit as far away as possible from her partners at the poker table. She joined Gaddi, who was talking with Mabel's sister, Rhett.

Rhett was several years younger than her sister, but the resemblance was apparent. "How long will you be visiting?" Carley asked.

"We'll drive back to New Orleans early Sunday afternoon," she replied. "Edgar doesn't like to drive at night."

"This has been such a lovely party," Carley commented. "I'm only sorry that I didn't get a chance to talk over old times with you."

Rhett reached out and put her hand on Carley's arm. "I'm so sorry about Lydia."

Carley's eyes misted. "Thank you, Rhett."

"And how is Morgan?"

Carley hesitated. If only she knew. "She's living in France, now. In fact, I plan to visit her within the next few weeks."

"Then, do give her my love."

"I certainly will."

Gaddi stood up. "If you two will excuse me, I must speak to Maxim before we leave."

Rhett and Carley looked at each other. Once Gaddi was out of hearing range, Rhett said, "Poor Alva. She had such high hopes for that girl."

"But she seems happy, doing what she does," Carley commented.

Mabel became the center of attention. With the help of Bascom, she first awarded the bridge and poker prizes. Bob and Sherrie were the winners of the top prize in bridge, while Rudy captured the poker pot.

No one actually cared about those, except the winners. More important were the beautiful little white silk boxes that Mabel gave to all women present, and the small leather boxes to the men. They were opened to a chorus of pleasing sounds, as the guests examined the contents—exquisite dragonfly pins for the women and harlequin tie tacks for the men.

Later, on the streets of Mobile, these little mementos, as significant as a Good Housekeeping seal, would indicate the people in a charmed group. After a certain period of time, they would be returned quietly to their little boxes, taking their places with other mementos, other times, in a closed coastal society as palpable as the scent of wisteria.

Luis stood beside Mable as guests filed out of the house. Eager to get to her car in the meadow, Carley said her good-byes and looked around for Gaddi, but she was nowhere in sight.

Standing impatiently near the steps, Carley was soon joined by Lucinda. "You must be waiting for your passenger," she commented.

"Yes, but she seems to have disappeared."

"So has Rudy."

"Gaddi said she needed to talk with Maxim, but I don't see him either."

A gruff voice joined in. "If he doesn't get here soon, he can walk back to Cavallegria." It was Boris.

Bruce sauntered by and gave Carley a peck on her cheek. "What a nice party. I learned enough gossip tonight to dine out for weeks."

"Just make sure you don't get food poisoning," Carley called after him.

Boris harrumphed. Lucinda shook her head. Then the three went back to watching and waiting.

The black limousine pulled up a few feet away, and the chauffeur got out and stood by the door. Luis, on his way to the limousine, stopped when he saw Carley. "Do you need a ride?"

"Thank you, no. I brought my own car. I'm just waiting for my passenger."

"I'll see you tomorrow, Boris." He leaned his head toward Lucinda. "Madam."

"Good night," she said, attempting a smile, but Carley could tell that she was decidedly angry.

Finally, Boris said, "I'm going on. Maxim can get a taxi." With that he began walking in long strides to the same meadow where Carley's car was parked.

Carley felt the same way about Gaddi, but, of course, she couldn't do that to her, however tempted. When Maxim, Gaddi, and Rudy finally appeared, only two cars remained in the meadow.

"I'm sorry," Gaddi said. "Were you waiting for me?"

"Yes. But Maxim, Boris has gone on. It looks as if you'll need to get a ride back on your own."

"We'll take him, won't we, 'Cin, honey?" Rudy said.

Lucinda evidently couldn't say no to Rudy. "All right," she agreed. "But you can take me home first, since Cavallegria is in the opposite direction."

Seeing the white boxes that Lucinda and Carley were holding, Gaddi said, "Wait. I haven't gotten my box." With that, she tripped up the steps and waited for Bascom to bring hers to the door.

Gaddi had a difficult time keeping up with Carley's fast pace to the meadow, where the old Cadillac stood alone. In silence, Carley started the engine and pulled out of the meadow onto the road. It was a long time before she trusted herself to speak.

Still, Carley was glad to have someone else in the car, since the ride back to town was quite a distance. She did not like to drive alone at night, and once Gaddi settled down, she was pleasant company.

By the time Carley dropped Gaddi at her house, it was almost two o'clock. "Thanks for the ride," she said, getting out of the car. "I'm so excited about tomorrow at Cavallegria. It's going to be a wonderful day."

Carley agreed. "See ya'," she said and then drove home.

By two-thirty, she was in bed. In less than six hours, Carley would be celebrating the success of her seven coastal gardens.

Despite all the odds, all the hitches, she had done it. She was well on the way to regaining a most satisfying career.

Chapter 29

*E*arly the next morning, even before daybreak, Carley heard her radio alarm go off, far too soon. It was a combination of bugles, bells, and lights flashing, followed by irritatingly loud music—designed by the manufacturer to wake the dead, and those who might be experiencing hangovers from the previous evening.

She groaned, but reluctantly climbed out of bed. There was entirely too much to do to risk a few extra moments of sleep.

The cats had already vanished to a safer place before the raucous sounds could puncture their sensitive eardrums. It seemed that they had this inward antenna that could pick up the vibrations in the air before humans could do so. In any event, Carley had noticed the same reaction to the old doorbell at the front door. Their ears always perked up a few seconds before it actually rang.

That morning, Carley needed more than one cup of coffee to start the day. But after the caffeine infusion, she was soon dressed and ready to leave. At the last minute, she took the dragonfly ornament and pinned it to her blazer, since Mabel was to be one of the guests, and Carley knew that she would be pleased.

The correct position for the pin would have been on the left lapel, but Carley had lost so many pins lately because of their encounter with her seat belt strap, that she had switched the dragonfly pin to her right shoulder.

Three passengers were riding with her that morning—Joie, who was designated as hostess for the Zen garden, and the two cats, who had served as models for Angela, one of the female artists. For two days straight, Angela had followed Li-Po and Cho-Cho throughout the estate, capturing their antics on film, which she later transferred to canvas.

The primary reason that Carley had volunteered their services had to do with her guilt at leaving them alone so much lately. They'd had enormous fun exploring the property. Now, they were to return to wander among the gardens to give what the artist had described as *atmosphere.*

As Carley got out the large kitty carrier, Joie came to the side door. "I'm almost ready," Carley called out. It took a few extra minutes to persuade the cats to get into the carrier, since they equated it with going to the vet.

The sun was barely over the horizon when she backed out the driveway. Since Joie was riding with her, Carley had wedged the carrier containing the cats in the back of the truck, making sure that it was secure and adequately sheltered from the wind by the partial cover.

"You look quite nice this morning," Joie said.

"Thanks. I decided to buy some new white slacks. If you notice, there's not a mark or grass stain to be seen."

Carley also complimented Joie on her own appearance. Dressed in a cheongsam of green silk, she had pinned up her dark hair with interlocking chopsticks. And around her neck she wore the second necklace she'd brought back from California—not the one that Carley had borrowed, to wear to the fundraiser.

Joie was of indeterminate age—younger than Gran, but impossible to tell how much. Carley knew that she used face cream made from crushed pearls, the concoction supposed to be good for wrinkles.

There was something so calm about Joie that, at times, she seemed almost enigmatic. Carley liked that quality during this stressful time in her life, when her own emotions seemed to be attached to her body like a yo-yo on a string—especially when it came to her feelings surrounding Evian Whitstone.

But this was a day in which she was determined to forget him, a day that she had thought would never come—when her landscape project was finished and she would receive the final payment for all the hard work of the past weeks.

Carley was glad to see that the lazy clouds, hanging above the bay bridge, were not rain clouds. The anchored ships in the distance—battleship gray—were clearly visible. Even that early in the morning, the fog had lifted and visibility was good.

Joie was interested in Mabel's soirée of the night before, so the two had a lot to talk about on their journey to Fairhope.

When they arrived at Cavallegria, the gates were already open and the signs to the guest parking area were in place. The port-a-potties had vanished, and in their stead were signs directing guests to facilities in the Warhol cottage for women and the adjacent Hockney cottage for the men.

Traveling along the sandy strip of driveway, Carley saw that the silk-screened flags on each side were also in place. However, the pedestals and easels closer to the house were empty—but not for long.

They gathered in the dining room, where a buffet breakfast had been laid out by the resident cook for all the artists and those on the working committee. That included Jake and Barnie, clean-shaven and wearing well pressed clothes. There was a look of pride on their faces, Carley thought, and she was pleased that Boris had consented to invite them in recognition of their services. Without the two, Carley could not have made the garden designs a reality.

They had also been assigned to stations for the day—Jake, to oversee the parking area near the orchard and to make sure the traffic didn't get too snarled, and Barnie, to transport guests by golf cart from the parking area, if they elected not to walk.

"You know," Barnie said, "this is the first time that I have ever been invited to see a completed project on a private estate."

"I hope there will be many more for us in the future, Barnie," Carley replied.

He grinned. "If you're asking me to be on your team, count me in."

Bob walked in with Boris. He immediately got into line for the breakfast buffet, and Carley noticed that Sherrie soon arrived at his side. She supposed that, as an invited guest, Sherrie had come at the same time as Bob, even though she'd had no part in the execution of the boathouse.

Curiously, Carley had gotten much of her animosity for both of them out of her system. Perhaps it had to do with Bob's confession of having made a mistake in marrying Sherrie.

Between the previous evening and this particular morning, Carley had also come to the realization of what a strain it had been, being married to Bob. And if Whit had done nothing else in her life, he had made her see how sterile her love life had been.

She felt almost ashamed as she recalled a day toward the end of their marriage, when she had come home from work. She was immensely happy, but puzzled as to why she'd felt such a sense of elation and freedom. Bob had gone out of town for the night. Could that have been the reason?

At the time, she had quickly buried that thought, for it suddenly smacked of things that she didn't want to bring to the surface for reflection.

She acknowledged Sherrie with a "good morning." Sherrie managed a grudging good morning in reply. Then, Carley diverted her attention to Joie, who said in a low tone, "Look at Consuelo's face."

When Carley turned to look at her, she became alarmed. Consuelo had a number of scratches on the left side of her face that could not be disguised by makeup

"Consuelo, what happened?" she asked, as she joined her at the table. "I hope the cats didn't scratch you."

"Oh, no. It wasn't the cats. I was taking a walk on the estate last night and bumped into some vines with thorns. The scratches will heal." She seemed quite unconcerned about her injuries, so Carley didn't pursue the matter.

While Joie, Consuelo, and Carley continued to eat breakfast, Maxim stumbled into the dining room. Carley felt even sorrier for him than for Consuelo. The bags under his eyes were quite prominent, and he looked as if he had been on a binge. He seemed particularly sensitive to the morning glare. Carley decided that his partying must have continued well past Mabel's social function.

After breakfast, the mad scramble began—to place the art works in the various gardens. However select the guest list might be, there was always the chance of a painting being stolen, so the artists had been assigned in shifts to oversee the various gardens.

Most had elected to sign up where their own works were being displayed. Once the art was in place, someone would be there at all times to watch over the finished examples of Boris's successful summer session.

The caterers from Baker's Dozen, Inc.—of orange-chocolate cookie fame—arrived next and soon set to work, transforming the long, utilitarian tables under the white tent into islands of beauty, with snow white tablecloths, fresh flowers, and trays waiting for the feast of little sandwiches, fruit, and numerous sweets of culinary wonder.

Smaller round tables held empty punch bowls, which would be filled at the last minute with a special concoction of juices and chilled champagne. After all, it was a day for celebration.

Another table had also been set up, to hold the maps to the seven gardens, descriptions of the various artworks, and the price list of those that were for sale.

The acrylics and watercolors could go home that same day with the purchasers, but the oils had not had time to season. They would have to be shipped later.

Once the boathouse had been finished and Jake and the crew had cleaned up around the extended site, Carley had finally ventured in that direction when she was certain that no one else would be about.

She had to admit that it was a vast improvement to the old one and its rotting pier. The structure, half in and half out of the water, had a high-pitched roof, a launching dock and two boat bays, where boats could come in out of a storm or escape curious eyes.

The steps up to the deck were wide, freshly painted with the type of marine paint that guaranteed protection for years to come. The inside was constructed of cedar, the space divided into several rooms, including a tackle room and a bath.

Carley recognized the slightly modified design as one that Bob had entered into a contest earlier. Today, of course, she would not go near it.

Soon, Carley could hear the noise of approaching cars into the estate. Barnie appeared with his first passengers— Mabel, Rhett, and Edgar, who had come quite a distance from the river plantation house.

Seeing her gift attached to Carley's blazer, Mabel gave her an extra warm smile. Carley noticed that both she and Rhett were wearing their dragonfly pins also.

But what a fashion contrast to Carley's business-like apparel. The sisters were dressed in pastel chiffon, with garden hats to match. Carley immediately thought of the Queen's tea party at the Court of St. James, which both sisters had attended years ago.

As a rather gruff host, not used to opening his estate to a number of people, Boris had asked Carley to help greet the guests. He was probably at a loss in putting names to the faces, she decided, and was relying on her to recognize them, since she had supplied many of the names on the official guest list.

Within a few minutes, Cavallegria was filled with

people. Edward, with his wife Jorja, Henry, Goose, Agnes, and Lizzie appeared. Then, surprisingly Alva came in her motorized scooter, accompanied by Gaddi.

"Well, young lady," Goose greeted Carley. "I want to congratulate you on a job well done. And on time, too."

"Thank you, Goose."

He leaned over and whispered, "Don't let me forget before I leave. I have a final check to give you."

"Oh, look at the lights along the pathway," Agnes exclaimed. "How clever."

Henry and Edward, not to be outdone, said, "We're proud of you, Carley."

She smiled. "I'm so glad that you could come. And I hope that you enjoy each garden."

Jorja, seeing the food spread on tables under the tent, was much more interested in eating than viewing the gardens. She darted quickly in that direction, with Edward directly behind her.

With such a spirit of conviviality, Carley was pleased that so many people had come. Besides those who'd arrived by car, others had taken advantage of the new pier and come by boat. Carley noticed that in that group were Martin Pemberton, the contractor, and several members of the architectural firm of Regan, Barnes, and O'Reilly, along with their wives.

Boris, growing visibly impatient at all the to-do, turned to Carley and said, "Why don't we get some refreshments? I think we've been standing here long enough."

"Well, I *am* thirsty," Carley admitted. It would also be good to find the shade, since the humidity had climbed steadily and promised to get worse as the day wore on.

While she was at the punch table, she saw the satellite TV truck approaching. Pleased, she quickly put down her punch cup and waited for the truck to stop and the crew to alight.

Carley had never had trouble interesting newspaper photographers to cover a special event, but it was always much harder to convince a local TV station to do the same. The reclusive Boris was the major factor, she knew, but at the same time, her landscapes would be featured, along with the artists' creations. So everyone would gain from the publicity.

"Good morning. I'm so glad you could come," she said, recognizing Flip English, the TV reporter with whom she had talked earlier.

She led him to Boris and, after a brief interview, Flip and the camera crew dispersed to the gardens on their own and Carley went back to the shelter of the tent.

Less than a minute later, Barnie's golf cart approached again. He had only one passenger this time—Lucinda.

Where was Rudy, Carley wondered. He usually accompanied Lucinda everywhere she went, but he was nowhere in sight. Quickly adjusting her puzzled look to a welcoming smile, Carley went out to greet Lucinda.

Even more guests began to arrive, so Carley was kept busy for the next few minutes. But when a black limousine appeared, it was Boris, himself, who left the tent to greet this particular guest.

"Good morning, Luis," Boris said, as the man Carley recognized from Mabel's dinner party the previous evening emerged from the vehicle. Almost immediately, the two men disappeared onto the terrace, rather than coming to join the others milling about.

Watching, Carley felt a little self-conscious, as Luis stood before Boris's large painting and began to view it from every angle. Would he recognize her as the subject? Deciding that it wouldn't be polite to keep watching, Carley turned her attention elsewhere. But she would have been even more self-conscious, if she had been privy to the private conversation taking place.

"Most unusual, Boris," Luis said. "Both the concept and the design. I like it very much."

"I thought you might," Boris replied.

"It's quite different from the one I saw in Amsterdam."

"Well, I had an intriguing subject. Feisty, but vulnerable at the same time. Quite a lethal combination."

"And you say that it's been sold?"

"Yes."

"Was it a museum or an individual buyer?"

"A private investor."

"Do you think that investor would change his mind if I offered twice the amount of the sale price?"

"Unfortunately, it's out of my hands. You'd have to take that up with the buyer."

"Then, let's contact him and negotiate," Luis replied. "I want the painting."

"Actually it's a woman. She bought it as a surprise birthday present for someone."

The celebration in the gardens that morning continued to have an air of excitement and conviviality, and Carley, who had kept her fingers crossed, couldn't have asked for any grander success. The weather had cooperated; Boris's half-hidden smile had indicated his satisfaction, and Carley, for the first time, relaxed.

It was then, just as she'd finally allowed herself a pat on the back for a job well done, that a bloodcurdling scream came from one of the gardens. Within moments, the glorious day disintegrated into a total disaster that threatened chaos on the entire estate.

Chapter 30

The screams had come from the aboriginal garden, its approach hidden from view by the surrounding bocage of wild vines and scrub trees.

From the time of the initial scream, guests had left the refreshment tent, the pathways to the other six gardens, and the art display on the front court. A stampede had erupted, with two of the photographers following the crowd.

Carley was in the middle of the stampede, being propelled forward, with no way of getting there first, to reassure the people viewing the bis pole for the first time. Inwardly, she was swearing at Wingate for having put the shrunken head on this ancestral pole, in the first place.

More than likely, it was Gaddi, or some other sensitive soul, who had emitted the noise that threatened to put a pall on the rest of the day.

Carley's description in the garden notes had evidently not been sufficient to take care of the hysterical reaction that was now taking place.

She realized what a mistake the committee had made in not having that garden site manned, as well. But she had been overruled by Boris and Wingate and, privately, she'd hoped that few visitors would find this out-of-the-way garden and, instead, stick to the more accessible ones.

Carley finally finished her sprint and began to work her way to the front of the crowd. "Ladies and gentlemen, please don't be upset," she began. "The bis pole is merely a work of art, derived from the New Guinea tradition of..." Suddenly, her voice failed her. She, too, let out a moan when she saw the pole in all its gruesomeness.

Instead of the shrunken head of a bush warrior, another severed head had been wedged in its place. Blood had dripped from the mangrove root to its base, and spread in a pool around the *Love-Lies-Bleeding* that Carley had planted only days before. While she stared, she couldn't help but think of the irony.

To make matters even worse, Li-Po and Cho-Cho had evidently discovered the site first. Carley bent over and scooped the cats into her arms. That was the instant when the blinding light of a photographer's flash went off, recording for every wire service in the country the picture that made Carley Burnside notorious.

"Who is it?" someone inquired.

Was she the only one who had recognized the face? Surely not. Even with the stark expression of surprise— the long hair, the structure of jaw, and the devilish eyebrows were a giveaway. Poor Lucinda. Someone had to find her to keep her from this gruesome scene.

Carley had watched enough TV police procedurals to know that someone would have to call the authorities. And it would be imperative for all the guests to remain on the premises. But not here.

"Please, everyone. Go back toward the house. I'm sure that the authorities will want you to remain on the property until they arrive.

"You can find seats in the dining hall, and for those of you who would like more privacy, the Warhol cottage is open for women and the Hockney cottage for men. The directions are on your maps."

Gaddi tugged at her sleeve. "Carley, I think Momma's having a stroke."

Across the pavers sat the motorized scooter, with Alva slumped in it. With the cats still in her arms, Carley went over and knelt down beside her. "Alva, can you speak?"

Barely," she said. "My one outing in ages and this has to happen to spoil it."

Carley was no doctor, but it seemed to her that Alva's condition was not nearly so serious as Gaddi thought, since her speech was quite clear.

"It's a shock to all of us," she managed to say, trying to keep her own voice steady. Turning to Gaddi, she said, "Can you get your mother back to one of the cottages? Someone there can call a doctor for her."

"I suppose so." With that, Gaddi took over the motorized scooter and returned to the pathway, while Alva kept protesting that she could operate the scooter on her own.

Carley was grateful when Goose appeared. He took over, securing the scene against those who wanted to get too close and trample on any evidence that might give some clue as to who had done such a deed.

"Boris is notifying the police," he said. "They should be here any minute."

Edward, Goose, and Henry kept the curious at bay. "Carley," Goose instructed, "go find Lucinda and take her inside Boris's house. I hate to do this to you, but you won't go to pieces like everyone else when you tell her the news."

By the time Carley reached the house, Joie was already looking for her.

"Please, Joie. Put the cats in their carrier and take care of them. I have to find Lucinda."

When she approached the refreshment tent, she saw that Lucinda was with Rhett and Mable. "So what was that noise all about?" Lucinda asked.

Carley didn't answer her question. Instead, she said, "Lucinda, will you please come with me?"

"What's wrong, Carley?"

"I'll tell you when we get inside the house."

Lucinda put down her champagne punch. "If you'll excuse me..."

"Of course," Mabel and Rhett agreed.

Carley noticed that Boris's painting had been removed from the front terrace and Luis was nowhere in sight. Neither was Boris.

Carley led Lucinda into the house and to the vintage living room that showed the luxuries of a by-gone era. Tiffany lamps, antique bergère chairs covered in dusty damask, well-worn Italian sofas with needlepoint pillows filled the room, with faded vintage pictures scattered about, and a large oil painting of a white-haired dowager, presiding over the mantel.

Lucinda took her place on one of the sofas. Carley sat down beside her and reached for her hand. "Lucinda, I have tragic news."

A tear rolled down her cheek. "It's Rudy, isn't it?"

"Yes."

"And he's dead." She didn't ask it as a question, but said it as an affirmation.

"Yes."

"I knew they would eventually get him. I knew it in my heart this morning, when I discovered that the boat was missing."

"The boat?"

"Yes. Once we got home last night, Rudy decided to run Maxim back here in the boat, rather than the car. I stayed awake until I heard the boat return, but then I'm afraid I drifted off to sleep. This morning, when I woke up, Rudy was missing and the boat was gone, too."

"Have you questioned Maxim?"

"Yes. He said that Rudy dropped him off and then started back immediately. And I believe him. You see, this isn't the first time that Rudy's changed his mind and stayed out all night," she confided. And then, with a sob, she added, "Oh, Carley, I tried so hard to protect him, but he was so reckless."

"Do you have any idea why anyone would want to harm him? Or who it might be?" Carley asked.

Lucinda shook her head. "He would never tell me. He said that I would be safer that way. He really did love me, Carley. In spite of what everyone said."

Kindness and sympathy caused Carley to agree.

"Where is... his body?" Lucinda asked.

Carley hesitated. "He was found in one of the gardens — the aboriginal garden." She wiped away a tear on her own cheek and swallowed hard to get rid of the lump stuck in her throat. She couldn't bring herself to tell Lucinda that his body was missing. That would be too much for her.

In relief Carley heard the sirens in the distance. The police and, more than likely, an ambulance were arriving. The front door opened; footsteps sounded across the foyer. When Carley looked to see who had entered, she saw Mabel and Rhett. "We'll stay with Lucinda. I'm sure you're wanted outside."

With that Carley left the living room of the mansion and walked out into the dappled light, into the melee of police cars, plain clothes men, and Evian Whitstone, glaring at her as if she were somehow to blame for what had happened.

"Go back into the house, Carley," Whit ordered, "and wait for me there."

This was an entirely different man from the one who had made love to her. He was impersonal, stern, and frightening. All charm had vanished and had been replaced with a rock-hard intensity that brooked no opposition to his order.

Carley rejoined the women in the living room, but it was not long before she was left alone. The police gave Rhett and Mabel permission to take Lucinda home. "Edgar and I will stay with you, Lucinda," Rhett said, "until your daughter can arrive."

"She's not speaking to me anymore, Rhett."

"I'm sure that Mabel can persuade her that you need her now, more than ever."

Much later that afternoon, when the refreshment tent had been taken down, when the guests had been interrogated and allowed to go home, and the entire area swept clean of all art and artists, Whit returned to the living room, where Carley had finally dozed in exhaustion.

Sensing someone nearby, Carley opened her eyes and found Whit leaning over her.

"I didn't mean to startle you, but now that things are beginning to settle down, I'd like you to go over every inch of the estate with me."

"Now?"

"Whenever you're ready."

"Joie—"

"I sent her home with the cats. Once we're through here, I'll take you back."

"Who *are* you?" Carley demanded.

"At this point, it doesn't matter."

"So you're an impostor."

"You might say so."

"I should have known. Anybody who chooses spring water for a first name has to be an impostor."

Whit laughed, but it did not sound humorous. "In my business, one name is as good as another."

Carley ignored his answer. "Where do you want to start?"

"Why not at the edge of the property, then make a circle, and work our way back to the house?"

"Are you looking for anything specifically?"

"The murder weapon, for one. And the rest of the body."

"I would have thought that the police had already combed the property for clues."

"They have, but it's a large estate. And you're probably better acquainted with it than anyone."

"Then, let's start at the wildflower garden in the orchard," Carley suggested. "The ground is fresher there than anywhere else."

From one to the other they went, traversing the acreage, with their heads down, while searching for anything out of the ordinary. Carley didn't feel like talking and Whit remained silent, as well, except to ask certain questions pertaining to the landscaping.

The fountain in the shell garden revealed nothing; the obelisk remained devoid of clues. From one end of the property to the other they walked, while Carley examined every site to make sure that nothing had been disturbed or buried beneath the flowers and shrubs.

They avoided the aboriginal garden, since the police had examined every inch of that site, and it was still marked off by the crime scene tape.

By late afternoon, Carley could think of only two places that remained to be scrutinized — the barn and the boathouse.

"Did you investigate the old barn across the creek?" she finally asked. "It's hidden beyond the willows. That's where Wingate stores his imported mangrove roots."

"Show me."

It took awhile to get to the small creek, cross the wooden bridge, and stand before the rustic-planked barn that had seen better days.

"It's probably padlocked. Do you need a warrant to break in, or can you open that lock, too, like the cottage door lock?" Carley inquired.

"Why are you so hostile, Carley? Do you think that this is enjoyable for me?"

"Since I really don't know you, I have no idea."

"Then, let's wait until this investigation is finished. When it's over, we'll discuss more personal matters."

He took a pair of latex gloves from the crime kit he was carrying, put them on, took out a pipe cutter and, within moments, the lock fell apart. He then relegated the padlock to a plastic bag and dropped it into the kit.

"Don't touch anything inside," he warned.

"It's a little too late. A week ago, I helped carry Wingate's sculpture out in a gray tarpaulin."

"So I'll find your fingerprints all over the place."

"Not only mine. Jake's and Barnie's, too. "

The light was meager in the barn, because of an overhead light that seemed to be out. While Whit left the door wide open and began to rummage around, Carley watched from the doorway. Several extremely large mangrove trees were visible, but she saw no sign of Wingate's tools or the gray tarpaulin.

"Looks like somebody has rearranged things," Carley commented, coming inside. "I don't see the tarpaulin, and the two unfinished poles seem to have been moved."

Whit said nothing, but continued to examine the barn from one end to the other, with his attention finally returning to the mangrove poles. With great effort he moved one and then another, to examine the dirt floor beneath them. He probed the area carefully, suddenly coming into contact with something metallic, buried in a shallow trough.

He scooped out more dirt. "Looks like I've found something," he said, finally drawing out a long machete from its burial site.

Jake's machete. Carley recognized it immediately. It was the one he always kept by his side, the one he had used each day to chop down anything in his way. The blade seemed to be stained with a reddish brown.

Carley, becoming ill, bolted out the door and ran to the bridge. No. It was impossible. Jake, her friend, her most loyal helper, could never have done such a wicked thing.

"Carley!" Whit called. "Carley!" No longer wearing the latex gloves, or carrying the monstrous crime kit, he rushed after her.

She looked at him with accusing eyes for having put her through such a traumatic discovery. When he looked as if he might try to comfort her, she moved away. This was a man that she didn't know and she wanted no sympathy from him.

 *Chapter 31*

"*D*o you feel better now?" Whit asked, waiting for her to recover.

"I'll manage."

"Then, let me gather up the evidence and we'll proceed to the boathouse."

"Please put up the machete, first," Carley requested. "I don't want to be anywhere near it."

"You recognized it, didn't you?"

"Yes, it belongs to Jake, my foreman. But I would swear that he had absolutely nothing to do with the crime."

"It hasn't been established yet, that it's the murder weapon, Carley," Whit commented. "That will be decided in the lab."

His words were small comfort to her as she waited for him to recover the evidence and return to the bridge. In silence, they walked back to the front terrace of the house, where Carley remained until Whit had put the bloodied weapon in the trunk of his car and locked it.

On the way to the boathouse, some of the solar lights had already turned on, marking the path toward the obelisk. With Whit beside her, she tried to ignore them, since they brought back memories of the storm and the night spent in the cottage. But as they passed the obelisk, Carley blurted out, "Did you know that you and Consuelo were being spied upon at the boathouse by one of the artists hiding up there?"

Whit suddenly stopped. "When was that?"

"One night when you were supposed to be out of town."

"You sound a little jealous, Carley."

"Just disappointed. You see, I'm new to this dating game. And I've been a bit naive. But not anymore. I've learned my lesson."

"Carley, there are things happening all around that I can't reveal to you. You'll just have to trust me for now."

"The stockbroker said the same thing before he absconded with Alva's mutual fund account."

Carley could see Gran shaking her head at her retort. As usual, she should have kept her mouth shut, but that was impossible. Her nerves were taut from all the stress of the past weeks, culminating in the vast tragedy of a day that should have held such joy.

Whit's mouth tightened, as if he were having a hard time remaining silent. Finally, he said, "Trust works both ways, Carley."

"I have no idea what you're talking about."

"Then, let's forget it for now."

Whit began the slow, steady examination of the boathouse, from the tackle room, where boating equipment had been stored, to each section. He investigated the rear access doors, the inside stairs from the boat bays, and walked along the berm to the new ramp. At one point, he scooped up some dirt and put in a plastic bag. Yet, nothing was visibly out of place.

"Tell me about your former husband," Whit said. "Does he make a specialty of designing boathouses?"

She spoke just as impersonally. "Not really. He's much more interested in designing commercial buildings, since there's more money in that. But about two years ago, he became rather obsessed with a boathouse design by Frank Lloyd Wright. The structure was never built, but it's in Wright's portfolio of his best architectural plans."

"So when Boris contacted the architectural firm, your husband would have been the logical one assigned to the job."

"Ex-husband."

He ignored her correction.

"Have you talked with Maxim yet?" Carley asked. "Lucinda told me that Rudy brought him back here in his boat last night."

"Yes. He was quite cooperative. But since Lucinda said that Rudy returned to Point Clear after that, then left again, we have no reason to suspect the man."

They stood on the observation deck and looked out toward the water, where the sun had shed rainbows of color from the clouds to the water in the undisturbed bay. Sea gulls, looking for food, called to each other as they soared past.

How beautiful and innocent the scene looked when, perhaps underneath the water's fragile surface, a horror waited to be discovered by some unsuspecting fisherman.

Finally, Carley could stand no more. "I'd like to go home now, Whit."

"Of course. It's been a long day for you. And there's nothing more we can do here tonight."

Whit had not arrived in his red Ferrari. Instead, the unobtrusive gray, suitable for surveillance, was similar to the car that had parked on her street for days.

As she climbed into the passenger side, she saw the headlights of another car coming down the drive.

"That must be Boris and Wingate," Whit said.

He edged his car to the far right to give the other car room to pass. Driving by, he acknowledged Boris but didn't stop. When Whit's car reached the front gates, Carley saw that a policeman had been placed on duty, to secure the area.

They left the private road, and Carley made no attempt to converse as Whit pulled onto the main highway headed back to Mobile. Finally breaking the silence, Whit said, "Are you hungry?"

Carley had no intention of prolonging the evening with him. "Yes, but I can wait until I get home."

218 • Frances Patton Statham

"Wouldn't you rather stop at a restaurant on the way?"

"No. That would take too long. Besides, I'm not eager to face a crowd, after what's happened."

To Carley's chagrin, her empty stomach made a rumbling noise, causing Whit to smile.

"Then, why don't I get some take-out, and we can sit in the car to eat."

"If you wish."

He ignored her less than enthusiastic response. He kept driving until they came to a row of fast food places and restaurants. "What appeals to you? Ribs or seafood?"

"Barbeque."

Whit pulled into the parking area of a brown-stained, rustic building, with a distinct odor of mesquite smoke permeating the air. "The food must be good here, judging from the number of people."

They were in luck. A car was pulling out of a parking place as they arrived. But suddenly, Carley didn't want to remain alone in the car. "I need to wash my hands," she said.

"All right. We'll go in together."

As soon as Whit parked, Carley opened the car door to get out. She wanted no gentlemanly display from this man, since their being together again was strictly business.

Once inside, Whit said, "I'll meet you back here," indicating the sign that pointed the way to the ordering line.

Carley took her time in the rest room, washing her hands and removing the slight smudge on her cheek. She had kept a tight grip on her emotions during the worst of the day, except for the brief moment on the bridge.

She'd always prided herself on being able to handle any emergency at the time. It was only later that her knees would buckle. But she was determined not to show any further weakness in Whit's presence, even though her face still looked pale.

By the time Carley reappeared, he was waiting patiently for her. They ordered, filled their drinks cups at the fountain and then returned to the car.

As she started eating, Carley realized how hungry she was. She attacked her food with gusto and, watching, Whit smiled at her.

She looked at him and grudgingly returned his smile. "Thanks. I'm beginning to feel better, now."

"I noticed that. And I'm grateful."

"For what?"

"For being a little less hostile."

"Was it that obvious?"

"Yep. So from now on, I'll know what to do when you get peevish with me. Just feed you."

She started to comment, but decided against it. There would be no *from now on*, but there was no need to broadcast her decision.

Afterwards, they crossed the bay bridge, took a side street and wound their way past the shopping center and past the deli where Carley usually stopped for cheese. After a few more stop lights, they arrived at the entrance to her own quiet, tree-shaded street.

"What a traffic jam," Carley commented. "I wonder what's going on."

"It seems the news hounds are waiting for you, Carley."

Her English Tudor house was surrounded by TV trucks, with bright lights illuminating the entire yard. Standing at her front door, a reporter was evidently broadcasting live.

Whit sped up. "Put your head down," he ordered. "I'm getting you out of here."

He kept driving, past her house, past the lights, and on down the street. Less than a minute later, he said, "It's okay now."

When Carley raised her head, she saw that they were at the end of the long street, where it intersected with another residential street. Whit turned right, in the direction of the expressway. "You can't go home, Carley," he said.

"Of course I can. I'll wait them out."

Whit didn't stop. "Tomorrow, maybe. But not tonight."

"Then take me to a motel. The Ramada Inn isn't too far away. I'll stay there tonight and Joie can come for me in the morning."

Whit ignored her. He passed the motel and kept driving.

"Where are taking me?"

"To the house on Dauphin Island. You'll be safer there."

"I don't want to go to Dauphin Island," she protested.

"You have no choice."

"If you think I'm going to spend another night with you..."

"You won't. You'll be spending the night with Consuelo."

"What?"

"For God's sake! She's my sister."

Images bombarded Carley's brain—the two dancing together at the party; the easy manner with each other. Except for the red hair, the two bore a remarkable resemblance. But just a few hours earlier, she had practically accused Whit of having an affair with his own sister. No wonder he'd been so short with her.

"You could have told me earlier."

"And ruin her cover?"

"You mean, she was in the gardens as a *plant*?" Carley laughed at her own joke, and then immediately became contrite. "Forgive me. That wasn't funny."

"No, it wasn't. But I forgive you."

So that was why Maxim's picture of Whit and Consuelo had suddenly disappeared, replaced by another of his works for the day. Consuelo couldn't afford for anyone to make a connection between the two. So what had happened to the painting?

"I'll have to call Joie to let her know where I am." She dug into her shoulder bag for her cell phone.

Before she could dial, Whit cautioned, "A scanner can pick up your call too easily. Let me call her for you on the scrambled line. I wouldn't want anyone else to learn of your whereabouts, especially since I went to the trouble of removing the bug from your truck."

"What are you talking about?"

"Someone has been following you, Carley. Were you aware?"

"I suspected it several weeks ago, but it was nothing that I could prove. Then, it seemed to stop. Do you know who it was?"

"We're working on it. Right now, we don't have enough evidence to accuse anyone with certainty."

He changed the subject. "So what is Joie's number?"

Carley told him, and soon she heard Joie's voice. "Joie?"

"Where are you, Carley? There's a madhouse out front."

"I know. I'm with Whit. He's taking me to his sister's," she explained, "to spend the night. Could you watch after Li-Po and Cho-Cho? I'll be home sometime tomorrow."

"Of course. How can I reach you?"

Whit could hear every bit of the conversation, since the speakerphone was on. Carley looked at him, waiting for an answer.

"Joie," he cut in, "she'll call you. Don't try to call her cell phone number. It can be traced too easily."

"I understand."

"See you tomorrow, Joie," Carley said. "And I hope you'll be able to get some sleep tonight."

"Don't worry about me. The cats and I will manage just fine."

When Whit and Carley arrived at the secluded house, it was quite late, all the inside lights were out with the exception of the ones in the aerie, and Carley was exhausted.

Whit stopped in the drive and, idling the engine, he used the phone again. "Connie, I'm in the driveway. I have Carley Burnside with me."

"Thanks for warning me," she said. "I wouldn't want to mistake you for a burglar."

After he hung up, Carley asked, "Would she really shoot you?"

"I don't know. But I wouldn't want to take the chance."

The garage door opened and as soon as the car drove inside, Whit closed it.

When Carley stepped into the hallway, she heard the elevator coming down from upstairs. Consuelo emerged, dressed in a blue silk kimono, with a small bandage to one portion of her face. But her hair was no longer a flaming red. It was the same dark color as her brother's. Carley hardly recognized her.

# Chapter 32

Carley was relieved that Whit did not stay. After he had briefed Consuelo on the events, he left again. He still had the machete in the trunk of his car, Carley knew, so he would have to turn it over to whoever was in charge of the crime. Carley also wondered if he were going to see to Jake's arrest.

She wanted to call Jake, to hear from him that he had nothing to do with Rudy's murder; to hear his explanation of how the machete had wound up in Wingate's barn. Of course, by doing that, she would be interfering with the investigation. Instead, she prayed that Jake had a good explanation and an airtight alibi.

"Let's find a bedroom for you," Consuelo said. "They're all on the second floor."

Carley gave no indication that she was familiar with the house. She followed Consuelo up the stairs, along the bridge, and down the hallway.

"You'll have to sleep here, tonight, in Whit's bedroom," she said. "The others aren't furnished—except for the one I'm sleeping in."

When Carley hesitated, she said, "It's all right. He won't be coming back tonight. And there're fresh linens on the bed."

Consuelo must have noticed how drained Carley looked. She became quite motherly, even though she was only a few years older. "Why don't you take a nice, soaking bath and then come downstairs for a cup of green tea?"

"That sounds wonderful." Anything, Carley thought, to delay climbing into the massive bed and remembering what a ninny she had been, falling so hard for someone like Whit.

"You didn't bring a bag?"

"No. I couldn't get to my house."

"Well, anything I have would swallow you. Maybe you could wear one of Whit's pajama tops to sleep in. He never uses them." She walked over to the armoire, pulled open a drawer, and began to look.

"Here we are. This ought to do." She unfolded a short-sleeved top of pale blue plaid cotton.

Consuelo left the bedroom, but she did not go down to the kitchen immediately. Carley heard the elevator going to the floor above, where Consuelo had been when she'd first arrived. Soon, the elevator returned to the main floor.

Not realizing that she had stood in the middle of the floor, listening, Carley left the bedroom and went into the adjacent bath, where she filled the luxurious tub with water.

Lying in the whirlpool tub, with the pulsating water massaging her tired muscles, Carley felt the tension of the day slowly disappear. She remained in the tub until the water turned cool.

A half-hour later, she found her way to the kitchen. Consuelo smiled when she saw her, dressed in Whit's oversized top.

They sat at the kitchen table and discussed the day's events. But Carley made no mention of Consuelo's other role at Cavallegria.

"I feel so terrible for the artists," Carley said, squeezing a sliver of lemon into her cup of tea. "They were banking on selling their art today, but I suppose it didn't happen."

"At least, *one* sold. You probably know by now that I bought Maxim's painting." Consuelo smiled. "I wanted to tell you about the family connection earlier, but, of course, that was impossible."

"Yes, but I'm still puzzled over the role of Dresnick. Is he really a chauffeur?"

"Whit will have to fill you in on anything else, Carley. Sorry. Would you like another cup of tea?"

"No, thank you. If you don't mind, I think I'll go on to bed."

Carley picked up her cup and saucer to take to the sink, but Consuelo stopped her. "I'll wash up. Just leave the cup on the table."

"Well then, good night."

"Good night, Carley. Sleep well."

Carley mounted the stairs again and returned to the muted beige bedroom. With a nightlight in the adjacent bath, and the door slightly ajar, Carley climbed into the lonely bed and, in the semi-darkness, she hugged the pillow beside her, while she settled down to go to sleep.

In an effort to put Whit out of her mind, she relived the day that she had first encountered her ex-husband Bob at Cavallegria, and seeing Jake—standing in the background, with a scowl on his face and his right hand on the machete. *Is he bothering you?* He'd had a murderous look in his eyes and, suddenly alarmed, Carley realized that she did not know Jake nearly so well as she'd thought. Could he be capable of actual murder? But what would he have had against Rudy?

She tried to hold on to that image, to think it through, but her body demanded respite from the long day, and she could no longer keep her eyes open.

It seemed to have become a habit lately—redressing in the same clothes. The next morning was no different.

Hearing movement downstairs and smelling the aroma of coffee, Carley hurriedly took a shower, got dressed, and walked downstairs to the kitchen. Surprised, she saw Dresnick and Consuelo together, talking and drinking coffee.

"Good morning, Carley," Consuelo greeted her. "Come and have some breakfast with us. You remember Dresnick."

"Yes. Good morning." Carley tried to hide her shyness at

seeing the man. Was her secret safe? Or had he told Consuelo what she had intended keeping to herself?

"Good morning, Ms. Burnside," Dresnick responded politely. He stood and pulled out a chair for her.

"Dresnick is going to take you back to town this morning. After breakfast, of course."

"That's quite kind of you."

Carley ate little, but drank two cups of coffee, before returning upstairs to brush her teeth and reclaim her linen blazer. Then, she was ready to leave.

"Thank you, Consuelo. I appreciate your hospitality."

Carley realized that she sounded much too formal, as if she were still thirteen years old and in Flo Timmes's etiquette class. But for her, it was an awkward situation.

"Glad I could help."

"I hope you don't mind riding in a plumber's truck," Dresnick said.

Carley suddenly laughed. "What, no limousine?"

"Not this time." He smiled and added, "Too noticeable."

So Dresnick backed the Jackson Plumbers, Inc. truck from the garage, and they began the trip back to Mobile and to Carley's house.

"The police chief is having a press conference this morning about the murder," Dresnick said. "Whit decided that would be a good time to get you back home. We'll be at your house a few minutes after eleven, so the church-going folks should be occupied, too."

"Have they arrested anyone yet?"

"No. But quite a number of people are being interrogated."

"Do you know anything about my foreman, Jake Fuentes?" Carley didn't want to mention the machete, but she suspected that Dresnick was already aware of it.

"He was brought in for questioning this morning."

Poor Jake. She decided that she would call Goose and ask his advice on a good criminal lawyer for Jake. It was the least she could do. But Sunday was a social time in Mobile.

Goose and Agnes usually went to church together and then met friends at the Club for lunch. It would be at least early afternoon before she could talk with him. That is, if they didn't go to a movie, too. Then, it would be much later.

"Where did you get the truck?" Carley inquired, breaking the silence.

"Whit requisitioned it."

"Oh." That didn't tell her anything, so she stopped asking questions.

A few minutes after eleven o'clock, they pulled into the driveway. Carley was relieved to see that the way was clear. "Thanks, Dresnick. You're a real gem."

"I'm coming in with you," he informed her. "I'm to re-key your locks and work on the sliding glass doors."

"You can do that?"

He grinned. "Piece of cake."

"And you think that's necessary?"

"Yep. Unless you want ex-husbands and other sundry guests to come in at all hours."

"Heaven forbid! So you know about that. Then go to work, Dresnick."

She left him to that chore and used the phone in the kitchen to call Joie. "I'm home, Joie."

"Turn on the television," Joie ordered. "And then call me back."

"Which channel?" Carley asked, but Joie had hung up.

Actually, it didn't matter which channel, since the news was the same. Other programs had been preempted, and there Carley stood — holding Li-Po and Cho-Cho, while the reporter gave the entire story of the previous day.

"Garden designer gets more than she bargains for." With all the publicity, people would have thought that *she* was the murderer. To make matters even worse, Carley decided that she had the typical "deer in the headlights" look.

Too gruesome to show. A celebration gone wrong. Those were the stock phrases used to describe the day. Her entire project had been marginalized. Where was a picture of Wingate,

228 • Frances Patton Statham

who was responsible for the whole thing? Where was a picture of Rudy? He was the one who had been murdered. And where was Boris—or the artists? Why did she have to bear the brunt of all this sensational publicity?

Dresnick quietly went about working on the locks and putting up a security bar at the sliding glass doors of her office, while Carley ignored the phone's continuous ringing. Once he had finished, he handed over the new keys.

"How much do I owe you?"

"Take that up with Whit," he said.

Carley thanked him, let him out the side door, and returned to her office.

Shortly thereafter, Joie crossed the garden and knocked on the sliding glass door.

It took Carley a minute to figure out the new security mechanism that Dresnick had just installed.

Welcoming Joie and the cats., Carley said, "Come in."

The phone rang again. She ignored it, until she heard Morgan's urgent voice. "Carley, if you're there, pick up immediately."

 Chapter 33

"Morgan, where are you? Where have you been?"

"I've been sailing in the Mediterranean with friends. But I'm at the millhouse now, Carley."

"Well, thank heavens. I thought you had disappeared for good."

"Let's not talk about *me*," she urged. "I just saw your picture on satellite television. What's going on?"

Carley groaned. "There was a murder yesterday at Cavallegria, the artist colony at Fairhope."

"Was that where you were restoring the gardens?"

"Yes. And I did a wonderful job. I don't deserve this kind of publicity."

"Well, it might be good for you to get out of Mobile until things quiet down. So why don't you come and visit me here? I'm starting the renovations on the house next week. You could design the gardens for me at the same time."

"I doubt if I could leave, Morgan, until the murder investigation is complete."

"It's not as if you had a part in it...."

"But my foreman might have. They're questioning him now. It was his machete that seems to be the murder weapon."

"Carley, I don't see how you can keep getting yourself embroiled in such trouble. I remember the time that you..."

"There's no need to bring up the past, Morgan. I have enough to worry about with this present situation without conjuring up stuff that happened a long time ago."

Joie was listening unabashedly to the conversation, and she smiled when Carley suddenly switched gears. "How is Cristina getting along at her new school?"

"I talked with her yesterday. She's adjusting well."

After another minute of conversation, they hung up. There were so many things that Carley had wanted to discuss with Morgan — most of all about Gran and the recent discovery in the attic trunk. But that subject would have to wait for another time.

The cats, demanding attention, had been rubbing against Carley's legs while she had talked with Morgan. So she stooped down and gathered them in her arms.

"Is Morgan finally settling down?" Joie asked.

"I doubt it. Another week or two and she'll be on the go again."

Carley motioned for Joie to follow her into the den. They sat down in Gran's two easy chairs to talk about the events of the past twenty-four hours. The cats jumped down from Carley's lap and raced into the kitchen to find their favorite spots under the hutch.

"By the way, I had the locks changed, or rather re-keyed. So I'll need to give you a new key before you leave."

"I'm glad you weren't here, Carley, with all the traffic and spectators yesterday. The noise went on until midnight, when people finally realized that you weren't coming home."

"Do you think that Lucinda got the same attention?"

"Not if she had her gates locked."

"That's one of the drawbacks in being in an older neighborhood like this one, with an open lawn between the house and the street."

"Have you thought about putting a surveillance camera at your door?" Joie inquired.

"Do you think I need one?"

"Well, it would certainly have caught the culprit who left the poisonous snake."

"But that's past history, Joie. Besides, it would be much too expensive. Since I have no idea how soon I'll get another job offer, I need to make the money last." Carley realized then that Goose had not yet given her the final landscape payment.

With the new house key in hand, Joie left to go back to the carriage house, and Carley returned to her office to check her e-mail.

She was amazed. The boxes were full, with job offers, with messages from strangers trying to sell her things. She even had one offer for her and the cats to star in a pornographic film together. There had also been five hundred hits to her web site—all because she had been in the wrong place at the wrong time.

For the next several days, the murder was the main topic of conversation for many Mobilians. Carley did not go out of the house during that time—even to the grocery store. But by Wednesday night, when the poker game resumed, the reporters had finally lost interest in her.

"I'll raise you another five," Carley said.

"I'm folding," Henry announced, throwing down his hand. He joined Edward.

Goose smiled. "Call."

They showed their hands. Carley's straight flush beat Goose's full house, and she claimed all the chips.

"You play just like Lydia," Edward complained, but Carley took it as a compliment.

Before beginning another round, they stopped for refreshments. It was during that time that the four felt free to talk. Goose had returned Carley's call the previous Sunday night. But since Jake had been released, after being declared a *person of interest,* Goose had felt that it was premature to hire a criminal lawyer, since he had not been officially charged.

"The machete was supposedly stolen from his truck," Goose said. "Now, they're looking at Wingate, since it was found in the barn he used for his poles. "

"Have they determined that the machete is actually the murder weapon?" Carley asked.

"It's almost certain. But they're waiting on Rudy's DNA to confirm it."

Henry, aware of Carley's concern for the artists' monetary loss that day, said, "It's strange how a little gruesome notoriety will cause such interest in the general public. I guess you've heard. They're bidding like mad on eBay for Angela's cat picture."

"No, I didn't know."

He continued. "And the other artists have been contacted, as well, with huge sums offered. It seems that lots of people want a piece of that tragic day."

Edward, putting down his beer stein, smiled and said, "Some artists, who never even *saw* Cavallegria, are getting in on the Internet sales, too."

Carley felt better about the artists' financial welfare. Hers was decidedly better, too, since Goose had brought her final check, which she planned to deposit the next day.

"How is Boris holding up?" Carley asked Goose.

"He's sorry that he ever opened his estate to the public. He was just beginning to rejoin the human race, when this happened. I'm afraid that he might become a semi-recluse again."

"Did you hear the rumor that his dock might have been used as a drop-off point by smugglers?" Carley asked.

"Yes, but I've heard a lot of rumors," Goose admitted, "although that is one of the wilder ones."

They all sighed, while Edward dealt another round of cards and the game continued.

Ever since her last conversation with Whit, Carley had tried to make sense of what he had told her about the bug on her truck. She had gone through so much grief, with the stalking, the grading equipment fiasco, the candy, the bogus note, and worst of all, the snake. So who had done this to her? The sooner the culprit was discovered, the better she would feel. Somehow, though, she equated all these mishaps with someone who had not wanted her to succeed with the Cavanaugh project. Now that it was completed, perhaps she was safe.

But what Whit had not addressed was why *he* had been following her, too. What had she done to gain the attention of an undercover agent, which she was almost sure he was? The only thing of which she was absolutely certain was that she had learned her lesson with strangers. She would never act so vulnerable again. Joie was right to have warned her about romantic pitfalls. As far as she was concerned, all her attention and energy would now be devoted to making her company a success. Evian Whitstone was a closed chapter in her life.

On Thursday, a surprised Carley received a call from Luis Delgado, asking her, as a landscape architect, to go to Biloxi with him to see the coastal property for which he was negotiating. It would be quite a boon, if he decided to award Burnside, LLC the contract for the landscape work. So she accepted his invitation.

Of course, the work would not be immediate—probably a year or so before it developed, but she had to think ahead, if her company were to grow.

But when he added, "By the way, pack a bag. We may have to stay a day or so," she had second thoughts.

Carley had not bargained for this kind of invitation. She hesitated. "Luis, I'm not sure..."

"It's all right, Carley. You will have a separate suite in the hotel for the weekend. This trip is purely business."

Carley felt a little embarrassed at her suspicions. But then he added, "My colleagues will be entertaining us, so bring some evening wear, as well."

Thinking about this second request, she finally decided that the advice was appropriate. Of course, his colleagues would entertain. He was merely being thoughtful to let her know ahead of time, so that she would be dressed properly.

One didn't show up at a cocktail party, wearing jeans. At least, in the South.

Her little black dress had seen far too many parties. Although she had sworn off Morgan's wardrobe, she felt that her twin wouldn't mind her borrowing from it just one more time.

Carley went upstairs and delved into the familiar closet. She had rather enjoyed wearing the colorful designer clothes, instead of her more conservative ones. Was she more like Morgan than she suspected?

In landscaping, she could be just as flamboyant with flowers as she liked. It was only in her personal life that she had felt the need to be conservative.

True, it would take a giant leap for her to enjoy the social world. But perhaps dressing better would put her more at ease. Maybe when she returned from Biloxi, she might go shopping for some new clothes. She certainly needed them.

Carley tried on a number of Morgan's dresses. Unsure of the number of events, she borrowed more than she felt necessary, putting in her luggage at the last moment a stunning lavender cocktail dress, with all its accessories.

Joie had left on a consulting job farther down the coast. Since Carley didn't want to leave Cho-Cho and Li-Po with the vet, she decided to call Gaddi to ask if she might feed them while she was away. Gaddi agreed immediately.

"I'll bring you the key," Carley said.

"Why don't I come over to your house, instead? It would help if I could get acquainted with the cats before you leave."

On Friday morning, before Luis was to come for her, Gaddi arrived. Carley showed her where she kept the cat food in the pantry, and then pointed out their special Friday treat of chicken livers, which she had put in the refrigerator.

Gaddi was in no hurry to leave. She watched while Carley finished packing.

"Golly, what gorgeous clothes," she commented.

"They're all Morgan's," Carley confessed.

Once Carley had zipped both the small case and garment bag, Gaddi said, "Well, I'd better be going." She took the key with her and drove away only minutes before Luis arrived in the limousine.

Posting a message for Joie on the refrigerator, to let her know where she would be staying, Carley walked to the front door just as the chauffeur was getting out. She was glad that it wasn't Dresnick.

The man took her bags from the foyer and placed them in the limousine, while Carley locked the front door.

"Thank you for being so prompt, Carley," Luis said, as she slid into the back seat beside him. "That's one of the things that I admire about American women. Besides their beauty, of course."

Carley merely smiled at him and said, "Good morning, Luis." She had been warned about Spanish men and their machismo. So, if he wanted to flatter her, that was fine. Just so he hired Burnside, LLC for his mammoth business project. That was all that she wanted.

Carley was so accommodating in conversation on the trip, that she felt certain Gran would have been proud of her. No smart mouth answers escaped her lips, the way they'd sprinkled her conversations with Whit.

The limousine was filled with exotic foods, Spanish wine, luscious cheeses. And later, when they stopped for lunch, she was impressed with the small, elegant restaurant that was off the beaten path—a wonderful little house with grape arbors and umbrella tables on a patio of terra cotta stone.

How different from the last meal she'd had with a man— a take-out of barbeque and fries. And how different the conversation. Luis made no mention of that tragic day at Boris's. But he had not gone over every inch of the estate, looking for clues, as she and Whit had done, so he was not nearly so involved. He had simply vanished—whisked away and, for him, that day appeared forgotten.

Luis was an old-world gentleman and quite charming.

Carley couldn't help but like him. As she ate, she was quite content to listen, to hear about his plans for the large hotel complex.

Contrary to what he had told Gaddi at Mabel's dinner party, he fully intended making it into a gaming hotel, with fine restaurants and headlining shows as an added attraction. Carley could visualize a fabulous landscape already.

They finished their leisurely lunch and then returned to the limousine. The trip from Mobile to Biloxi usually took a little over an hour to travel, but Luis did not appear to be in any hurry. With twenty-six miles of spectacular beaches to enjoy, it seemed almost irreverent to speed past the lush, tropical scenery.

Carley watched the familiar landmarks begin to appear along the sparkling Gulf. One after the other, the hotels on the strand came into view — each one a more impressive monument to financial power and privilege than the previous one.

As she recognized the name of the hotel where they would be staying, the Beau Mirage, the limousine slowed but did not stop.

When Carley turned to Luis in a questioning manner, he said, "I hope you don't mind, Carley. There's been a last minute change of plans. We'll be staying, instead, at a friend's private estate for the weekend."

 *Chapter 34*

" *I* don't think so, Luis."

"What's wrong, my dear? Don't you trust me?"

Why did men always ask that same question? This was the second time within days that Carley had heard that familiar retort. "Trust has nothing to do with it, Luis. I left word where I would be staying. And I'm expecting several important calls."

"Did you not bring your cell phone with you?"

Getting no reply, Luis seemed rather upset. "Turn around, Martin," he ordered the chauffeur. "We'll have to leave Ms. Burnside at the hotel."

With that decision, Carley realized that she had lost any consideration for the landscaping contract. But other things were more important—her own skin, for example. She did not know Luis well, and although he had been a guest of Mabel's, there was also the possibility that a murderer had been one of her guests, too.

Carley waited in the limousine while Luis went inside the Beau Mirage hotel. It did not take long before he returned with a key and a bellhop to take her luggage. "If it's suitable, Martin will come for you at six tonight." Once again, he had that rather distant coldness in his voice.

Carley smiled, even though she didn't feel like doing so. "Then, I'll see you tonight."

Following the bellhop into the hotel, Carley rode the elevator to the eighth floor.

"Your suite is all the way to the end of the corridor," the bellhop informed her.

Carley would not have been surprised to have been given a room next to the icemaker after her challenge to Luis's plans. She had certainly become much more cautious in her personal life. If that offended Luis, though, she was sorry.

After she had unpacked and hung up her clothes, Carley still had several hours to while away before evening. She took the elevator to the lobby, to browse in some of the shops. Seeing the exorbitant price tags, however, she lost interest. She decided that she would have more fun throwing away her money on the nickel machines in the casino.

Carley bought twenty dollars worth of nickels—her limit— and sat down on one of the black bar stools in front of one of the machines. When all the nickels were gone, she would go back upstairs to her suite and watch TV.

She struck up a conversation with a rather oversized woman with a small butterfly tattoo showing above her blouse. "You here for pleasure?" the woman asked.

"No. On business."

"I come every weekend. Beats staying at home by myself."

"Do you usually win?" Carley asked.

"It comes out about even."

While the two were chatting, a bell sounded from Carley's machine. A flood of nickels spilled out. She tried to catch them in the large cup, but it overflowed, with coins falling onto the floor, as well. Immediately, other hopefuls turned around to see who had hit the jackpot.

"Some people have all the luck," the woman beside her said, bending down to help Carley retrieve the stray nickels.

Embarrassed by all the attention, Carley said, "I might as well stop while I'm ahead." She took the heavy horde of nickels and cashed them in for dollars—three hundred dollars worth. Then, she took the elevator to her suite.

On the way up, she kept thinking that the money she had just won would help to pay for her lodging. She did not expect Luis to pick up the tab.

A few minutes before six o'clock, Carley was in the lobby and waiting for the limousine. She was surprised when Luis, himself, came in.

"You look lovely, my dear," he commented, as he greeted her.

"Thank you, Luis."

There was no hint of coldness or animosity in his voice this time. Carley was relieved since she had not known what to expect after her refusal to go along with his change of plans.

Uncertain as to the formality of the evening, she had worn an apricot colored dress, trimmed in turquoise. With a matching jacket, it was simple in design; yet had that certain something that spoke of fine tailoring. It was perfect for a summer's evening on the coast, without being ostentatious. Morgan surely had a flair for selecting her clothes.

Luis guided Carley to the waiting limousine, and they sped off. "We'll be having cocktails at Manon's," he informed her. "Then, dinner with friends at one of your fine old Southern plantation houses, called Ravineau."

"Not with Betsy and Tom!" she exclaimed.

"Yes. Do you know them?"

"Betsy and I were in the Queen's Court together. Is that where you're staying?"

When he nodded, she said, "Oh, Luis, I'm so sorry to have acted such a prude this afternoon."

"It was my fault. I should have mentioned it. But the invitation came at the last minute and I was not aware that you knew them."

They had not traveled far when Luis said, "It's still not too late for you to check out of the hotel. I could send Martin back to retrieve your luggage and bring it to Ravineau."

"But I'm already unpacked."

"A maid can repack for you."

"Then, it's fine with me. I'll look forward to being with Betsy again."

They arrived at the upscale restaurant, Manon's, where a private room had been set aside for the cocktail party. Evidently, Luis was to be the host, and he and Carley were first to arrive. "I'd like for you to help me greet the guests as they come in," Luis requested.

"I'll be happy to do so."

Luis then excused himself to discuss the final arrangements with the maitre d', while Carley remained in the room.

The restaurant possessed an unusual reputation, with an air of romantic mystery surrounding it. It was said that Manon Lescaut, herself, had escaped from France with her lover, the young Chevalier des Grieux. But Puccini, who had written the opera about her had evidently not been aware of the bayou countryside; for the composer had poor Manon dying of thirst in a desert, while des Grieux was searching for water. So much for geography!

The room, as Carley looked around, was decorated in pale blues and ivories, with a touch of apricot and gold on the ceiling. It was ironic that the outfit she had chosen to wear looked as if Carley might have had this room in mind when she'd dressed for the evening.

Luis soon reappeared. He seemed to be in a good mood. And he certainly looked the picture of sartorial splendor, with his foreign-cut silk suit, white shirt, and well-polished black shoes.

Carley had never cared for the grunge look and pants falling down below a fellow's underwear. But neither was she exactly enamored with the other extreme. Yet, here she was, dressed to match, courtesy of her sister Morgan.

Her contemplation vanished as the first guests arrived — Betsy and Tom.

No introductions were needed. Betsy squealed when she saw Carley, and they fell into each other's arms, while the two men smiled at each other over this warm display of affection.

"What's this about your staying at a hotel?" Betsy demanded. "You know our home is always open to you."

"Well, I've reconsidered. If the invitation is still open, I'd love to stay with you."

"Then, it's settled."

Luis did not mention that he had already sent Martin back to the hotel for Carley's luggage.

Soon, the room was filled with strangers, mingling and partaking of all the delicacies. Bartenders made equally exotic drinks, and the atmosphere was one of conviviality and loquaciousness.

Carley had mentally picked out several of the business partners, even before they were introduced. She was well aware of that aura of power surrounding certain people, a hubris that one senses, as recognizable as the slightly antiseptic odor of doctors.

"Now, who is this lovely young woman, Luis?" one of the men asked, with a sly look.

"She's my landscape architect, Ms. Carleton Burnside."

Carley cringed, hoping he had not been following the news lately. He merely acknowledged the introduction, but several times during the party, he glanced in her direction, as if he were pondering where he had seen her.

By eight o'clock, the cocktail party ended. Only a limited few had been invited for dinner later. Within a few minutes, the room was empty of all but Betsy, Tom, Luis, and Carley.

"We've made a compromise, Luis," Betsy said. "Dinner will be served a little after nine. I know that's early for you, but late for us Southerners."

Tom chuckled. "I had a hard time persuading Maum to wait that long. Usually, she has dinner on the table promptly at six-thirty."

Carley smiled at the mention of Maum, who had been a fixture at Ravineau for years. She remembered how intimidated Betsy had felt soon after her marriage to Tom.

But since she had never voiced any interest in the culinary arts, Betsy had soon made peace with the woman who claimed the kitchen as her own.

"I'm quite flexible," Luis assured them both. "Regardless of the hour dinner is served tonight, I look forward to our time together."

Martin, the chauffeur, was outside and waiting. He had Carley's luggage in the limousine. Once Luis settled the bill, they were ready to leave Manon's for the drive to Ravineau.

One of the few Greek Revival mansions that had survived from the mid-1800s in that area, Ravineau was lucky to have been requisitioned as a Union hospital, thus guaranteeing its safety. But the state, itself, had not fared so well, with many in that nineteenth century generation never coming home from the battlefields, including Tom's great-great- grandfather.

But the young widow and her two children had survived the war and, gradually, over the next hundred years, the old house that had once been such a part of history had finally reclaimed its legacy of grace and beauty.

Down the canopied avenue of oaks the limousine traveled. Twilight had descended on every side, but the welcoming lights in the distance were a reassurance that all was well. The Doric columns and the pedimented portico emphasized the strong architecture of the three-story mansion, flanked by the addition of two wings that had not been an original part of the house. It was Tom, himself, who had added the wings a few years previously.

The limousine stopped. Betsy was on the porch to welcome Luis and Carley, and to give instructions to Martin, since he would also be staying on the estate, in a little guesthouse.

"Do come in, you two," Betsy said, and led the way into the double parlor, where a few guests were already assembled.

Luis remained in the parlor, while Betsy took Carley upstairs to one of the bedrooms. "I didn't dare say anything at the cocktail party, Carley, but you've certainly been in the news. Have they caught whoever killed that man?"

"They have several suspects, but I've really been kept in the dark on the investigation."

"It's a crying shame that you've been subjected to such publicity."

Carley wanted to forget what had happened and just enjoy being with Betsy. "Sometimes, good things come out of horrible circumstances. Because of all that notoriety, I have more job offers than I could possibly get around to in the next ten years."Carley did not mention the downside.

"Well, I must say that I'm impressed that you've caught the attention of Luis Delgado. Tom's been trying to interest him in a land deal for the past three years. So where did you meet him?"

"At a dinner party. At Mabel Eldrin's. You remember her, don't you? From our Court days?"

"Of course. Is she still giving out those little presents at her parties, as if she were still Queen of Mardi Gras?"

Carley nodded. "Dragonfly pins, this time. Eighteen carat gold. I heard that the police found one at the murder scene. But no one's admitting to losing it."

"Interesting. Well, I won't breathe a word to the guests tonight."

"Thanks, Betsy."

They left the bedroom and walked down the stairs to rejoin the others in the parlor.

 *Chapter 35*

When Carley walked into the lavishly decorated parlor, she recognized a few people from the cocktail party at Manon's.

In addition were a local judge and his wife, Maggie. The older couple were particularly good friends of Tom's family, Carley discovered later, and lived on an adjoining property. The judge, Truett Archibald, was also Tom's godfather.

The evening went well from the very beginning. Maum outdid herself on the dinner, and Carley could tell that Betsy was enjoying her role as hostess to a rather august group.

Betsy was the perfect wife for Tom. But Carley knew that she would never be comfortable in that situation.

She needed to have a life of her own, beyond her husband's. Yet, she was amazed at how well Betsy maneuvered in that milieu — of politics, society, and power.

Perhaps, in her own way, Betsy was just as talented as any other woman who was career oriented. More importantly, she had chosen her own path.

Once dinner was over, the men went to the billiards room to discuss business, leaving the women to return to the parlor. This arrangement was completely different from Mabel's party of the week before.

During the evening, Carley mainly listened to the reciting of news about local people she didn't know. Yet, somehow she welcomed this insularity.

Whether out of disinterest or a politeness not to bring up anything unpleasant—at least about the people who were present—they did not ask her a single question about the tragedy in Fairhope. They merely maintained a superficial conversation, laced with laughter and brandied coffee.

But during the conversation, Maggie Archibald kept looking at Carley, as if she wanted to speak with her. Finally, when Carley went to the powder room, Maggie followed, catching up with her.

"Carley," she said softly, "I have debated all evening as to whether I should speak privately with you or not."

"What about?" a surprised Carley asked.

Maggie looked around, to make sure that no one could eavesdrop. "It's about your grandmother. You see, my husband Truett is in a position to hear things that most people don't ever hear. In all my married years, I have never breached his confidence. But in light of what is happening around you, I think you should be aware of past rumors."

As they entered the powder room hallway, another guest was already there, repairing her lipstick at the large, ornate mirror. Seeing her, a frustrated Maggie whispered, "I'll talk with you later."

Carley was relieved that the conversation had been cut short. She didn't want to discuss Gran and her shadowy past. She wanted to remember her as a loving grandmother with no secrets to hide.

By the time she returned to the large front parlor, it was almost twelve o'clock and the men had rejoined the women. Within ten minutes, the couples, including Judge Archibald and Maggie, began to leave. Soon, only Luis and Carley remained with the hosts.

"Can I get you anything?" Betsy asked a few minutes later.

"Not for me, thank you," Carley said, trying to stifle a

yawn. "It's been a lovely evening, but I think I'm ready to say good night."

Luis looked over at her and smiled. "In Spain, the night is just beginning. When you come to Barcelona, Carley, I will have to introduce you to another way of life."

Betsy, seeing the look on her face, said, "Well, we're not in Spain tonight, Luis. So if you two will excuse us, I'll say good night, too."

The men stood as the two left the room. "Until tomorrow," Luis said.

"I'll turn out the lights when we come upstairs," Tom assured Betsy.

As Carley and Betsy began to climb the stairs, Betsy, in a low voice murmured, "I gather that you and Luis are not sleeping together."

"Absolutely not. This is a business arrangement."

"I just wanted to make sure. But I saw how he looked at you tonight. And I hear that Spaniards make wonderful lovers."

"I'm not in the market for a lover," Carley protested.

"Play your cards right, and you just might become a *señora* in a big *casa*, with all that lovely money to spend."

Carley laughed. "You're already dreaming, and you haven't even gone to bed."

Betsy gave her a hug and then disappeared down the hall to the master suite wing.

During the night, Carley heard a steady, soft rain on the roof. For her, it was always a soothing sound, like the music of the ocean tides, or the flute-like zephyrs that teased the rows of palm trees so fragilely anchored to the sand. And it helped to lull her into a deep sleep.

By early morning, she awoke, refreshed. For a short time, Carley remained in bed—lazily stretching and watching the rays of sunshine making sparkling patterns on the far wall and then traveling around the room like a group of shadow puppets performing for an audience.

Ravineau had a sense of timelessness about it—as far removed from the events of the past weeks, as if Carley had stepped into another world that was protected from reality. Then, a knock at the door shattered that illusion.

"Carley, are you awake?"

"Yes."

"Breakfast downstairs in a half-hour," Betsy called out.

"Thanks!"

Carley climbed out of bed and began to get ready for the day ahead. Since it was to be a business day, she dressed in her official uniform of white slacks, shell, and navy linen blazer with her heraldic logo on the pocket. She wanted no one to mistake her for Luis's latest love interest.

Breakfast had been laid out on the sideboard, and she was the first to arrive in the dining room. She poured herself a cup of coffee and sat down at the table. Within moments, Tom and Betsy joined her.

"We won't wait for Luis," Betsy informed her. "Since he doesn't have breakfast this early, Maum has taken coffee to his room."

Carley nodded. "So what time do we leave to see the properties, Tom?"

"About ten-thirty," he said. "The three of us will meet Luis's other partners at the Pavilion, and then go from there."

"Just the three?" In surprise, Carley looked at Betsy. "But you're coming, too, aren't you?"

"Oh, no. I'll be far too busy, getting ready for tonight. At the Club."

It was to be a huge social event, with the hope of introducing Luis and his partners to the movers and shakers, who could smooth the way to the finalization of the land deal and its subsequent boost to the coastal economy. Of course, it all hung on Tom's success in swinging the deal. If things went wrong, and the day did not turn out successfully, another face would be put upon the event. Regardless, the party would still take place.

"Luis says that he admires your work, Carley," Tom said.

"You mean the gardens at Cavallegria?"

"Yes."

"That's surprising. He left in such a hurry on Saturday that I didn't think he'd had a chance to look around."

"Well, he evidently saw enough. He told me that he values your opinion, which is also a little surprising."

"What do you mean?"

Tom laughed. "Men—particularly Latino men—have a hard time seeing women in any position but one."

"Now, Tom," Betsy scolded. "Stop sounding so naughty."

Carley smiled at the lighthearted sparring between husband and wife. Then she changed the subject.

"I understand that an architect will be in the group today. Do you know which one?"

"It's an oriental name—Ibee Sey," Tom informed her. "But his first name is pronounced like the initials, E.B, and his last name like *Oh, SAY can you see.*"

Carley laughed. "That's easy to remember."

She served her plate from the buffet—fruit, scrambled eggs, country ham with red-eye gravy, mullet that everyone referred to as *Biloxi bacon,* and biscuits, made fresh that morning. "Luis is really missing a morning feast," she commented with enthusiasm.

"Some people are not up to such a substantial breakfast this early," Betsy defended. Carley, seeing that she was eating little of the bountiful Southern breakfast, began to wonder if Betsy might be pregnant again.

Realizing that she had seen no sign of their small son, Thomas Winston Pettigrew, III, Carley said, "Where is Trey this morning?"

"Oh, he's spending the weekend with Gramma," Betsy answered. "He created such a commotion the last time we had important guests, that we thought it might be safer if he went to visit her for a day or two."

"He climbed one of the live oaks during dinner, and we had to call the fire department to get him down," Tom explained.

"...And the party wound up on the front lawn, watching the spectacle," Betsy finished.

"I never did get that same group together again," Tom added, shaking his head.

By ten o'clock, Carley was back downstairs. Luis was sitting in the parlor, reading the morning newspaper. "Good morning, Luis," she said, walking into the room.

"Good morning, Carley."

He started to rise, but she held up her hand. "Don't get up." He paid no attention to her request.

"Would you like part of the newspaper?" he asked, once she was seated.

"Yes, I would. Whatever you're finished with."

She couldn't help but smile when she saw how he was dressed. His attire was almost identical to hers—navy blazer and white slacks. So much for trying to distance herself professionally. They looked like one of those lovey-dovey couples who always dressed alike everywhere they went, she decided. But it was entirely too late to change.

Carley silently browsed through the paper to see if any new leads to the murder had been reported. There was only one small article on an inside page, which didn't report anything new uncovered in the investigation.

Newsprint rubbed off on her hands, so shortly before ten-thirty, Carley went to the downstairs powder room, while Luis went back upstairs. By the time they both returned to the parlor, Tom was waiting. They were riding with him to the Pavilion, since the limousine had gone ahead to the hotel to pick up the architect.

Betsy stood on the porch and saw them off for the day.

By leaving after the main rush hour, they avoided the busy morning traffic. During the ride, the three talked little.

Finally, to break the silence, Carley said, "Luis, tell us about the architect that we'll be meeting this morning."

"He's from Hong Kong, but he designed a hotel for me in Singapore about five years ago," Luis said. "So he understands the effects of tropical climates and humidity on buildings, just as you, Carley, understand the effects on landscaping."

She smiled at the compliment. But she was well aware of his rationale. A well-known landscape specialist had recommended *kudzu* as a good ground cover in one of his columns several years previously, prompting his amused Zones 7-10 audience to send him pictures of trees and telephone poles completely inundated with the voracious strangler.

Carley had always enjoyed being part of an entire design team, working with architects and draftsmen during the creative process for a property. Yet, she knew better than to get her hopes up about this project.

If nothing else, she would just enjoy the day and not look beyond it.

The Pavilion was a pleasant, casual addition to the coast, separated from the busier thoroughfare, and claiming a direct access to the beach. With its white, sparkling roof and its Gulf side screened to catch the prevailing winds, the facility was a favorite place for private meetings and parties. When they arrived, Carley saw that several cars were already parked, as well as a caterer's van.

Once inside, Carley understood why Luis had asked only for coffee that morning. A fabulous brunch had been arranged, more to the Spanish taste. She was surprised that she was hungry again so soon after breakfast. One day her metabolism would betray her, but until then, she might as well enjoy what Providence had provided.

Tom was a charmer. Like a successful politician, he engaged each man, making him feel as if he were the most important person in the room.

Everyone who had been invited was present, with the

exception of Ibee Sey. The limousine had not arrived from Beau Mirage, the same hotel where Carley had originally checked in.

Even the short time that she had been around Luis, she was aware of his displeasure when his plans were not going according to the script. Feeling his impatience, she hoped that the delay would not jeopardize Tom's presentation. The schedule to view three different properties in one afternoon was a rigorous one.

Finally, after consulting with Tom, Luis said, "Please begin your brunch. Mr. Sey seems to have been delayed, so we will commence without him."

Carley took a plate and walked around the buffet — choosing a slice of melon with prosciutto, a small tortilla de patatas, and something called horchatta de almendra, a sweet drink that was supposed to be the drink of the gods. She was glad that all the food names had been listed.

In the screened alcove facing the water, a table had been set up, with several places at one end labeled with a small reserved sign. Carley chose the opposite end, and soon the other places around the table began to fill up. While waiters took additional orders from those already seated, many of the guests were kept busy, trying to hold onto their napkins, as the ocean breeze swept through the room. Carley finally tucked one corner of her napkin into her belted slacks, but the breeze continued to lift the corners of the tablecloth, even though they were weighted down by strands of seashells.

"How many hurricanes have you had this year?" one of the partners next to Carley asked.

"We had a tropical depression, with quite a bit of rain," she replied. "But as for hurricanes, we've had none so far this year."

Carley was quite aware of the significance of his question. No one would want to invest in property that might be swept away at any moment.

Just then, the door to the Pavilion opened to reveal a

rather harried man of about sixty. He sought out Luis, who rose to greet him.

"I'm sorry to be late, Luis. There was a murder at the hotel during the night, and the entire eighth floor was blocked off this morning for an inordinately long time."

Carley was shocked. Another murder so soon after the first one? She was glad that she had not remained at the hotel. She could have been caught in the same situation as Ibee Sey.

Being near one crime scene was more than enough. She had no desire to repeat the experience. Otherwise, the authorities might begin to suspect *her*.

 *Chapter 36*

Carley blithely went through the rest of the weekend without any hint of the maelstrom generated by the second murder.

After brunch, the business people moved into another room that could be darkened for Tom's presentation of the three properties. Tom's partner, Eben Madison, controlled the lights and the videos. Watching the visuals, Carley silently congratulated Tom on his imaginative performance, always an important part to any sell.

Luis and two of his partners, Rondell and O'Shaunessy, watched each segment and, at intervals, conferred with each other. Conspicuously absent was Judge Archibald, but Carley gathered he worked best behind the scenes. Still, his influence was felt with the presence of the local county commissioner and representatives of the Gulf Coast Chamber of Commerce, who spoke on variances, tax breaks, and business perks.

Carley and Ibee Sey sat together. They were more interested in the impact to the shoreline and topography information. Being the only woman in the room had its disadvantages. Carley had already been dismissed by several of the locals as just a tag-a-long, with no particular influence or expertise. But she was content to remain in the background and not voice her opinion one way or the other.

When the time came to leave the Pavilion to view the

first property, Tom said, "Carley would you like to ride with me?"

"Why yes, thank you."

Luis intervened. "Tom, I think it would be more convenient for Ibee to go with you. I'm sure that he has a number of questions to ask you. Carley can ride with me."

Tom immediately acquiesced. So did Carley. One did not go against such a request, especially with a lucrative deal hanging in the balance.

The limousine's engine was running and the air conditioning had cooled the interior by the time Luis and Carley climbed into the vehicle.

A blinding glare had enveloped the entire landscape, and they both sought their dark glasses to avoid the damaging UV rays.

"Are we the only two riding in this limousine?" Carley inquired.

"Yes." He reached over and took her hand. "Why did you not come and sit beside me at the table?"

"Because I saw the reserved cards at that end," she answered.

"One of those was for you."

"Oh, I'm sorry," she said, gently removing her hand to return her glasses case to her purse. "I wasn't aware."

"You are a talented and beautiful woman, Carley. To me, one asset is as important as the other."

In a teasing manner, she said, "Then, I will need a signal from you, Luis, to let me know which asset you prefer on which occasion."

He laughed, reached over to take her hand again, and said, "This should tell you my preference at the moment."

She did not dare remove her hand from his a second time. His action made Carley realize that she was not prepared for this new phase in her life—as a vulnerable single woman. She had already made mistakes, but she was hoping not to add to them that weekend.

In fact, she wasn't even sure as to Luis's marital status.

What if he had a wife and six children back in Barcelona? It might not make a difference to him, but it would certainly make a difference to Carley.

Twenty minutes into the trip, they came to the first property to be seen and evaluated. It had finally been approved for development after an impact study showing that the benefits would outweigh the potential harm.

They left the limousine and joined the others, already out of their cars. "Luis, I'm going to walk over the property on my own," Carley warned him. "Tom will expect to take you and your partners on his personal tour."

He did not object. So while the men gathered in a group, Carley walked toward the beach, where sea oats swayed in the breeze. As she looked out toward the horizon, she thought of the short distance to Horn Island and its wilderness landscape of sand dunes, slash pines, and saw palmettos. Then, she turned her back to view the property from the perspective of the beach. In any oceanfront or Gulf front property, she considered the view from the water equally important.

Carley didn't know why she didn't care for the site. She merely had a gut feeling that something was wrong. Was it merely a reminder of her unpleasant experience on the nearby barrier island? Or was there something else? It was not often that she had a sudden aversion to primal land.

To try to overcome this aversion, Carley left the beach and began to follow the way to the stakes that had been set up to mark the four corners of the property. Scrub trees and palms erupted in various combinations and levels, with an undulating rhythm that she had once seen on a particularly ugly golf course. But that had been the fault of the designer, not the grader of the land.

"Oh, Ms. Burnside," a voice called. It was Ibee Sey. He waved to her and she began to walk to meet him.

"What do you think of this property?" he asked.

Carley hesitated. "I think I would have to see the other two sites before I voiced an opinion."

He smiled. "So you do not care for it either."

"I didn't say that, Mr. Sey," she quickly refuted. "Besides, you have much more expertise. I would be interested in what *you* usually look for in a property."

"I'm a product of the East, and so I follow certain ancient methods for choosing the best. To me, this site is not the best."

Carley suddenly smiled at him. "Mr. Sey, I have a friend who is a feng shui expert—Joie Chang. If you are going to be in the area for a while, I would love for you to have dinner with us one night next week."

"She is Chinese?"

"Chinese-American."

"Thank you. It will be my pleasure."

Luis started walking in their direction, so the two hurried to meet him. On the way, Carley felt rather smug. Ibee Sey was single, well mannered, and probably lonely. So was Joie. They were about the same age. Carley was sure that they would like each other.

"We're ready to leave," Luis informed Carley. "Why don't you wait in the limousine while I have a few words with Ibee?"

She walked up to the paved street, where the chauffeur was sitting, with the vehicle door open. When he saw Carley, he immediately turned on the air conditioning. It had been so hot that Carley had shed her jacket, but once inside, she placed it over her shoulders.

About five minutes later, she and Luis followed Tom's car. The others came behind the limousine. Carley felt as if she were in a funeral procession, since the cars traveled together until they reached the next site.

"Are you planning to have a golf course, Luis, along with the casino hotel?"

"Why do you ask?"

"Only because these two tracts of land are adjacent to each other."

"I suppose that *is* something to be considered."

The moment Carley stepped out of the car, she felt the energy of her surroundings. Just as she started to wander away, Luis said, "Not this time, Carley. Stay with me," he requested.

The words he spoke sent a shiver down her spine. They were the very words that Whit had used that night at Dauphin Island. The remembrance brought such a longing in her heart that it was difficult to remain in control of her emotions.

Ibee joined them, as well as Rondell and O'Shaunessy. They listened to Tom, while he expertly led them into seeing what could be done with that particular property. The site needed little selling. It was so obviously first rate. Ibee looked at Carley and smiled.

Then, Luis said, "I understand that the third tract is adjacent to this one. If my partners and I decided to purchase both, what kind of deal could we expect?"

His question took Tom by surprise, but he recovered quickly. "I'm sure that we could work something out that would be advantageous to both parties."

"Ibee, do we have your blessing?"

The architect nodded.

"And Carley?"

"Absolutely."

"Then, there's no need to take up anymore time," Luis commented. "My partners and I will get together to come up with an offer for the two adjacent properties."

Carley realized then that, although Luis had the two other partners to consider, he was the one who made final decisions. He had just made the decision to cut the afternoon short. It was hot and uncomfortable, and Carley had an idea that Luis was ready for some shade and an afternoon drink. Or perhaps he was used to a siesta, when going out for the evening.

They gave up the limousine to Ibee, to return to the hotel, while Tom took Luis and Carley in his car back to Ravineau.

When they arrived, Tom did not get out of the car. "I have to go into the office for a short while," he apologized. "Can you two make yourselves at home, until Betsy gets back from the country club?"

"I'm sure we can," Carley replied.

"Get Maum to make you some lemonade," he advised. "She puts a little extra um-pah in her recipe."

Carley laughed. "Will do."

"Sometimes I do not always understand your American idioms," Luis said, holding the screened door open for her.

"Tom meant that Maum sometimes slips a little gin or vodka in the lemonade."

Luis smiled. "Ah."

"I'll see if she's in the house." Carley walked through the long hallway and into the kitchen, but Maum was nowhere in sight. So she fixed two glasses of ice water and brought them back to the parlor. "Looks as if we'll have to wait on the lemonade."

"Then, perhaps I'll have time for a shower," Luis replied.

"I think I'll do the same. It's been a hot afternoon."

They both went upstairs with their water glasses in hand. "See you later," Carley said, nonchalantly opening the door to her bedroom. But she didn't feel comfortable being alone in the house with Luis.

She walked into the bath, turned on the water and almost immediately turned it off again. She needed time to think, and she had missed running for the past few days.

She climbed out of her slacks and shell and pulled on her jogging clothes and running shoes. But before she had a chance to get downstairs, she heard Luis knock on her bedroom door.

"Carley," he called softly in a seductive voice.

There was no mistaking what he had in mind. What was she going to do? Turn on the shower again and pretend not to hear him? She wasn't ready for this escalation. She frantically looked around for escape. The French doors on the little balcony outside her room were slightly ajar. But the bedroom was on the second floor.

Carley decided that if Trey could climb up a tree, surely she could climb down the ancient wisteria vine that was twisted around the banisters of the balcony. She tested it for strength and then shimmied down the trunk.

Once on the ground, she started running. By the time she returned from jogging around the plantation, Betsy should be back from the club. She prayed that, in the meantime, Luis would not discover her duplicity. Too much was at stake for Tom and Betsy.

Forty-five minutes later, she returned from her run. Betsy and Luis were sitting on the front porch and drinking lemonade. "Hi, you two," Carley called out, taking the towel from around her shoulders and wiping the perspiration from her face.

"So that's where you've been," Betsy said. "Luis and I thought you might have been kidnapped."

"Just my regular jog," Carley explained.

"Well, come and have a glass of Maum's lemonade."

"Sounds lovely."

Betsy got up from the chair and poured another glass. With the lemonade in hand, Carley perched on the banister opposite them. "So what time are we leaving for the club?" she asked.

"Eight-ish," Betsy replied. "Oh, here comes Tom." She brightened at the sight of her husband.

"You're just in time for a little refreshment. Do you want the plain, or the um-pah?"

He grinned and gave his wife a hug. "Need you ask?"

When Carley glanced over at Luis, he winked at her. He was in a good mood again.

 *Chapter 37*

After the run and the refreshing drink, Carley remained in the shower for a long time, letting the cool water soothe her emotions as well as her muscles. With little exercise for the past few days, she could now tell the vast difference in the way she felt.

Thinking of all those good endorphins permeating every cell in her body, Carley smiled. At the same time though, she felt a little perturbed at her juvenile response to Luis's knock on her door. She was thankful that he had not noticed the scratch on her arm from the flight down the wisteria trunk.

Getting out of the shower, she blew her hair dry, leaving its styling until later. And then she took a siesta of her own, relaxing on that late summer afternoon, while the bees buzzed around the racemes of blossoms on the balcony and gathered the nectar for their survival.

The house was unusually quiet during that hour. Yet, as Carley drifted in and out of sleep, she felt a calming sense of relief and of letting go of all the negative things that had happened. It was a welcomed mood that she did not want to give up. But then, the jarring of her alarm clock caused it to vanish.

Reluctantly, she climbed out of the canopied bed and went to brush her teeth.

* * *

Maum was straight out of another era, and she kept to that same creed, slipping into the room to leave a little tray of food and drink, since they would all be eating late that night. As Carley used her electric rollers, she felt like Scarlett O'Hara gnawing on a chicken bone before the picnic.

Later, dressed in Morgan's lavender cocktail dress, she took out the matching amethyst necklace and earrings that had once belonged to her own mother. They were so beautiful that Carley wondered why she had waited such a long time to wear them again.

After she had fastened the clasp of the necklace, she swept up her sun-streaked hair in a more sophisticated manner and gathered it into a soft chignon at the nape of her neck. On impulse, she went onto the balcony and cut a tiny wisp of wisteria to pin into the chignon.

Later, oblivious of everything but the graceful workmanship of the handcrafted railings and the faded old French wallpaper clinging to the curved, inner wall of the staircase, Carley floated down the carpeted treads to the entrance hall below.

Luis stood still and watched her descent. "Quite impressive," he said.

"Yes, it's a beautiful old staircase," Carley agreed. "So few of the originals are left."

Luis took her hand and kissed it in a gallant manner. "You are not really a carbon copy of your sister, are you?"

"Not quite. I'm right-handed, and she's left-handed."

From that time on, he treated her in a careful manner, less intimately, more delicately. Carley wasn't sure what had caused him to back off, but she was grateful. And it made the evening much more pleasant.

Tom, Betsy, Luis, and Carley rode in the limousine to the country club, passing down the familiar avenue of oaks and traveling toward that sweet scented approach of immaculate greens and sand traps, until the club, itself, emerged like a sparkling white monument of wood and stone.

It was more than a typical Saturday night at the club, for Tom had reserved the main ballroom for dinner and dancing. Once inside, Carley could see Betsy's handiwork in the flowers and table arrangements, with party favors at each place.

"The men look so handsome in their white coats, don't they?" Betsy said, after they were seated. "But I guess this will be one of the last times they wear them until next year. Labor Day is almost here."

"That seems so arbitrary," Carley replied. "Especially with another six weeks of scorching, hot weather."

"But fashion dictates." Betsy sighed.

A spirit of conviviality swept through the room. Crowds gathered in small, animated groups and then mutated into other postures—sitting, standing, dancing, eating, listening, talking.

Later in the evening, when Carley was on the dance floor with Tom, he said, "I don't know what you said to Luis today, to get him to buy the two properties, but I want to thank you."

"I really didn't do anything, Tom. *You* were the one responsible for convincing him. I was most impressed with your sales pitch."

Tom laughed. "To tell you the truth, I thought I would be lucky to sell one of the tracts of land. Not *two*."

The music stopped and they went back to the table. The others on the dance floor soon joined them. But with the next dance, Carley was in Luis's arms.

As they were dancing, he casually said, "I hope that scratch on your arm will heal soon."

"Oh, it's nothing."

"You're quite lucky, you know."

"How so?"

"You might have broken your lovely neck climbing down from the balcony."

Carley gasped. "You saw me?"

"Yes."

"And you're not angry with me?"

"Far from it. I think you're adorable."

Carley relaxed and enjoyed the rest of the dance. She

even danced with Ibee Sey. He was a small man and wore round glasses that gave him the slight appearance of a barnyard owl, but oh, so polite.

Tom and Betsy, with his partner, Eben Madison, must have invited half the county. Betsy was in her element, and Carley, seated again at the table, thought what a complementary match in that marriage—something that she had longed for, but never attained.

Not that she was envious of Betsy's lifestyle. Carley knew that would wear thin in a short time with her. What she longed for was an equal partnership, an equal respect for diverse talents and creativity. Would it ever happen? Or was it just a dream no more attainable than a glass slipper?

She found her foot tapping to the music and Luis took note. He held out his hand for her and they wove their way to the dance floor again. But the music soon changed to the same boogie-woogie that she had danced with Rudy at the Grand Hotel.

The spell was broken and reality had reaffirmed itself. "Luis, let's sit this one out, please," Carley suggested.

He acquiesced immediately, but instead of going back to the table, he led her on to the verandah.

"Are you all right?"

She took a deep breath. "I *will* be in a moment or two."

"I suppose that I was much too hopeful that the murder at Cavallegria would not intrude on this weekend. "

With his words, Carley realized that he had not completely dismissed the tragedy.

"That's it, isn't it?"

"Yes. The music reminded me. I'm sorry."

"Carley, if you need to get away for a while, I have a house in—"

"No, Luis, but thank you."

"You would have the place to yourself. I would not be there, unless you asked me to come." Luis cleared his throat. "The timing is all wrong tonight, I admit, but Carleton

Burnside, I want you to be aware of my intentions. I plan to court you — but I'll wait until you're ready."

With the noise of the music in the background, he continued.

"My wife and I have been legally separated for the last five years. Since she is Catholic, she does not want a divorce, and I saw no need to force the issue, until now. When I return to Barcelona, I'm going to begin the procedure for an annulment. So consider yourself duly warned of my intentions."

"And children? Do you have children, Luis?"

"No. But I hope to in the future."

Carley merely nodded. "We'd better go back inside, Luis. Our hosts will wonder what has happened to us."

The party wound down at 1:00 A.M. Since Luis was taking a connecting flight out of Mobile less than eight hours later, to link up with Iberia Airlines back to Barcelona, they did not linger in the parlor after they reached Ravineau.

For the four of them, there would be no lazy Sunday morning in bed with a leisurely breakfast — only coffee and Danish, and a mad rush of the limousine to reach the airport. Carley would see Luis off and then be taken home by the chauffeur. Despite everything, the weekend had been a welcomed respite from all that had happened earlier.

Somewhere along the way, Tom and Luis had made plans to hammer out the final purchase agreement for the property, to be done by long distance. It was just a matter of negotiation. And Betsy and Carley promised that they would not wait so long to see each other again.

Ibee, the architect, would remain for at least another week, becoming familiar with the coast and viewing other establishments in the area. He had talked of compatibility with the surrounding buildings. That was something that Joie would understand, and Carley was looking forward to getting the two together.

That Sunday morning came far too soon for her. Carley groaned as she rolled out of bed. But within a short time, she was showered and dressed. Except for a few last minute items, her luggage was packed, as well.

When she walked downstairs, Luis was already in the dining room and pouring himself a cup of coffee.

"Good morning," Carley greeted him.

"Good morning," he responded. "Coffee?"

"Yes, please."

He handed her his own cup and poured himself another. "I wish you were going back with me," he said. "To Barcelona."

"When will you be returning to America?" she asked, attempting to keep the conversation on an impersonal level.

"As soon as possible. But as I said last night, I have certain personal business to take care of."

Just then, Betsy came into the dining room. She was dressed in a light caftan and had little makeup on her face. She appeared sleepy, but in her hands she carried a tray of warm Danish buns. "Today is Maum's day off. Hope you don't mind the meager fare."

"The buns smell wonderful," Carley commented.

Betsy poured herself a glass of orange juice and joined the two at the table. "Tom has gone to the guesthouse to make sure that the chauffeur is awake. He should be back in a few minutes."

She had no more than said it, when Tom, dressed in sweats, returned. "Martin will bring the car around in about fifteen minutes, Luis."

"I want to thank you both for your hospitality," Luis said, smiling. "You have something quite special here."

"Then, you must come again," Betsy urged. "But I can't promise you that it will always be this quiet. Trey, our little boy, lives here, too. And before next year, he'll be joined by a little brother or sister."

"Oh, Betsy, congratulations!" Carley responded.

"And to you, too, Tom," Luis said. He then looked at Carley in an intimate way.

Hoping that neither Tom nor Betsy noticed his glance at

her, she quickly averted her eyes to the remainder of Danish on her plate.

A few minutes later, just as Carley was closing her suitcase in the upstairs bedroom, Betsy appeared at the open door, with an envelope in her hand. "I almost forgot, Carley. Maggie asked me to give this to you."

"Thanks, Betsy." In a hurry, she slipped the sealed envelope into one of the side pockets of the suitcase and zipped it shut. There would be plenty of time to read the note later.

Within a few minutes, Tom and Betsy stood on the porch and waved good-bye, as Luis and Carley climbed into the waiting limousine.

As it disappeared down the avenue of canopied oaks, with their strands of Spanish moss swaying in the slight breeze of the morning, their Sunday morning newspaper still lay unopened on the foyer table.

When the limousine reached the outskirts of Mobile, Martin turned off the main road and followed the signs to the airport.

Security in the smaller regional airport was much easier to navigate than in an international one. After Luis checked his luggage, Carley remained with him. On that Sunday morning, there were not many passengers. Perhaps that was why, after she had shown her identification, that Carley was given a pass to the gate to see Luis off. The boarding had already started.

"I'll call you when I arrive," Luis said. He took her hand in his and before she knew it, he leaned over to kiss her good-bye. It was a slow, lingering kiss, with a promise of future involvement.

"Have a safe trip, Luis."

He smiled and joined the line of first class passengers, while Carley watched until he disappeared.

On the way through the airport, she walked by a newsstand, where the Sunday newspaper was on prominent display. Large, bold headlines beckoned her closer. **Landscaper Murdered at Hotel.**

A curious Carley stopped to read the sensational news. As she recognized her own name, her heart gave a decided lurch against her rib cage.

The woman identified as Carleton Burnside of Mobile was discovered bludgeoned to death in her suite at the Beau Mirage Hotel in Biloxi on Saturday morning.

A well-known landscape architect, she had recently completed restoring the gardens at Cavallegria in Fairhope, the scene of another recent murder. Authorities have not decided if the two murders are related.

Carley raced to the waiting limousine. She had to get home, to correct this error before it spread further. She was not dead. She was alive.

But then, how could such a tragic mix-up have happened? Who was the dead woman? Why had she been murdered? And why, in heaven's name, had someone mistaken the other woman for Carley?

 *Chapter 38*

"*M*artin, I have to get home as quickly as possible."

"Is anything wrong, Ms. Burnside?"

"Yes. A terrible mistake has been made, and I need to correct it immediately."

She offered no further explanation, but sensing her urgency, Martin sped up, navigating the streets on that quiet morning with an expertise of a race car driver, while keeping his eyes open for signs of a half-hidden police car.

Sitting rigidly upright in the back seat, Carley dialed Goose's number. It rang until his answering machine picked up. "Leave a message—"

"Goose, this is Carley. I'm on my way home. I've just seen the newspaper, but it's not true. I'm very much alive." She hung up and then tried to call Joie. No one answered.

Was there anyone else that she needed to call? Henry? Edward?

She had no idea where Whit was, or how to get in touch with him. And there was no need to call Morgan until later, if at all. Her twin would have no idea of what had happened, and it would only worry her.

It was then that the unpleasant realization dawned on her. If she had really died, how many people would be truly grief-stricken? New friends, such as Luis? Old friends?

Carley thought about Bob's wish not to have children so soon in their marriage. What devastation she'd felt when her own parents had died in the automobile accident. But at that time, she'd had the loving arms of Gran to rush into and she'd never let her down. Yet, she would never want the same sadness for her own child.

Carley roused herself from such maudlin thoughts. *Hey, you're alive,* she thought. *Stop thinking this way.* Then, just as quickly, she remembered that another woman had died in the very room where she had been registered.

Was someone still out to get her? Carley had thought she was safe after the successful completion of the Cavanaugh project. Was there something else then, completely unrelated, that was propelling this vendetta against her? Did she unknowingly possess some vital information that someone was determined to erase? When the news came out that she wasn't the one who was murdered in the hotel suite, would she then be in more danger than ever?

The limousine finally turned onto her street but when her English Tudor house came into view, Carley saw that a strange car was parked directly behind her truck, and the driveway had been blocked off. With nowhere to park except curbside, Martin kept the motor running while he retrieved her luggage.

"Just set the bags on the front steps, please," she requested.

He did so, and then drove on.

Carley struggled with the new set of keys to open the front door, and then dragged her luggage into the foyer. But once inside, she stopped and listened. Someone was in the house—more specifically, in her bedroom. She could hear them. It couldn't be Gaddi, because the car in the driveway wasn't hers. And Joie certainly wouldn't be riffling through her things.

Furious that someone had invaded her house, she picked up the poker from the living room hearth just as a tall figure emerged from the bedroom, with Li-Po and Cho-Cho following. Carley didn't know who was more surprised.

"What are you doing in my—?"

"My God! Is it you, Carley?"

She dropped the poker. She was standing face to face with Whit.

"Who did you think it was? Morgan?"

His haunted look suddenly changed to joy. Several steps later, he had taken her in his arms and begun kissing her in a most satisfactory manner. "I've gone through hell these past twenty-four hours," he confessed, "thinking that you were dead."

"Well, as the old Mark Twain line goes, '*the news of my death was greatly exaggerated.*'"

Whit's relief turned into anger. "Where *were* you?" he demanded.

"At Betsy Pettigrew's house, outside Biloxi."

"God, you gave me a scare."

"I can say the same for you. But you haven't answered my question. What are you doing here?"

"I came looking for clues to catch the SOB that murdered — or rather *thought* that he was murdering you. Dresnick is heading the investigation at the hotel. For the first time in my career, I couldn't bear to look at a dead body."

Carley didn't know who was more vulnerable at that moment. Before she knew it, she was back in his arms. Forgotten was her resolve never to be so susceptible to her emotions again. They had been away from each other for too long, and as they reached the bedroom, they impatiently began to shed clothes, inhibitions, and sanity.

She and Whit clung to each other as if they could not bear to be apart. In his exquisite lovemaking, the question that she had asked herself earlier was answered. Someone cared that she was alive.

Their hunger for each other took its own good time for fulfillment. The hours passed in a varied tempo of passionate murmurings, a heightened awareness that erupted into desire and consummation, and then surfeit, exhaustion, and sleep.

Much later, as Carley experienced that slow return to

wakefulness, Whit, already awake and watching her, said, "Carley, how did everything get so screwed up? Why were you registered at the hotel, but staying somewhere else?"

She yawned and stretched before she replied. "I checked into the Beau Mirage on Friday, thinking I would remain there for the weekend. But then, Betsy's invitation came, so I checked out after only a few hours."

She propped herself on one elbow and gazed into Whit's extraordinarily blue eyes. "Are you sure that I was the intended victim? Why couldn't it have been the one who checked into the same suite after I left?"

"No one else checked in. You were the only one listed in the register," Whit countered.

He furrowed his brow and said, "I'll have to contact Dresnick and let him know that he has an unidentified body on his hands."

"Couldn't he tell, just by looking, that it wasn't me?"

"The face—" Whit hesitated. "But I won't go into that."

Then Carley remembered the description that had been used by the newspaper reporter—*bludgeoned* to death. Carley shuddered.

"Have you talked with anyone about this mistake?" Whit asked.

"I called and left a message on Goose's answering machine. Why?"

"It might be advantageous for the next few days if you remained dead."

Carley thought about her invitation to Ibee Sey. "I can't do that. I've already issued a dinner invitation to a visiting architect. He knows that I'm alive."

"Cancel it."

"Is that an order?"

"If I said that it is, would you follow it?"

She hesitated. "Give me a good reason."

"To stay alive."

"That seems like a good reason."

While Carley had been in the throes of lethargy, Whit

had evidently been planning the strategy for the next few days. He would contact Goose and ask him to remain mum before setting into motion the mourning for the deceased Carley Burnside.

But what bothered Carley was that Whit did not seem surprised that someone was out to get her. Did he know something that he was not telling her? He was full of questions, yet revealed little, himself.

"Why is all this happening, Whit? Do you have a single clue?"

He finally said, "I think that you're sitting on something in this house, Carley, that is a major threat if it ever becomes known."

"I have no idea what it might be, unless—" Carley wasn't sure that she wanted to confide the information that she'd found about Gran in the attic trunk

"Unless, what?"

"First, I need to ask you a question. Are you and Dresnick with the CIA?"

"Not exactly."

"Interpol? FBI? Or maybe international thieves?"

Whit laughed. "We're on the right side of the law, if that makes you feel better."

If Gran had been involved in something underhanded, she was now beyond the reach of any authority. "Then, I have something to show you, once we shower and get dressed. You can use this bath and I'll go upstairs."

"I have a better idea. Let's shower together."

"That won't start anything again, will it?"

"You never can tell. But I'll try to behave."

Later, when they were dressed and Carley had pulled her wet hair back in a ponytail, she led Whit up the stairs and into the attic. She closed the door to keep the cats from entering and getting so dirty from the dust. She did not want to bathe them again, especially after she had just paid a hefty sum to have them groomed at the ritzy cat boutique downtown.

Opening up the trunk in the far corner of the attic, Carley said, "I hope I'm not compromising Gran's memory by allowing you to see these." She took out several of the expired passports and, under the scrutiny of the light, Whit examined them carefully. He smiled and said, "I have a number of these, myself, done by a similar expert."

"What are you talking about?"

"Your grandmother was in the spy business, Carley."

"I can't believe that," she protested. "She was always a model citizen and very patriotic."

"Stop worrying. She was on our side." Then, he added, "But these are all quite old. Where are the more recent ones?"

"These are the only ones I found."

"No. There're others. She became active again after you and your sister grew up. She must have been privy to some damaging information on certain people, and something that you've done recently has caused them to think that she passed on that information to you."

"Is that why you were following me? You thought I would lead you to that information?"

"It started out that way," he admitted. "I had no reason to think that this assignment would result in my falling in love with you."

While she was trying to assimilate this confession and to decide whether to feel betrayed, the doorbell rang.

Carley crept toward the door and pushed it slightly ajar to listen. The front door opened, and she heard Gaddi's voice. "Here, kitty! Here, kitty, kitty."

Carley quickly closed the door. "It's Gaddi," she whispered, "coming to feed the cats. What should we do?"

"Remain up here until she's gone. Turn out the light."

Carley tiptoed toward the wall switch, flipped off the light, as well as the attic fan. Turning around in the dark, she promptly bumped into Whit.

He put his arm around her and they stood there, immobile, waiting for Gaddi to feed the cats and then leave.

They would not be hungry since Carley had already fed them. She hoped that Gaddi wouldn't notice.

The time stretched into minutes and, without the fan, the heat began to rebuild under the eaves.

"How long does it take to open a can of cat food?" Whit complained.

"Maybe she's also taking care of the litter box."

"No. I think she's coming up the stairs."

Carley heard the telltale squeak of the fourth tread, too. What possible reason could Gaddi have for coming up to the second floor?

It didn't take Carley long to realize her motive. She remembered how interested Gaddi was in Morgan's clothes when she was packing.

Hearing the unzipping of garment bags in the bedroom below, she said, "I think she must be trying on clothes."

"I could gladly wring her little neck," Whit responded. "I'm already sweating like a perp under hot lights."

Carley giggled at his comment, but was immediately shut up by a kiss. What seemed like eons later, Carley heard the front door close. It took less than a minute for them to flee from the attic.

They had no sooner gotten down to the second floor landing, than Carley looked out to see a silver Lexus parked on the street. She heard someone at the front door, attempting to unlock it. But since Dresnick had re-keyed the locks, the old keys were obsolete. Carley watched from behind the sheers on the upstairs window as Bob, her ex-husband, jiggled the lock and then, finally giving up, he went back to his car and drove off.

"Probably looking for your will," Whit commented. "I hope you changed it after the divorce."

"No. It didn't occur to me. I'll need to do that immediately."

Within a short time after they had come downstairs, a taxi stopped, and Joie got out with her luggage on wheels. She disappeared down the drive toward the carriage house.

"You certainly do have a lot of traffic for a dead person," Whit commented.

"I'll have to call Joie."

"Will she be able to keep your secret?"

"Of course."

Carley waited to give Joie time to get settled and then she dialed her number. "Joie, it's me. I hope you're not too shocked to hear my voice."

"No. Why should I?"

"You mean, you haven't seen the newspaper?"

"I've just gotten home, Carley, after an exhausting trip."

Ten minutes later, Carley opened the side door. It was not often that Joie showed emotion so readily, but she hugged Carley immediately. "So what's going on?" Seeing Whit, who was pouring himself a second glass of ice water, she acknowledged him, also.

The three sat at the kitchen table while Whit and Carley explained the tragic events of the weekend and asked for her help in keeping their secret.

"I'm going to slip out of the house after dark, Joie. Whit's taking me to another location for several days. So I hope you'll look after things while I'm gone."

Joie agreed, but she remained in the kitchen, making no move to leave before Whit. Once Carley returned to the kitchen, after seeing him off, Joie finally said, "Carley, I guess it's time for me to give you the key."

"What key?"

"The one to Lydia's safety deposit box in New Orleans. Your grandmother cautioned me never to part with it, unless someone came after either you or Morgan."

"Does anyone else know about this?" Carley questioned.

"No. I'm the only one. That's why I didn't want to say anything until after Mr. Whitstone had left."

"You mean you don't trust Whit?"

"I have no view, one way or the other. I just felt that it was safer this way. It will be entirely up to you as to whether you want to tell him."

276 • Frances Patton Statham

Carley was dumfounded at Joie's revelation. Goose had made no mention of a safety deposit box. Evidently, its contents were so secret that Gran had kept the box's existence even from her best friend and executor.

Carley did not relish being the target of a dangerous, unknown enemy. Perhaps the information in Gran's safety deposit box would provide a clue as to the danger she was facing, before the assailant could strike again with more deadly aim.

 *Chapter 39*

So many questions needed to be answered, but Carley was in no situation to discover the entire truth about anything, being stranded in the "safe house" on Dauphin Island.

One small bit of good news from Whit was that Jake had been released from custody for the moment. Carley had Goose to thank for that. He was still on the list of suspects, however, since his machete had proved to be the murder weapon. But the machete had been wiped clean of any fingerprints, and Jake had sworn that it had been stolen from his truck. More importantly, he had been given an alibi for that night by Angela Ramirez, the artist, who had finally come forward.

Carley had wondered at the time how Jake had arrived so early on that Saturday morning. Now, she knew. He had spent the previous night in Angela's cottage.

Boris and Wingate were no longer in residence at Cavallegria. The police had given them permission to close the main house and go on their sabbatical after such a strenuous season.

Carley grieved for the care of the new gardens. She was hoping that Goose had hired a caretaker for the property in Boris's absence.

As for Lucinda, she had gone to stay with Rhett and Edgar in New Orleans for a while. It was quite sad that Rudy's body was still missing and that Lucinda's daughter was still estranged.

Joie had promised to get in touch with Ibee and invite him, on her own, for dinner. Since she'd had no contact with Joie after she'd been given the key to the safety deposit box, Carley was out of the loop on that, as well. It seemed that life was going on all around her, while she was stuck on Dauphin Island.

For three long days she had fixed unappetizing meals and watched the news on TV. She did not have access to a local newspaper, and even her cell phone had been denied her, for fear that someone in cyberspace could pick up a conversation from it.

With nothing else to occupy her time on that early Thursday morning, she resorted to peering through the telescope in the aerie and watching the boats ply their way up the bay. Soon, that became boring, too.

Whit was nowhere to be found. Neither was Consuelo. Carley felt as if she were a prisoner, unable to go for her usual run, unable to go near the dock or the water, for fear of being seen. She was definitely becoming stir crazy.

How did she know that this disappearing scheme was going to work? One conversation, one slip, and the whole affair could be jeopardized, even though the few who knew that she was still alive had been sworn to secrecy.

All at once, Carley remembered the note that Betsy had given her from Maggie. It was still in a side pocket of her luggage. So she went to the bedroom, pulled down her luggage from the closet shelf, and retrieved the envelope.

There were no names attached, either hers or Maggie's. If anyone else happened to see it, the note could not be traced.

"I'm so sorry that our conversation was cut short. I'm taking a dreadful chance in writing this note, so as soon as you read it, please destroy it.

"As I mentioned, my husband is in a position to hear things that the general public is never aware of. Because it could not be proven beyond a doubt, no indictment was ever made. But certain people feel sure that your grandmother was murdered in the hospital. A man in a white coat was seen leaving her room that night, but he was not anyone on duty. So, be extra careful, my dear. There are forces out there that are still up to no good."

"Oh, Gran," Carley whispered, a sob catching in her throat. Yet, in view of all that had happened, Carley was not surprised. Maggie's note merely corroborated what she had suspected for some time. With tears in her eyes, she tore the note into bits and flushed down the toilet.

Now, it seemed more imperative than ever to discover what Gran's safety deposit box in New Orleans contained. She could not bring Gran back. But perhaps, she could finish what her grandmother had begun.

What if she sneaked into New Orleans, removed the contents, and got back before Whit had a chance to suspect that she had slipped confinement? She could get there before the bank closed and then have all weekend to examine the papers.

If by chance, someone recognized her, she could always pretend to be her twin, Morgan. In true-life circumstances, Morgan, as her next of kin, would be arriving for her graveside services, scheduled for Friday morning, with an Episcopal memorial mass set for Sunday.

Signing to gain access to the bank box would be no problem, since Joie had told her that both her name and Morgan's were on the card, along with Gran's signature and authorization. She could sign Morgan's name instead of hers.

Almost immediately, she realized the flaw in that plan. She had no identification to prove that she was Morgan.

Carley sighed. She would have to use her own name and hope that no one at the bank knew that she was supposed to be dead, like Gran. After all, New Orleans was far enough away from Mobile and the surrounding area for names in the news not to make much of an impression.

Suddenly, another problem occurred to Carley. Transportation. Both her Toyota truck and Gran's Cadillac were at home, and she couldn't get a rental car without showing her driver's license, which would leave a trail.

But had Whit not left the plumber's truck in the garage, in case of an emergency?

By 9:30 A.M., Carley was bouncing along on the road to New Orleans.

Freedom always felt invigorating after being imprisoned and, with the fresh air and bright sun to tease her, Carley began to make plans to leave the safe house for good.

She decided that she would pose as Morgan and go to her own funeral. That way, she could return to her house. If Whit had contacted Morgan at Milly-la-Forêt, then there would be no chance of her arriving in Mobile and fouling up her plans.

Several hours later, Carley exited I-10 and drove into New Orleans. Colorful bougainvillea climbed along the wrought iron balconies. Splotches of missing paint on the old street lamps indicated that they had seen better days.

She had always loved New Orleans—its Vieux Carré, its Garden District. Even smelly Bourbon Street. Sadly, though, like Venice, the city was sinking into the silt. Also, the termites were attacking everything in sight. And as usual, in a doorway on Canal Street, a rumple-clothed old man was still sleeping off the excesses of the night before.

Past Jackson Square, Carley found the street where Banc Algernon was located. Parking was always at a premium, so she began searching for a parking place within walking distance. When she finally found one several blocks away, it was well past twelve noon.

During the extreme heat of Southern summer days, some of the banks still observed the European tradition of closing two hours for lunch. Banc Algernon was one. The sign on the locked entrance told Carley that it would reopen at two o'clock. That meant that she had an hour and a half to waste before retrieving the contents of the safety deposit box.

Disappointed, she decided to find an obscure place for

lunch. She would also have to move the truck to another spot afterwards, since she didn't want to get a ticket. If she still had time on her hands, she might browse in several of the antiques shops. Of course, she couldn't buy anything. She would have to save her cash for gas and lunch. She certainly couldn't use a credit card.

Carley avoided her favorite places to eat and tried, instead, to find a small, dark, hole-in-the-wall. But entrances to restaurants in the city were deceiving. The small, dingy brick entrance she chose suddenly expanded into a brightly-lit brick courtyard, with umbrella tables.

She did not have to wait long. A table suddenly opened up with the departure of a young couple with a baby. Following the hostess, Carley put on her dark glasses again, not so much to avoid the glare, but to make it more difficult to be recognized, however remote that possibility.

She had no more than sat down and begun to look over the menu, when a voice called out, "Morgan?"

Carley nearly dropped her menu.

Seated several tables away were Rhett, Lucinda, and Edgar.

"Rhett, is that you?" she asked in an unsteady voice.

"Yes. Do come over and join us. You shouldn't be alone at a time like this."

Carley hesitated, but she knew that she could not refuse. She caught the waiter's eye and signaled that she would be joining the other table. Immediately, Carley drew in her breath and tried to assume Morgan's persona.

"You remember Lucinda, don't you?" Rhett said. "And Edgar, of course."

Carley nodded. "Hello."

"When did you arrive?" Edgar inquired.

"Late last night."

All three were so solicitous. "We're planning to be there tomorrow to support you," Rhett said. "But what a tragedy."

Thankfully, the waiter came. She was extremely hungry, but in the circumstances, it would not be appropriate to stuff herself. "I'm really not very hungry," she commented. "I think I'll have the small Cobb salad."

"Anything to drink?"

The others were drinking wine. Before Carley could answer, Edgar said, "You must have some Merlot. It will be good for you." He took over and ordered for Carley. "Waiter, please bring another glass and another bottle."

It was going to be awkward, eating with her left hand, but Rhett was quite observant. When her salad arrived and she began eating, the fork slipped out of Carley's hand and landed on the floor. "I'm so clumsy," she apologized, while the attentive waiter brought another fork.

Lucinda reached over and patted her other hand. "That's all right, dear. Grief will do that to you. It's been happening to me all week. I even spilled my wine at dinner last night." Then she added, "Did Carley write you about my darling Rudy?"

"She...she called me and told me. I'm so sorry, Lucinda."

"You know how talented Carley is—or was. She was going to design my gardens after she finished at Boris Cavanaugh's estate."

"I didn't know that."

"Actually, she didn't either. I won the bid at the auction."

"But I thought—" Carley stopped immediately.

Lucinda smiled. "I used a little subterfuge. She had turned me down earlier, so I arranged for a bidder to call in that night at the fundraiser. I even bid against myself a number of times, so she wouldn't suspect."

Lucinda suddenly lost her animation. "But I guess it doesn't matter now. With Rudy gone, I plan to sell the place and move back to Mobile."

In the silence that followed, Rhett said, "How is Cristina?"

"She's fine, thank you. She's already at school in Switzerland. With the renovations going on at Milly-la-

Forêt, I thought it best to give her a stable environment for this year, at least."

No one inquired as to what she was going to do with the Mobile house.

Carley looked at her watch several times, and when she felt that she could leave without offending anyone, she asked for her check.

"No, absolutely not. You're our guest today," Edgar insisted.

"Well, thank you. That's certainly gracious of you." Carley knew it would be futile to argue. "Now, if you'll excuse me, I need to—" What excuse could she give to rush away? "—to shop for something appropriate to wear to the services."

"We understand," Lucinda sympathized. "Last week, Rhett and I visited nearly every shop in town. But it's so hard to find anything black that's still cool enough to wear in all this heat."

"I have an idea," Rhett said. "We'll go with you to shop." She then turned to her husband. "Edgar, why don't you wait for us on the bench outside?"

"That's really not necessary," Carley said.

"Of course it isn't *necessary*, but we can save you a lot of time, since we already know where you might find something simple but elegant."

While Edgar was left to pay the bill, and then to wait on the bench for their return, the three women walked out onto the street. Rhett and Lucinda took over, steering Carley another block until they reached one of the expensive little boutiques, where she had never shopped.

The two older women seemed to be familiar with the saleswoman. "Francine, our dear friend needs something suitable to wear to a relative's funeral," Rhett began.

"So we immediately brought her to you," Lucinda added. "The Contessa Bramante."

Carley could tell that Francine was impressed with the title, and she groaned inwardly. The saleswoman would be bringing her the most expensive outfits from the back room. No rack clothes for the countess!

"Let's see now," the woman said, eyeing her up and down. "A size six in American clothes. Am I correct?"

"Correct."

Rhett and Lucinda became the critics as Carley tried on several black outfits. She didn't dare look at the price tags. But two ensembles fit her perfectly — one, with a piping of white that gave relief to the somber black — and the other, a two-piece tunic style, in a linen blend.

"They're both quite smart on you," Rhett said.

"Which do you prefer, Morgan?" Lucinda inquired.

"I can't seem to make up my mind. Perhaps I can think about them and come back later — "

Francine interrupted. "Contessa, why don't you take both? You can decide at home and then return the one you don't wear." The salewoman was well aware that she had probably sold both dresses and there would be no returns.

"I'll have to go to the bank to exchange some money first. I left Paris in such a hurry."

Lucinda spoke up. "Francine, why don't you just put the two on my account, and we can settle later."

"Oh, no, Lucinda. I couldn't let you do that," Carley protested.

In the end, Carley walked away from the shop with a garment bag containing the two ensembles that she couldn't possibly afford. But she had to get away. She had overstayed her parking.

Edgar, as instructed, was sitting on the bench in front of the restaurant. "Can we give you a ride to your car, Morgan?"

They would probably expect to see Morgan's notorious Jaguar, but it was in storage. Carley couldn't let them see the plumber's truck.

"No thank you, Edgar. It's quite near." She hugged both Lucinda and Rhett, and fled down the street.

By the time she reached the truck, a parking ticket was

already lodged under a windshield wiper. She snatched it off, unlocked the truck, placed the garment bag in the seat beside her, and drove off to find another space.

Carley felt like a fugitive as she entered the bank, with the empty canvas bag she had borrowed from the safe house. The lunch and the shopping had completely unnerved her. But gathering her courage, she walked to the desk and smiled.

Holding her breath, she produced her driver's license and the security key for identification, all the time praying that the banker would not be familiar with her name, except as a customer. Finally, the woman returned her credentials and with a second key, escorted her into the vaults.

"How long do you think you will be?" the woman asked.

"Only five minutes."

"Then, press the buzzer when you're finished."

"Thank you."

Carley did not take time to go through the various items. Instead, she dumped the entire contents into the bag. She put back the empty box, waited a few minutes, and then pressed the buzzer. When the vault reopened, she murmured her thanks and escaped from Banc Algernon.

Carley didn't think that she could ever become a bank robber. The situation was so stressful that once she reached the street, she was breathing more heavily than she ever did on any morning run. And she felt that every person she passed on the street was eyeing her suspiciously, even to the sightseers going by on the trolley car tour.

Her only stop was for gas on the outskirts of the city, so she made it back to Dauphin Island in record time.

When Carley pulled into the garage, she saw another vehicle parked in the second space. Cautiously, she slung the garment bag over one shoulder and, with the other bag containing the contents of the safety deposit box in her left hand, she inserted the key to unlock the door into the house.

It opened suddenly on its own. Blocking the entrance, an angry Whit demanded, "Where in the hell have you been?"

 *Chapter 40*

" Shopping. I've been shopping," Carley repeated.

"Don't you realize how dangerous that was, to blow your cover?"

"If you could just stand aside and let me in, then we can discuss it like two rational people."

Whit moved to allow her into the house. He took the garment bag, but Carley held on to the small canvas bag. They walked into the great room that faced the water.

Before she had a chance to defend her actions, Whit spoke. "What do you have on your face?"

"Makeup. I was being Morgan today, and dressed accordingly."

Carley realized then that he was used to seeing her in a more natural state. "And that brings up a decision I made this afternoon."

"Go on."

"I've been thinking of this private interment scheduled for tomorrow. Everyone will be expecting Morgan to come to her own twin's funeral. So I plan to go as Morgan."

At first, Whit was silent. "I had already come to that conclusion," he finally said. "That's why I'm here — to take you back home."

"Good. I'll pack my bag. At least I'll have the cats to keep me company there."

He looked at her and smiled. "Besides feeling abandoned, is there anything else that you want to get off your chest?"

"Like what?" She certainly didn't want to tell him about her trip to the bank.

He stood there, not saying a word and acting as if he were waiting for some confession from her. Finally, she dug into her shoulder bag. "You might take care of this parking ticket."

When she handed it to him, he frowned as he examined it. "So you've been to New Orleans."

"Yes. And I bumped into friends who thought I was Morgan. So I didn't blow my cover."

An hour later, Carley was back at her house. Whit did not linger. He was still miffed with her for causing him such anxiety. He also had a lot of damage control to do, now that the body in the hotel suite had been identified as the young maid who had packed Carley's bag — a college girl who was blonde, too.

Knowing that the suite was paid for, she had evidently decided to sample a taste of the good life, including sleeping in Carley's Versace nightshirt, which she had conveniently neglected to repack. But she didn't deserve what happened to her, and Carley felt sad about it — even sadder that the girl was officially listed as a missing person in order to protect Carley. Her family must be frantic with worry.

When she checked her answering machine, Carley discovered three calls from Luis — each one a little more frustrated at her not being home to speak with him personally. Carley regretted not being able to call him back, in case her phone was tapped. But pretending to be Morgan, she did call Joie.

Within a few minutes, the woman was at the side door. She did not bring Li-Po and Cho-Cho with her. Joie took one look at Carley and said, "I thought you were in hiding."

"You mean, you knew it wasn't Morgan on the phone?"

She brushed aside the question. "So tell me why you're back."

"I've decided to go to the funeral as Morgan."

"Then, I need to tell you about the catered luncheon buffet I've arranged for tomorrow."

"Like the one we had for Gran?"

"Yes. People would expect it—to come here to the house, to grieve and reminisce about you after the funeral. I've already contacted Baker's Dozen for the food."

It was a touching gesture, so like Joie to orchestrate. "Thank you, Joie, for thinking of that," Carley said. Then she added, "Would you like to ride in the funeral limousine with me tomorrow?"

"No. I have too much to do here in the house. But Father Luke will give the invitation at the service. He'll be coming to the house later, too."

Joie did not linger. "I'll see you tomorrow," she said, and left the same way she came.

Carley had been surprised to see a black-ribboned wreath hanging on her front door. She assumed that Joie had been responsible for that, too. Or it could have been Whit. Curious to read any snippet about the upcoming service, Carley walked into her office, turned on her computer, and went online.

The digital version of a newspaper was never as satisfactory as a newspaper you could hold in your hands, so she wasn't sure that she would find anything. But once she clicked on *obituaries*, her name popped up.

Reading a short profile of your own life from someone else's viewpoint, Carley decided, was like reading about a stranger. People have a tendency to sort personalities into narrow, one-dimensional pigeonholes. Her obit followed the same pattern, with one exception—the nature of her unexpected death. She was gratified to see the final paragraph. *In lieu of flowers, the family has requested donations to be made to the Mobile Botanical Gardens.* That was a nice touch. At least, the gardens would benefit from her supposed demise.

That afternoon, Carley was extremely curious about Gran's papers, which she had taken from the bank vault. Yet, at the same time, she procrastinated in looking at them, for once she started down that path of discovery, there would be no turning back.

Putting it off for a while longer, Carley gathered together the items she would need the next day—shoes, purse, and some semblance of a hat and veil to go along with the dress. When Dresnick came for her in the funeral limousine, she did not want to keep him waiting.

She took the tunic dress from the bag and looked at the price tag for the first time. "Six hundred dollars!" she protested out loud. She had never spent that much for a dress. Why, she could have bought ten new pairs of slacks for that amount. She looked at the price tag on the other ensemble, the one with white piping. It was fifty dollars more.

Rhett and Lucinda had shanghaied her. Since the only black dress she possessed in her own wardrobe was the after-five one that she had worn to Mabel's dinner party, Carley was stuck with wearing an expensive dress that she didn't want. She would need to reimburse Lucinda as quickly as possible with money that she would rather use for something else.

By eight o'clock, she was finally ready to devote her entire attention to Gran's papers. Carley dumped the contents of the bag onto the kitchen table and began to sort, separating typed documents from handwritten notes. The first one that caught her eye was a letter that Gran had addressed to both granddaughters.

My dear Carley and Morgan— If one of you is reading this letter, then I know that I'm no longer with you and that you are in danger because of me.

I served my country well and I have no regrets about that. Neither do I regret those marvelous years that you were both in my care. I treasure each one, in watching you grow into beautiful young women, so capable and talented –

By that time, tears blinded Carley's eyes, and she had to stop reading. She got up to get a tissue and blow her nose. A few minutes later, she began reading again.

The more she read, the more alarmed she became. It was true. Carley was sitting on a powder keg, getting ready to explode.

Gran had evidently been tracking a smuggling ring that had been operating between Havana and the Gulf Coast. But then, when she was zeroing in on the money trail, she had been pulled off the case suddenly and reassigned. But that had not stopped Gran. Suspicious of her removal, she had kept digging on her own. An anonymous document warning of her activities confirmed her suspicions. There was a mole in her division. And here was the evidence to confirm it, all except the name spelled out—only the initials, E.W. Evian Whitstone? Could the mole possibly be Whit? Was he the one who had slipped into Gran's hospital room that night? No, that wasn't possible. The very idea struck Carley with a sudden chill.

But had he not appeared on her doorstep and immediately intruded into every aspect of her life? And had he not followed her to begin with, to Ocean Springs? How did she know that he was not the one to have put the bug on her truck?

She had assumed that all the actions against her—the surveillance, the roadblocks, the scare tactics, had been an attempt to keep her from executing the landscaping at Cavallegria. But then, there was Rudy's murder, and later the attempt to murder her. So, what if all these events were not merely coincidences, but had some commonality? Could Whit possibly be at the core of all of them? But no. The very idea was too troubling even to think about. The initials belonged to someone else. After all, he had admitted that Evian Whitstone was not his real name.

Just as she was trying to fit the various pieces of the

puzzle together, her front doorbell rang. Startled, she grabbed up the papers, stuffed them back into the bag, and hid it in one of the kitchen cabinets.

While she stood in the middle of the floor and quietly listened, the doorbell rang again. With its persistence, Carley realized that the person was not going away. She crept toward the front door, to look through the wide-angled peephole. Although the view was half obscured by the wreath, Carley saw enough. It was Morgan. But Morgan was supposed to be in Europe.

Carley unlocked the door and opened it only partially.

"Do let me in, Carley. I've been standing out here for ages." She turned to the waiting taxi and waved it on.

The outside sensor had come on, bathing the front steps in light. Carley tried to remain out of its glare, while Morgan struggled with her luggage. Carley was not happy to see her at this particular time. "What are you doing here, Morgan?" she asked.

"Is that any way to greet your twin? Especially on the eve of your funeral?"

"Well, hurry and come in, so I can shut the door."

Once Morgan was inside, Carley became more hospitable, giving her a hug.

"You *know* I've missed you, and I'm really happy to see you. It's only that your coming has upset a lot of plans for tomorrow. Didn't you get a call, asking you to remain at the millhouse?"

"I don't necessarily obey strangers, Carley. I had to come and see for myself what's going on. After all, I'm your older sister."

"Only by seven minutes," Carley allowed.

Morgan ignored her comment. "Besides, I started thinking. If you were really dead, then, of course, as your nearest relative, I would be expected to attend your funeral."

"The plan was for me to go, pretending to be you."

"That won't be necessary, since I'm here."

Carley knew that Morgan was every bit as stubborn as

she was. There was nothing else to do but let the real Morgan attend the services. So opening a bottle of wine, Carley poured a glass for Morgan and then pulled out a cold beer for herself.

The beer reminded her of the Wednesday night poker game, which had been called off. She felt guilty that Henry and Edward would be grieving for her, with Goose unable to tell them what had actually happened. But she would make it up to them as soon as this awful mess was cleared up.

Morgan sat in the den with Carley, where she gradually relaxed from her trip. During that time, Carley filled her in on the procedure for the next day, describing the people she might meet, as well as her lunch and shopping excursion in New Orleans with Rhett and Lucinda.

Later, they went upstairs to Morgan's old bedroom. While she unpacked, Carley changed the sheets on the bed and put fresh towels in the bath. When they had both finished, Morgan said, "Let's see the dresses that you bought."

They went back downstairs and into the master bedroom, where Carley pulled the two purchases from the closet. "Lucinda put them on her tab, so I'll have to take one back to the boutique and pay her for the other."

"Aren't there two events—the interment and then the memorial mass?

"Yes, but..."

"Then, if they fit, I'll need both."

"I can't afford both," Carley said.

"Don't worry. I'll reimburse Lucinda."

The price tags did not seem to bother Morgan. "I think you're finally becoming more discerning," Morgan commented, viewing the dresses. " —now that you're single again."

She took her time trying on both dresses and looking at them from every angle in the three-way mirror. "Yes, both will be quite satisfactory." But when it came to the accessories, she declined everything except the hat, which had come from her own closet, anyway. It was the one she had worn to Gran's funeral.

"I bought a new pair of shoes and handbag in Paris," she said, "before the flight. So I'll use those."

Morgan had taken one of the final flights on the Concorde from Paris to New York. She lamented its imminent demise, complaining that overseas flights later would be just as exhausting as her connecting flight from New York to Mobile. After bringing Carley up to date on Cristina's world, a tired Morgan was ready to say good night.

Still confused over Gran's papers, Carley failed to inform Morgan of her relationship with the now questionable Whit, as well as her trip to Banc Algernon.

"Be sure to wake me in plenty of time tomorrow morning," Morgan called after her, taking the dresses upstairs with her.

"Okay," Carley replied. "Good night."

When Morgan had disappeared, Carley made sure that all the doors were securely locked. Then, she tiptoed into the kitchen to retrieve the bag that she had hidden.

Closing her bedroom door, so that her bedside lamp would not shine into the hallway, Carley climbed into bed and began to reexamine the trove of papers.

As she read them, Carley decided that there were enough pieces in place for her to finish Gran's investigation. That was the least she could do. The final proof was buried somewhere on the desolate and uninhabited Horn Island. But exactly where? The island was fourteen miles long and three miles wide. Without a marker, it would be impossible to find what Gran had suspected.

Just before she was ready to turn out the light, a paper shifted, slid along the comforter, and floated to the floor. When Carley picked it up to put in the bag with the other papers, she saw that it was the same scrap of paper that had dislodged itself from the others in the kitchen.

Carley had never communed with anyone on the other side. But lately, she had dreamed of Gran, and it was getting ridiculous in the number of shiny pennies that she had found throughout the house. Was Gran trying to communicate with her, to tell her something?

She looked at the paper in a different light, staring long and hard at the marks that she had taken for doodles, with no meaning. The more she looked, the more convinced she became that the markings were important.

Carley got out of bed again and walked barefooted to her office, where she pulled out the map that she had saved from her first excursion to Horn Island. Putting the two papers side by side, Carley saw a resemblance in con- figuration, even though the scale was completely different.

With Morgan's unscheduled appearance , that altered her plans, leaving her free to disappear and explore on her own.

If Walter Anderson, the artist, could row a skiff by himself the twelve miles to the island, then surely she could take the same trip in a motor boat.

The more Carley thought of it, the more excited she became. It would be easy to rent a boat as Henry had done, but then run it across the Sound herself, using a navigational chart.

And so, with the decision to leave by dawn for Ocean Springs, Carley set her clock, switched off the bedside lamp, and waited for sleep to come.

Chapter 41

Carley was not so foolish as to embark on her trip without leaving a clue as to where she was going, in case something happened. Only, it could not be in an obvious place.

When she and Morgan were teenagers, they had started the tradition of leaving messages impaled on the long, slender spout of Gran's decorated watering can, and placing it in the middle of the kitchen table. Because of it, Gran always knew where they were. Carley decided to use that ancient message center again.

This time, however, she would not place it on the table for just anyone to see. Instead, after writing the note, Carley put the watering can back in its place on top of the tall hutch, amid the pottery collection of antique rabbits and eggcups.

Then she left the new key to the house in plain sight—on the breakfast mat beside Morgan's coffee cup, where she was sure to find it. It was too bad that Gaddi still had the other key.

That morning, before the sun rose and before she woke Morgan, Carley dressed and then gathered together bottled water, two candy bars, bug spray, sturdy gloves, and her waterproof camera. She placed them into her backpack and, selecting a sharp shovel from her gardening equipment, she put all the gear in her truck.

Walking back into the house, she climbed the stairs and knocked on Morgan's bedroom door. "Morgan, it's time to get up. Are you awake?" Carley heard her groan. "The coffee's made, and there's juice in the refrigerator."

"I don't think I can get up this early. Call me in about twenty minutes."

Carley opened the door. "Morgan, I can't do that. I'm going to disappear for the day. So you're on your own." She watched until Morgan tossed aside the sheet and sat up, rubbing her eyes. "Good luck," she added and closed the door.

As the sun began its morning journey from the east, Carley began a journey of her own, retracing the trip that she and Joie had taken together to Ocean Springs. So much had happened in that length of time between journeys, including the two murders—Rudy's and the woman who'd been mistaken for her.

A slight, early morning mist caused her to turn on the windshield wipers at intervals. But she was glad that no storms had been forecast for the day. It would make it much harder to cross the Sound in choppy water.

During her drive, Carley tried to forget the charade that she had left behind. Perhaps it was just as well that Morgan had chosen to come. She would make a much more convincing display of grief. But would Whit suspect the switch? And what about Joie's reaction? Carley had wrestled with calling her again, but then decided against it.

The traffic began to get worse as a steady stream of cars, trucks, and SUVs entered the highway from the side roads and intersections. Carley passed by a number of familiar businesses and restaurants until she reached *Giverny's*, the restaurant where she and Joie had stopped for lunch. This time, she continued driving.

It was there, on that day in July, that Whit had first appeared, and then later at the *Sea Horse*, where he had spied on her from another table. Gran's information about the mole still bothered her. Had Whit really fallen in love with her, or had he used her vulnerability as an excuse to insinuate himself into her life for other purposes?

That morning, she seemed to be suspicious of everybody, even Gaddi. Her dragonfly pin had disappeared, and Gaddi was the only other one, besides Whit, who'd been in her house while she was away. She also couldn't forget Gaddi's strange behavior at Mabel's dinner party. It had been almost as disconcerting as the undercurrent that had existed between Maxim and Rudy.

Carley was not the only one to have noticed the animosity between the two men the first part of the evening. Lucinda had noticed it, too. But then, Rudy had offered Maxim a ride home that night, even though it was out of the way. It didn't make sense.

Carley had always felt that people had an inherent goodness about them and that when they showed less than stellar qualities, that it was a temporary aberration. But Morgan was different. "Grow up, Carley," Morgan had advised. "Some people are rats and always will be. So you need to protect your rear."

In view of recent happenings, Carley now leaned the same way. But she didn't like the feeling and would be glad when her worst suspicions were dealt with and finally put to rest. Only then could she get back to some sense of normalcy and return to what she loved — designing gardens.

By the time she reached Ocean Springs, Carley regretted that she had not started earlier. She had no idea how long it would take, but she knew that she had to get back to shore before dark, since the small craft would probably not have adequate running lights.

At least she would not have to worry about what was going on in Mobile. In a few minutes, Dresnick would be coming for Morgan, and her twin was perfectly capable of playing out the charade.

Carley did not return to the docks where she had taken the excursion boat to the island. Instead, she drove to the commercial area of the cove, where the barge had anchored and where Henry had rented his boat from Tullie's Bait Shop and Rental.

She pulled into the parking area and searched for a spot that was partially sheltered from the road. Because of its bright color, the truck stood out and, with her painted logo on the side, it was easily identifiable. She eventually found an empty space between two large SUVs.

As she walked into the rustic shack, filled with pungent odors of mullet, tackle, and sundry aromas that she had no wish to investigate, Carley saw Tullie, the owner, bringing a small bait barrel from the back room.

He looked as if he had stepped out of a seafood commercial; his salty swagger at odds with his rather obvious paunch.

Business was slow at mid-morning, and only one other person was inside. Tullie seemed glad to have another customer, so it did not take long to negotiate the rental of the boat. For good measure, Carley purchased a clam bucket and rented an orange life jacket, along with a compass.

As she placed her gear and shovel into the boat, Tullie hovered. "Now, you're sure you know about the shallows," he said. "Wouldn't want you to run aground."

"I've got my chart," Carley replied.

He untied the bow spring line and Carley took it in. Then, he remained on the wooden pier and watched while she cast off. On the second attempt, the motor started, and she got underway, heading for the channel between the buoys.

If it had not been for the seriousness of the trip, Carley would have enjoyed the outing. There was a calmness about the water that morning, with the seagulls soaring overhead in formation and then parting, to dive into the channel for an unsuspecting fish. Even the pelicans, so clumsy on land, were graceful in their flight.

Bob had been the sailor in the family. She was an amateur, so Carley consulted the compass. She wanted to make sure that the boat did not yaw, since she was facing the eye of the wind.

There was a certain risk in this venture, with the added danger of having to tie up at Horn Island's main dock. If she had possessed the stamina to row across, she could have come aground on a much more secluded area of the island, and no one would be aware of her intrusion.

A half-hour later, the island came into view, as if it were floating on the surface of a distant sea of azure blue. Carley kept to the course visually, watching the island grow in perspective, gain shape and texture gradually from the meager duality of sand and dark foliage to its full force of multiple glittering prisms of color. Variations of white, yellow, gray, chartreuse, and hunter green at sea level combined with the blue of herons and the ebony of cormorants claiming the skies below the clouds.

She drew in her breath at such wild beauty as her hands guided the tiller, bringing the boat about into a safe haven under the dock. After securing the line around one of the pilings, she sat for a few minutes in silence — content to say a word or two of thanks for having made it safely to the island.

Now came the tricky part.

Gran was certain that the smuggling ring had gotten rid of its main cache before the Coast Guard closed in on them. When they were arrested one nautical mile from the island, only a few boxes of contraband Havana cigars were seized. But with their previous records, that was enough to send the culprits to prison for a short time.

Like so many criminals sitting on a fortune, they were probably biding their time until parole and until the moment they could dig up what they had buried. Gran seemed to think so. What that illicit fortune was, Gran had not given any indication.

Millions of dollars of heroin, cocaine, and dirty money were smuggled into the country annually. The whole illegal process was like a sieve. When one hole was plugged, two more took its place. But Gran had been determined to plug up this one, evidently without the help of other fellow agents, until it was too late for the turncoat to warn the culprits of the sting.

But how had she come into possession of the map? Carley remembered the conversation at the poker table about the trip to Cuba for the sister city conference. Had that been a cover for Gran to meet with someone there?

Regardless, Carley now had the map that showed several possible locations for the buried treasure.

Carley shouldered her backpack and began the trek inland, passing by the same spiny cacti and sticker bushes of the previous jaunt. At intervals, she stopped to drink from the water bottle and to spray more bug repellent on her clothes.

Sidestepping obstacles and watching for dangers of the reptile kind, Carley followed the path marked on the map, past the bogs and marsh grass until she approached the south edge of the inland lake.

How singular! Almost in the same spot where she'd found the idle machinery on that Sunday in July, she noticed that someone had been digging again. Curious, she removed her backpack and began to examine the soft ground. Then, she started digging with her own sharp garden shovel.

The overhead sun was unrelenting in its punishment. But a stubborn Carley continued digging. Was this the place where the smugglers had chosen? But with the evidence of fresh digging, was she already too late?

After an inordinate amount of time, she finally hit something with her shovel. But it was far too soft for treasure chests or boxes.

Kneeling down, she began to remove the earth around the area with her gloved hands. Like an archaeologist, she carefully smoothed away layers of dirt until a piece of cloth finally emerged. It looked like part of a canvas tarpaulin.

A chill swept over her. This wasn't the treasure at all. Carley gasped in dismay when a human hand appeared, and she became ill when it dawned on her as to what or who might be wrapped in the cloth.

As unsettling as it was, she went back to removing more earth. Formal clothes, vaguely familiar from that gala evening at Mabels' slowly came into view. With that pungent and nauseating sweetness of death fouling the air, she finally uncovered the awful truth—a headless torso. Carley swallowed the bile in her throat and, with trembling hands, she took the camera from her backpack to record the crime.

It would be so easy to stop the search and go back to the boat, but she stifled that initial urge to flee from the scene. She was here, and she had to finish what she had come to do. But at that moment, she was sorry that she had come alone.

Then, from a distance, she heard someone call her name. She was *not* alone, after all.

"Carley, where are you?" the familiar voice demanded.

She did not answer. She picked up her gear and began to run, to find some place to hide.

But the voice seemed to be following her. "You can't get off this island," it warned. "Your boat's gone—adrift in the Sound by now."

If that were true, and he had cut off any means of escape, then she could only run, to seek a hiding place in this alien and hostile environment. But once hidden, how long could she hold out before he found her?

Think, Carley, think! she told herself. The marsh? No, not with all the quicksand. The ponds? Not unless she wanted to be alligator meat. The only place she could think of, that offered even a semblance of safety, was at the other side of the island.

"Don't be stubborn, Carley," the voice taunted her, sounding even closer. "Answer me."

Urgently, she began to lighten the weight from her backpack— throwing out items in various directions, until only her bottled water was left. If he stopped to investigate, perhaps that would slow him down and give her more time. Finally, she tossed the backpack, itself, into the marsh, where a large alligator, hoping for a meal, immediately lunged. Now there remained only her water and her last defense — the shovel.

If she had been performing in a Greek drama, the gods, about this time, would be sending down a chariot from heaven to rescue her. But this was real life. Carley Burnside could expect no supernatural intervention by the gods. If she were to survive, she would have to save herself.

# Chapter 42

Under the rotting, overturned boat, surrounded by tangled vines and weeds, Carley hid. She had been careful to disturb the vines as little as possible.

She could still hear his voice, alternately patient and then angry. Closer, and then farther away. Back and forth he went, as if he were playing a game in which he was sure to be the winner.

"I only want the map, Carley. I know you have it."

Of all the people that she'd suspected, she never would have chosen Barnie Overton. He had been so helpful, subleasing the grading equipment and even working with her at Cavallegria. But had that been a ruse, also? Had he done it to keep his eye on her, thinking that she might lead him to the coveted treasure?

The visibility from beneath the old boat was meager, and it took great effort not to make a sound when a spider crawled up her arm. Quickly brushing it off, Carley realized that things could have been worse. What if it had been a snake, instead—like the one sent to her earlier?

For a number of minutes, she was aware of nothing but her own ragged breathing. No taunting voice in the distance; no overt activity of breeze or tide disturbed the silence, Then, she heard the flapping of wings as birds flew from the presence of an approaching human being. She had a sinking feeling that Barnie had found her hiding place.

Carley strained to see through the tiny window afforded

her by the crack in the rotted wood of the hull—sensing more than seeing.

Then, so near that she could have reached out and touched them, she caught a glimpse of Barnie's familiar tan leather work boots. He kicked at the old hull, causing her to grit her teeth to keep the sound that was lodged in her throat from erupting.

Despite the cramp that had invaded her leg muscle, she was poised to fight for her life, although it would be difficult under such uneven odds. She waited for Barnie to overturn the wreck. But then, in all the waiting, a strange thing happened. The man uttered an oath and then seemed to back off.

For the next half-hour or so—Carley couldn't see her watch to gauge the true time— she remained where she was. But the heat was sweltering and she had to decide whether she would rather suffocate, die of heat stroke, or risk finding another hiding place.

Listening for any indication that Barnie might still be near, she finally crawled out from under the hull. The man was gone and, in relief, she took a long, deep breath of fresh air.

With her gaze centered on the Sound, she longed to see a Coast Guard cutter on patrol, or some fishing boat plying the waters. Even then, any vessel would be too far out to see her distress signal.

Her only hope was to circle back and try to reach Barnie's boat while he was still searching. Then, he would be the one stranded on the deserted island.

Carley crept along the sandy beach, carefully darting between the dunes of sea oats or taking up a position behind a pile of driftwood. She waited, listened, and then darted again until she faced that area of water known as *The Horseshoe* on the navigational chart.

It was there, about fifty yards offshore, that she saw her rental boat adrift in the water. So Barnie had been telling the truth. He had cut the boat loose from its mooring. But it was now stationary—evidently caught on something in the shallow water.

Carley had the storm, Isidore, to thank for that, for stirring up the sea floor, as so many hurricanes and tropical depressions did, playing havoc with underwater cables, pipelines, and snagging errant bow lines.

Suddenly aware of movement behind her, she turned. Barnie stood only about thirty feet away, cutting off any escape to the dock. She could see the triumphant grin on his face. He was holding a gun, yet he didn't fire. Perhaps he was afraid a gunshot would bring the Station Ranger to investigate. That was predicated, of course, on whether one were actually on the island.

Then, again, maybe Barnie was merely guessing about the map. He couldn't be sure that she hadn't stored the information in her head. He would need her alive long enough to show him the location of the hidden contraband.

He kept walking slowly toward her, diminishing the distance with each step. Carley had only one recourse of action left. She kicked off her shoes and took a running leap for the water. If she could reach the rental boat, then she could untangle the line and head back to the mainland and safety.

"Don't be an idiot, Carley," Barnie shouted, as he suddenly realized what she was planning. "You'll never make it."

The current was deceptive. With her clothes weighing her down, she fought to keep from being swept back to shore. The more strokes she took, the farther away the boat seemed.

For a while, she stopped struggling and began treading water until she could find another burst of energy to press forward. When something alive touched her foot, she panicked. She began to swim for her life with every ounce of adrenaline she could muster.

Carley decided that, when contemplating death, one's mind doesn't have time for flashbacks, to wallow in past sins of commission and omission. At least, that was the way with her. She had only one goal on her mind, and she was swimming toward it.

The sun vanished behind the clouds, and the breeze picked up, viciously slapping the waves against her face and body. By the time she finally reached the boat, with her heart pounding in her chest, she was too exhausted to do anything beyond clinging to the stern of the boat.

When she finally gathered enough energy to tumble headlong into the boat, she heard the telltale motor of an approaching craft. Her hopes plummeted as she desperately began to tug at the bow line, caught on the underwater debris.

Then another craft appeared on the horizon—a Coast Guard cutter— and with it, a megaphone warning that reverberated over the water. Even with the distortion, Carley would know that authoritative voice anywhere. As the cutter advanced, she also recognized three other familiar figures standing on deck—Goose, Edward, and Henry.

In response to the warning voice, Barnie's boat suddenly changed course. But instead of giving chase, the cutter's motor died and a dinghy was lowered over the side.

As the dinghy approached her disabled boat, Carley shouted, "Go after Barnie. I think he's the murderer."

That brought no response. The dinghy, containing Whit and Dresnick, continued in her direction until it came abreast of the stranded boat.

Seeing Whit's mobile device, Carley said, "Why don't you tell the cutter to go after Barnie?"

"He won't get far," Whit replied. "Another cutter in the Sound is already giving chase."

"Well, it seems that you got here just in time. My line is caught on something. Can one of you help me cut it loose?"

"You're not going anywhere in that boat," Whit announced. "You're coming with us." He held out his hand and, reluctantly, she took it. He then turned to Dresnick. "Now, let's head back to the cutter."

"We can't leave the island now," Carley protested, with her teeth chattering. "I found Rudy's grave, and from Gran's map, I think I know where the smugglers buried their treasure. I haven't come this far just to go back empty-handed."

Dresnick looked at Whit and waited for him to make a decision. "I'll have to clear it with the Coast Guard," he finally said. There was considerable discussion back and forth.

In the end, a doubtful Whit said, "All right, Carley. We have less than an hour. I hope you're not going to embarrass us any more than you already have."

After they had tied up to the dock, she said, "If you don't mind, I'd like to recover my shoes and shovel first. They're still on the beach."

Carefully she avoided the prickly cacti, while the three walked along the sandy beach until they reached the stretch where she had left them. As she tied her shoes, Whit took possession of the shovel. "First, show us where you found the body," he said.

She led them inland, toward the lake and then stopped about fifteen feet from the shallow burial site. "It's over there," she said. "But you two go ahead. I don't think I want to see it again."

After they had taken note of the scene, the two men stood and talked quietly. Carley deliberately ignored their discussion and instead, watched the activity in the sky — clouds moving at a rapid pace, like geese rushing to get somewhere before the sun went down. With the allotted time on the island ticking away, Carley felt that same sense of urgency. Impatiently she waited for Dresnick and Whit to rejoin her.

"It's Rudy, isn't it?" she inquired.

"More than likely," Dresnick answered.

"Now, may I see the map?" Whit asked, changing the subject.

Carley pulled it from her pocket. But the salt water had

done its damage. The ink had run, and the map was illegible. "I'm afraid it's no good," she apologized, handing him the spoiled piece of paper. "But I think I know where the treasure is hidden."

"Then, lead us to the place."

Carley, watching for alligators, gingerly retraced her route until she reached the rotted hull of the old boat that had been a victim, itself, perhaps of past storms. "I'm almost certain that this is the site. Under the wreck."

"I hope you're right," a doubtful Whit said, eyeing the weathered old paint-chipped timbers that looked as if they might fall apart at any moment.

A large snake, enjoying the last vestiges of the sun, began to slither from its perch on the boat. Had its presence earlier caused Barnie to back off?

As a landscape architect, Carley had always had to deal with wild creatures; for after all, she was the one to invade their natural habitat. But it was ironic that the poisonous snake hidden in the florist's box was intended to do her harm, while this one might have saved her life.

As Whit raised the shovel to dispose of it, Carley said, "Wait. Let it go."

"Remember, this is a wild life preserve," Whit reminded her, as he proceeded merely to lift the snake and deposit it a distance away.

"But where there's one, there's usually a second one," Dresnick warned.

For that reason, the two men were cautious in turning over the wreck of the boat. The wood, to no one's surprise, fell apart. The ground under it, however, revealed nothing more than a slight indentation made by Carley's body earlier.

With only a few minutes left before they would have to return to the dinghy, Whit and Dresnick took turns digging. As each shovelful of earth and sand began to mount higher and higher, the sun began to sink lower and lower.

Just when Carley had become the most dejected, in case

she had miscalculated, the edge of a box came into view.

"There's definitely something buried here," a surprised Whit announced.

Carley crossed her fingers and waited. When the metal trunk was completely uncovered and lifted from its hiding place, she felt a great disappointment.

It didn't look as if it might be something people would die for. It was even less impressive than the buried trunk that had belonged to Wingate.

After Whit pried open the lid, Carley peered inside. The trunk contained a cache of small wooden cigar boxes—the same kind that she had seen, decorated as pocket books with sequins, in the expensive little boutique where Rhett and Lucinda had taken her.

"Cigars. Cuban cigars. What a wasted effort."

Whit laughed at her disappointment. He held out one of the boxes. "Take a cigar," he suggested. "And roll one open."

Carley looked at him as if he were completely mad. Nevertheless, she followed his suggestion. She selected one, slid the signet band off, and began to tear apart the mildewed brown tobacco. The cigar disintegrated in her hands, and brown stones resembling teardrops fell to her feet.

When she stooped to pick them up, she said, "They look like rough diamonds."

"You're absolutely right," a satisfied Whit said, smiling. "They're blood diamonds—worth a fortune."

Then it dawned on her. With Gran's help, she had discovered one of the illegal trade routes from diamond mines in Africa to dishonest buyers in America. She had read how certain contraband diamonds had gotten their name—through a legacy of blood shed by numerous mining victims under a murderous dictator.

"So this is how the diamonds got into the country," Carley said in awe. "Hidden in Havana cigars."

Dresnick smiled at her and then spoke to Whit. "You

think we could inveigle her to join our group? She's more like her grandmother than ever, don't you think?"

"Absolutely not!" Whit replied. Then he turned to Carley. "You should stick to gardens, Carley Burnside. Otherwise, you'll be the death of *me.*"

 Chapter 43

When one attempts to walk back the cat, or unravel a mystery, starting from the end and tracing all the happenings back to the beginning, some loose ends refuse to tag along. But that unraveling can be done at leisure.

Carley's more immediate concern when she returned home was in repairing relationships, particularly with Morgan.

"How could you do this, Carley?" Morgan demanded. "Both Joie and I have been frantic for hours. We thought you had vanished from the entire universe."

"It's not as if I didn't leave a note to let you know where I was going."

"It's a good thing that I finally remembered about the watering can. Otherwise, you'd still be up a creek without a paddle."

"That's not far off the mark, Morgan," Goose agreed. "Only, it wasn't a creek. It was the Mississippi Sound."

Goose, Henry, and Edward, who had alerted Whit of her disappearance, were still feasting on the remains of the funeral luncheon, which they had forgone earlier in the day. Whit and Dresnick joined them.

Goose's remark seemed to diffuse the conversation.

"I'm really, really sorry that I caused anybody to worry, especially *you*, Morgan."

Her apology seemed to mollify her twin a bit. So while

the rest of them continued eating, Morgan went upstairs to pack.

Carley's three poker buddies left first. She gave each of them a hug. Then, there remained only Whit and Dresnick.

"We have a lot to talk about, but that can wait until tomorrow," Whit said. "I think we've all had enough excitement for one day."

Carley agreed. She was extremely tired.

In the days that followed, as all the pieces of the puzzle began to fit, and both Barnie and Maxim Tourkay were apprehended, Carley and Whit began to enjoy being together again. She forgave him for tracking her so unmercifully during those earlier days, and he forgave her for having such doubts about him. And at the next Wednesday Night Investment Club meeting, she also gained a new insight into the relationship between Gran and her three longtime friends.

"We knew what Lydia was doing," Henry confessed. "We were all planning to help with the sting, once the smugglers got out of prison."

"We were the only ones that she could really trust," Edward added.

"I guess we may never know who the mole is, though," Goose said, with a tinge of regret in his voice. "And he's still out there, somewhere."

Carley couldn't understand why Gaddi had teamed up with Maxim and Barnie. Perhaps she had been around criminals too often in her prison ministry, or maybe she saw an opportunity to get out of her genteel poverty. Carley was certain that she never meant to be a party to Rudy's murder. But now, for the next year, at least, she wouldn't have to travel far for her prison ministry, since she would be in the Tutweiler Prison for Women, herself.

As for Sherrie, she was admonished severely for her tactics in attempting to sabotage Carley's work at Cavallegria, and Rocky Donovan lost his P.I. license.

After all these events had been brought to conclusion, after Rudy and the murdered maid had received proper burials, and Morgan had returned to France, taking her entire wardrobe with her, Boris Cavanaugh and Wingate gave one of the best dinner parties that had ever taken place at Cavallegria.

Because of the scandalous publicity, the artist colony, with its restored gardens became nationally famous, and Wingate's bis pole was now considered one of the seven wonders of the Gulf Coast.

On the night of the party, Carley was surrounded by people who wished her well. They were all there—Goose and Agnes, Edward and Jorja, Henry, Lucinda, Rhett and Edgar, Mabel, Consuelo, Dresnick, Tom and Betsy.

Joie was there, too, with Ibee Sey. He seemed to be in no hurry to return to Hong Kong. With his international reputation, he was thinking of opening an office in Biloxi, giving Regan, Barnes, and O'Reilly stiff competition in the architectural field.

The only one missing was Luis Delgado. He was a problem that would have to be dealt with in the future. But at least, he had been successful in purchasing Boris's painting from Lucinda, to be used in his new casino lobby. She no longer needed the surprise birthday present for Rudy. But she did get back her boat that Barnie had stolen.

Later that night, when the party was over, Whit and Carley passed through the gates of Cavallegria and turned toward home.

"I'm curious, Whit. Is this red Ferrari actually yours, or was it requisitioned like the plumber's truck?" she asked.

"Would it make any difference to you?"

"None at all."

Whit laughed and confessed, "It's mine."

"Oh? And what about the house on Dauphin Island? Do you own it, too?"

"I bought it, but since Connie likes it so much, I've signed it over to her."

Carley was silent for a moment. It was most unusual for someone in the spy business to be so wealthy. Shrugging, she finally said, "Poor Lucinda. I can't believe that Rudy was murdered, just because he overheard a conversation in prison."

"I think there was a little more to it, than that."

"But I still can't believe Barnie and Maxim were capable of trying to kill me at the hotel."

Whit hesitated. "They had no hand in that murder, Carley. Compared to the mole who has infiltrated our organization, they're just petty thieves who squabbled among themselves. But regardless, I think you're safe now."

"Well, that's a relief."

When they arrived at the English Tudor house, with its window boxes filled with glorious fall mums, Whit parked the Ferrari in the circular drive. He unlocked the door and they went inside.

"I'll be down soon," he said, planting a light kiss at the curve of her neck. He proceeded to walk upstairs to Morgan's old room, where the king-sized, walk-in closet was now filled with Whit's clothes.

Downstairs, Li-Po and Cho-Cho opened sleepy eyes when Carley entered the bedroom. "Sorry, fellows, but we have company. I think you should sleep in your hammocks tonight."

She and Whit had less than a week left, and then he would be off to other worlds, tracking down criminals, including the one who had murdered her grandmother Lydia, and probably the hotel maid. But she still wasn't sure of Whit's real name, or his supposed connection to the Whitstones of Metairie. And she wondered if years from now, the old trunk in the attic would contain other expired passports, other aliases, as companions to Gran's collection.

In the wee hours of the morning, Whit held her closely. "I'll never be able to stay for long," he lamented. "And my coming and going will be erratic. When you grow tired of the arrangement, all you'll have to do is tell me so."

"Bring up the subject again in another millennium," Carley murmured sleepily. "After all, I have more than enough to keep me busy while you play James Bond."

Carley was now on a retainer, to work with Ibee Sey on the Biloxi project. She also had Lucinda's new property in Mobile to design, and then Morgan's at Milly-la-Forêt. And there was always the Wednesday Night Investment Club.

"But promise me one thing, Carley," Whit said.

"What is that?"

"Try not to get into trouble while I'm away."

But that was highly unlikely. Carley's adventures had just begun.

§

About the Author

Frances Patton Statham is an award-winning artist, musician, writer, and lecturer. She received her undergraduate degree, *magna cum laude,* from Winthrop University, with a double major in voice performance and music education, a master of fine arts degree from the University of Georgia, and an honorary doctorate from World University.

Listed in such biographical works as *International Who's Who of Authors and Writers, World Who's Who of Women, International Who's Who of Intellectuals,* and *Personalities of the South,* Statham lives in metro-Atlanta.

Acknowledgments

In 2002, prior to Hurricane Katrina, Mobile friends invited me to help celebrate that city's 300th anniversary. Experiencing Mobile's living history gave me a vast appreciation of that region's French and Spanish culture, from its founding to the present day.Then, traveling along the Gulf Coast from Mobile to Dauphin Island, Ocean Springs, Biloxi, Pascagoula, and other towns, I felt quite fortunate to have seen the Gulf Coast before the devastation.

So many of the landmarks mentioned in this novel, such as the Walter Anderson Museum in Ocean Springs, Mississippi, were victims of the flooding. And beautiful, wild Horn Island has been closed to the public because of hazardous materials unearthed. But as the region struggles to regain its beauty, the strong sense of place—of the Southern Azalea Trail— will always remain in fondest memory.

To Emily, Helen, and Sue, I wish to thank them for sharing a tour that was both educational and fun. Although *Murder, al fresco* is a contemporary work of fiction, the historical past was always beside me, giving me a better understanding of the present.

I hope you enjoy the story.

Frances Patton Statham